GRASPING FOR STARLIGHT

REALM OF FAERIE
WATER'S DOMINION
EARTH PROVINCE
AIRY REACH
FIRE'S TERRITORY
Sunken Palace
The Big Narwhal
Indigo Isles
Portal Ball
Maborough Lake
Beryl's Grove
Goddess Pinery
Eristald
The Good Inn
Briar Burrow
Noh Waterfall
Mistral Summits
Lah Waterfall
Portal Ball
Zephyr Ravine
Yellow Lizard
Boling Springs
Thorne Volcano
City of Thorne
Scorched Wilds

PRONUNCIATION GUIDE

Aarae - A-ray /ˈɑːreɪ/

Aleksandr - Alix-ander /æləksˈændər/

Brynn - Brin /brɪn/

Cylan - Sy-lin /ˈsaɪlən/

Datalis - D'-taliss /ˈdætəlɪs/

D'ashil (human) - D'-shill] /dɑːˈʃɪl/

D'asim (Faerie) - D'-sim /dɑːˈsɪm/

Elowyna - Ello-weena /ˌɛloʊˈwiːnə/

Enamir (Earth) - Enna-meer] /ˈɛnəmɪr/

Eris - Air-riss /ˈɛrɪs/

Eristald - Air-riss-tald /ˈɛrɪstæld/

Etaldin - Eh-tal-din /ˈɛtɔːldɪn/

Fyodor - Fee-oh-door /ˈfjodər/

Hanli - Han-lee /ˈhænli/

Ilduy (Hello) - Ill-doo-ee /ˈɪlduːi/

Ilmore (Goodbye) - Ill-mor /ˈɪlmɔːr/

PRONUNCIATION GUIDE

Indis (starlight) - In-diss /ˈɪndɪs/

Indis Hahom (starlight's chosen)
- In-dis ha-hom /ˈɪndɪs hɑːˈhoʊm/

Inohryil (Otherworld) - In-or-yill /ɪnˈɔːrjɪl/

Iraforn - Eye-ra-forn /ˈaɪrəfɔrn/

Maelin - May-lin /ˈmeɪlɪn/

Mari - Mar-ree /ˈmɑːri/

Nahil (expression of anger) - Na-hill] /nəˈhɪl/

Niha (Air) - Nee-ha /ˈniːhɑː/

Nysyll -Nigh-sill /ˈnaɪsɪl/

Onhma (be careful) - On-ma /ˈɒnmɑː/

Rinah (Fire) - Rin-a /ˈrɪnɑː/

Thorston - Thor-sten] /ˈθɔːrstən/

Velyna - Velleen-a /ˈvɛlɪnɑː/

Wyna (Water) - Win-a /ˈwɪnɑː/

Xerses - Zer-seez /ˈzɜːrsiːz/

Y'nilsa (Soul's Smile) - Ya-nillsa /jəˈnɪlsə/

Zayndru - Zane-droo /ˈzeɪndruː/

Contents

FORTUITY OR FATE?

I t's hard not to live in fear when you're pretty sure your whole blood-line is under an evil curse, but Mari was trying to see the bright side of things. For starters, it wasn't raining today.

The warmth of the sandy beach loosened the tight muscles in her back as she settled into her beach towel. The public beach was empty this early in the morning—just the way she liked it. Quiet and peaceful sunbathing by the ocean quickly became her idea of a perfect morning.

Sunbathing was as close as she'd ever get to the water though; Mari had never learned to swim. She was pretty sure she'd had a cousin who drowned once—another victim of the Dawson Family Curse, as Mari liked to call it—and that was enough to convince her to leave the swimming to the fish and ducks.

The Dawson Family Curse had been on her mind a lot lately after the recent death of her uncle and legal guardian, Jacob Dawson. He'd lost his battle with cancer at the ripe old age of thirty-three, making Mari officially an orphan. There were times that this fact brought on a crushing loneliness that she was sure she could never overcome. Other times, she was relieved that there was no one left to lose; no more heartache to live through.

These recent events brought eighteen-year-old Marianne Dawson to the seaside village of Eastport. She'd purchased a small, one-bedroom cabin in the forest just outside of town and, for the time being, she was happily living off of the remaining proceeds from the sale of her uncle's home and belongings.

The August sun was getting hotter as the morning went on, but the cool breeze rolling off the waves kept Mari comfortable. Gulls called out greedily as they caught their breakfasts, the slapping of the waves muffling their cries as the water came to shore.

Mari dug her hands deeper into the sand beside her, letting the grains fall through her fingers slowly before picking up another handful and repeating the process. She was at ease here. Only recently had she learned to find some contentment in her own company.

Although she found it hard to believe in any God that would allow so much unnecessary death and pain in a person's life, Mari took a moment to pray to anyone who might be listening.

"Even if I'm doomed to die in my prime," she whispered, "please let the rest of my short life be this calm and easy."

On her hand's next pass through the sand, her fingertips brushed something smooth and cold. Thoughtfully, she closed her hand around the hard object and pulled it up.

Mari sat up, blinking the sunspots from her vision, and found a gray stone in her palm. She brushed away the rest of the sand and turned the oblong stone over, examining the perfectly circular hole that ran through the middle of the rock.

It was a very unusual stone and for that lone reason, Mari decided it was coming home with her. She'd always had a "magpie eye" as her late father used to say when Mari would bring home pocketfuls of little stones or leaves or other treasures she'd found.

Car doors slammed shut behind her. Mari turned to see a few small families dressed in beach attire piling out of their vehicles. She took this as her cue to leave.

After shaking out her towel and shoving it, along with her cool new rock, into the canvas bag she'd brought, Mari pulled her t-shirt over her bathing suit top and tugged jean shorts on. She tied up her ashy brown hair in a bun on top of her head and slipped on her broken sandals before starting down the road toward town.

She focused on the gravel crunching beneath her bicycle tires, putting distance between herself and the children as they shrieked with joy, diving into the ocean behind her.

Her pace slowed as she entered the historic downtown of Eastport. She felt a smile creep onto her face as she saw the shop she'd been eyeing for a week now finally had its "open" sign displayed.

She jumped off her bike, walking beside it until she reached the door of the quirky storefront. The exterior was brick and every inch of wood—including the door and the trim around the windows—had been painted a deep purple. Thick, green vines grew up the side of the shop, clinging to the textured wall and disappearing over the roof. The small garden beds below the large windows were lovingly tended, blossoming with a variety of flowers and grasses. Along the top of the edifice, gold lettering proudly proclaimed *Madame Zarena's Metaphysical Shop.*

Mari had been enticed by the interesting objects and trinkets she could see from the window as she rode past, but until today she had assumed that the store had gone out of business since no one had been around in quite some time.

Slowly, she pulled open the door and the jingle of tiny bells announced her entrance. Second to the noise, she noticed the smell of the shop; an indescribable and thick mixture of incense, oils, and plants filled the air. Mari inhaled deeply, her eyes fluttering closed for a moment.

"Hello," A kind old voice said.

Mari opened her eyes. "Hello." she addressed the old woman who stood, hunched, behind the counter. "This is a beautiful store you have here."

"For beautiful customers," the woman replied with a smirk.

Mari chuckled and began to look around. In stores like this, with small and breakable objects, Mari felt the need to keep her hands tucked close into her chest. The last thing she needed was to break an overly expensive trinket and have to pay for it.

Her eyes took in the hundreds of crystals and gemstones, polished and raw, that lined each shelf. Some were carved into pillars or hearts, and others looked the way they had when they came out of the earth, minus some of the dirt, of course.

Dried herbs and flowers were sold in glass jars or in bundles that hung from the ceiling. Some of the plants had been pressed for their oils that were for sale in tiny amber bottles, carefully labeled and neatly stacked. Atop another table near the back were boxes of tarot cards, pendulums, and other witchy tools that Mari enjoyed looking at but wouldn't begin to know how to use.

Finally, her gaze landed on the back wall of the store that housed floor-to-ceiling cases filled with books. The more modern and recently published books were near the bottom shelves, while it seemed the older, thicker, leather and cloth-bound tomes were carefully out of customer reach near the top.

Now, she allowed her hands to run freely over the wares. The books were comforting to hold and the scent of their new pages made Mari inhale a bit deeper. Perhaps she would buy herself one of the guidebooks to the local plants in the area to help identify some of the wildflowers near her cabin.

"Looking for anything in particular?"

Mari jumped, not hearing the old woman approach behind her. Hand on her thumping heart, she turned and smiled.

"I don't think so."

"Books tend to find us when we most need them, don't you think?"

"I suppose so."

Expecting the old shop owner to go about her business, Mari returned to perusing the bookcase. Defying those expectations, the store owner simply stayed put, staring at Mari with a thin smile on her thin lips.

"Um," Mari began, feeling pressured, "is there anything you'd recommend?"

The old lady slowly began to shuffle towards a door on the east wall.

"Come with me."

Confused but not distrustful of such a frail-looking woman, Mari put down the book she'd been inspecting and did as she was told.

The woman led Mari to what appeared to be a small kitchen that hadn't been renovated since the 1960s. The nicotine-stained walls and cracked, orange plastic chairs only added to the vintage feel, along with the yellow-flowered wallpaper and the green-flecked floor tile.

The magic of the store began to fade away as Mari sat at the mundane kitchen table. The woman had gone to the cupboard and pulled out two porcelain tea cups.

"Oh," Mari tried to say politely, "I'm not sure I really have time to sit and have tea with you…"

The old lady ignored her. After fiddling on the counter for a moment, she came back with two steaming cups of tea balancing on white saucers.

Mari decided to make conversation if she was going to be stuck here for a while. She smiled up at the woman and took a sip of her tea.

"So, are you Madame Zarena?"

"My name is Serena, but people are more attracted by a more foreign-sounding name." Serena took a sip of her tea as well.

"I'm Mari. I just moved here a few weeks ago. I had my eye on your shop since the first day I caught sight of your purple door."

"Why have you come to such a small and secluded town? A vibrant young girl like yourself? You should be out, enjoying life!"

Mari shifted in her seat and took another sip, stalling. Typically, she tended to overshare and be a bit off-putting to those around her. It wouldn't be a lie to tell Serena that her whole family was dead and she was trying to hide from the Dawson family curse, but it might make the old woman uncomfortable.

"Small towns are safer. Peaceful. Don't you agree?"

Serena scoffed, "There is more hiding around this town than you might think."

A second later, Serena's wrinkled hand shot out, snatching Mari's cup from her hands after she'd taken her last sip. Mari let out a small startled noise but relinquished the cup and saucer with a small whisper, "Thank you for the tea."

Serena turned Mari's tea cup over onto the saucer. A small tap on the bottom of the cup, and Serena set the porcelain aside. She thoughtfully studied the soaked tea debris that lay scattered on the saucer.

When Serena looked up, she met Mari's gaze. Mari held it for a moment before the urge to look away overwhelmed her and she shot her eyes down to the mess on the plate.

"What burdens you, child? It looms over you, night and day."

Mari felt herself start to blush and tried to play it off with a chuckle. Forcing nonchalance into her tone, she smiled, "Oh you know, just your typical family curse!"

Sarena did not waver. She held the same concerned gaze that searched Mari's face. "Curses are nothing to laugh about."

"Well, it," Mari stammered, "it's not a *real* curse. Just something my therapist said I made up at a young age to help my young brain make sense of all the tragedies in my life." Mari silently kicked herself for oversharing, once again.

Serena was silent for a moment longer before standing and smiling sweetly, "I know just the book for you!"

Mari was stunned; she'd forgotten that her request for a book was what had led her to the kitchen with Serena in the first place. She obediently stood and followed the woman from the old kitchen and back into the store.

As hunched over and withered as Serena's body was, she was still fast on her feet. By the time Mari had rounded the corner, Serena stood with one of the cloth-bound books from the very top shelf, holding it out to Mari.

Mari took the book, looking between its time-worn cover and the space on the shelf nearest the ceiling where it had sat.

"How did you get that down so quickly?"

"Eris, the Seelie Goddess," Serena began, ignoring Mari's question, "is known for her love of humans and has been known to break many Unseelie curses that may befall them."

"Sounds like an interesting story!" Mari carefully opened the pages that had yellowed with time.

"You'll find, near the middle, instructions on how to visit Eris your-self. She'll unburden you."

Mari nearly scoffed and made a sarcastic comment about how the pope himself probably couldn't help her with a fake curse, but then she saw in Serena's eyes that the old woman truly believed in this Goddess and her curse-breaking abilities.

"Of course, yes, I... appreciate that. Very much." Mari clutched the book close to her chest. "How much do I owe you for it?"

Serena scoffed and waved a hand dismissively, scurrying over towards the shelves on the other side of the store.

"You'll need these, too." She tossed some polished stones in a small cloth bag and placed it on top of the book in Mari's hands. "And," Serena handed her a small glass jar filled with dried tea and herbs, "it's always a good idea to have a cup of tea before a long journey." The old woman's eyes sparkled, "how fortuitous that you wandered into my shop today!"

Mari was officially stunned into silence. She could only manage a smile before heading up to the counter to pay for her goods, which she now felt she was obligated to purchase.

"I will only accept payment in the form of stories from your adventures," when Mari began to protest and reach for her wallet Serena held up a hand and added, "I insist."

Knowing full well that there would be no adventures, Mari only smiled brighter and took her opportunity to head for the door.

"Thank you very much, Serena. You've been very kind and it was really nice to meet you."

Still reeling from her whirlwind experience with the old woman, Mari loaded her new treasures into the canvas bag that sat in her small basket on the back of her bike and hurried home.

2

UNEXPECTED ENTRY

That night, Mari was determined to unpack a few more boxes—a task that she'd been putting off ever since she moved in. As soon as she finished, Mari sat down with Hank—a smoky-colored stray tomcat she had rescued a year ago—and opened the book Serena had given her.

She was careful with the old pages that had weakened over the decades and examined them thoroughly before gently turning them over. It didn't take her long to notice that this book was handwritten. A few more pages in she realized this had been someone's journal that they titled: "An Adventurer's Guide to the Realm of Faerie."

There was no author listed. The thought crossed her mind that perhaps Serena had written it. Maybe that was why she was so insistent that Mari take the book; simply to get the story read by someone.

The beginning held a few pages about why someone might want to travel to the Realm of Faerie in the first place—promises of "magic and wonders beyond comprehension" —and then a few pages more on how to keep yourself safe while there.

The author warned about two different alignments within the Faerie Realm: Seelie and Unseelie. The Seelie were "the kind ones that you may consider friends" while you'd do best to "avoid Unseelie at any cost."

Her interest was piqued, though her eyelids were beginning to feel too heavy to hold open. Even Hank had passed out, curled up beside her. She would only read a few more pages tonight, then a few more in the morning.

Next to a group of illustrations including mushrooms growing in a circle, summer flowers, sparkling gems, and an oblong stone with a hole through the center, a paragraph was written in a heavy hand. For this passage, the author appeared to purposely use ink that was thicker than the text surrounding it, implying that this was of greater importance.

If you feel you are sufficiently prepared for such a journey as the one to the Realm of Faerie, the road there is not a difficult one. With a seer's stone and belly full of summer herbs, give an offering to a Faerie circle and you'll be granted passage to the Realm of Faerie. What you'll encounter when you get there, however, I cannot guarantee will be to your liking. It is not often that the folk find themselves with willing and knowledgeable guests, so perhaps they will welcome you with open arms. However, if you find yourself in Unseelie lands... may good luck and courage find you.

———— · ✦ · ————

A few days later, the book and the Realm of Faerie out of sight and out of mind, Mari was elbow-deep in cleaning and unpacking the last of her boxes. The thought of finally having a cozy place to settle in and make a life for herself was giving her a seemingly endless amount of energy.

After finishing up the last box in the bathroom, Mari decided to take a short break and brew a cup of tea from the herbs that Serena sent her with the other day. She took a sip, smiling to herself as she remembered the old woman's antics in the shop.

The tea was delicious, a lightly floral black tea with a hint of citrus beneath it all. It was sweet enough, too, with just a touch of honey. Mari savored a few more sips before tidying up the space around her. She noticed the bag that she'd taken with her to the beach a few days ago lying half underneath her couch and bent to pick it up.

A tiny *clink* of a hard object hitting the floor drew her attention downwards. Mari bent to see the odd stone with the hole through the center of it that she'd found in the sand—she'd all but forgotten about it. Next to it lay the tiny cloth bag of gemstones that Serena had given her. She picked them up, putting the bag of gems into her pocket with one hand and toying with the stone with her other hand.

In her peripheral vision, a little gray ball bolted across the grass outside. She turned her attention to her living room window, finding that Hank had gotten out and was viciously chasing grasshoppers in her backyard.

She tucked the stone in her jeans and ran outside to catch her cat. Mari made kissing noises to try to get Hank's attention but he was much too focused on his prey. Not so focused, however, that he couldn't escape her grasp when she came up behind him.

"Hank!" She scolded.

The mischievous cat was enjoying this game he'd started to play—letting her get close and then sprinting away at the last moment, but never going farther than her line of vision.

Mari continued to chase him into the surrounding forest where, eventually, the cat stopped in a glade, licking its paw and giving Mari time to catch up. At last, Hank didn't protest as she picked him up, stroking his fur and scolding him lovingly.

As she turned around, ready to go back home, she realized with a pit of anxiety growing in her stomach, that she'd gone a bit too far into the forest to see her cabin anymore. Her eyes searched the trees looking for familiarity, when she saw a perfect little trail of brown flat-topped mushrooms growing in a curve around her.

The sight brought forth the memory of the illustration in Serena's book. The drawing had been next to the part that read: *with a seer's stone and a belly full of summer herbs, give an offering to a Faerie circle, and you'll be granted passage to the Realm of Faerie.*

Her hair was swept up in the warm summer breeze that rustled through the leaves of the hardwood trees around her. Nature was alive and thriving, a symphony of birds chirping, cicadas buzzing, and squirrels leaping from branch to branch. The yellow sun filtered through the leaves above, its rays casting patches of golden light all around.

Everything was peaceful there, full of life and beauty, and yet the nagging tug of anxiety wouldn't leave her body. The unnerving feeling of missing something—like walking into a room and forgetting what you went there for—pulled at her mind.

Her hand found its way into the pocket of her jeans and closed around the cold stone and small bag of gems. With an involuntary shudder, she realized she had nearly everything she needed to perform the ritual that Serena wrote about.

Mari ran her fingers over the stones in her pocket. Mostly, she thought this ritual the book described was nothing but fantasy and superstition. Yet, part of her lept at the thought of a chance to free herself from the fear and worry of her family curse. If she really was cursed and if there was some magic out there that could help her, why shouldn't she try?

She turned to Hank, "What's the worst that could happen? It's just a story in a folk tale, after all."

Mari threw a couple of gems to the ground—unsure of how exactly to give an offering to a circle of mushrooms in the first place—then she picked up the porous stone from the beach and held it to eye level, examining it.

As she did, she caught a glimpse of something large and dark through the hole in the stone. A gasp flew from her lips and she jumped backward, looking over the stone in her hand to find nothing there. Curious, she held the stone up to peer through the hole once more and found a large wooden door visible directly ahead of her.

The door, covered in moss and crumbling as it decayed, stood alone where it had not been only a moment before. It had a thick, rusted knocker with an equally rusted frame holding the structure upright.

"Was that there when we got here?" Mari could hear the shaking in her voice and held Hank a little tighter.

Mari took a deep breath, the tugging feeling in her mind only growing stronger. *You're afraid of everything, Mari,* she told herself, *be brave for once.*

With her cat still in one hand, the stone in the other, she approached the door and pulled it open, jumping backward in case something pounced on her from the other side. However, no Faeries or monsters were hiding behind the door. Past the old threshold, she found nothing but more forest stretching out in front of her.

She chuckled at herself, sighing a breath of relief. Feeling silly and grateful that no one was around to see her, she smiled at Hank.

"I think that's enough adventure for one day."

The cat meowed and wriggled free of her grasp, sauntering through the open door, and disappearing completely. Mari had already begun moving after the cat before she could register that he had vanished, and tumbled through the doorway herself. Between one blink of her eyes and the next, Mari found herself cloaked in a blinding white light and falling to the ground below.

A moment later she was lying on the forest floor, her eyes shut tightly, her neck and back aching from the fall. She groaned, rubbing her sore muscles with her hand.

"What is it?"

"I'm not sure but... I think it's *human.*"

Her eyes shot open at the sound of voices around her. Staring down at her was a face wrinkled in confusion. It had two eyes, a long nose, and a wide mouth all in the correct places, but surrounded by green, wrinkly skin on a head topped with two long, floppy ears that hung down next to its face.

Mari screamed, loud enough to hurt her ears. She scrambled backward, terror and confusion consuming her thoughts. Her back slammed into a tree, and she stared at the scene in front of her.

Four screams echoed her own and the creatures that had been examining her jumped backward as well. Mari's hands searched blindly until they closed around a fallen branch. She held her flimsy weapon out in front of her shouting at the startled creatures.

"Stay back! Leave me alone!"

Mari desperately looked for the door she had just stumbled through, but there was no sign of it anywhere. Her head whipped back towards the creatures in front of her.

No one moved. The little green one had hidden itself behind a tree. Two taller creatures, one covered in thin brown fur and the other hovering above the ground with tiny transparent wings protruding from its back, held each other as they stared on in shock that mirrored her own.

A rustling of leaves to their right drew everyone's attention away from Mari as Hank appeared, meowing plaintively and heading toward the fourth figure that stood alone and closest to Mari.

He was a boy, tall and very normal-looking despite his snow-white hair and pale gray skin. He bent down to retrieve the cat, who was happy to receive a scratch between the ears. Hank thanked the boy with a rumbling purr.

"Put my cat down!" Mari's heart pounded in her chest as the boy turned his dark eyes on her.

He did as he was told and held his hands up in surrender.

"It's all right," his voice was slow and soft, "we aren't going to hurt you."

"What are you?" Mari was breathing heavily, her words coming out in quick pants, "Where am I?"

"Put the stick down," the boy said, "we can help you."

"Alek, *onhma,* be careful," the brown-furred girl turned her attention toward the boy, her tone warning.

"Answer me!" Mari shouted.

"It's been a very long time since there's been a human here," the boy—Alek—said. "How did you get to the Realm of Faerie? What's your name?"

"Realm of Faerie?" Mari breathed, her mind reeling, "You mean, it's real? I... I didn't think..."

"You can call me Alek," he offered, with a smile. "These are my friends," he gestured behind him, "Velyna, Aarae, and Fyodor."

"I'm sorry we scared you," Fyodor, the little green one, stepped out from behind the tree, wringing his hands nervously in front of him.

"We were just out for a walk," the female with the brown fur, Velyna, said shyly, "and you appeared out of nothing."

"I'm Mari," she said hesitantly, still holding her stick out in front of her, though her heart rate was beginning to slow and her breathing along with it.

"Who's this?" The winged girl, Aarae, was smiling and had picked up Hank who was thoroughly enjoying all of the petting and love he was receiving.

"That's Hank. My cat."

"He's sweet," Velyna had joined in the petting and Hank purred even louder, sounding like a small engine.

"Alek, we should leave," Fyodor spoke up, louder than before.

Alek took a step closer to Mari, ignoring his friend, "Are you okay?"

She flinched in response. "I have to get home. I can't be here."

"Okay," Alek spoke quietly, trying to keep her calm, "it's just..." he looked at his little green friend and then back to Mari, "well, we can't do anything here, in the forest. Let's get you back safely to my house."

"No." Mari began to protest, then sighed. With a growing feeling of hopelessness, she was beginning to see that these people—if they could even be called *people*—might be her only chance at getting home.

"We truly won't hurt you," Alek said again, "please trust us. We only want to help you." His companions stayed quiet but didn't seem to disagree.

"Why?" Mari locked gazes with Alek, "Why help me?"

"Alek, my friend," Fyodor stepped forward, "the danger you'll be in if it's discovered that you have a human in your home..."

"Think about the danger *she'll* be in if she's *not* in my home." He took his eyes off Fyodor and addressed his friends as a whole, "it's the right thing to do. It's what our late queen—what our Goddess—would want. We mustn't ignore the call of our Goddess when it literally falls at our feet."

They looked amongst each other for a moment, contemplative. Mari wasn't sure what she'd prefer they decide. Ultimately, staying safe was the most important thing to consider at the moment, and based on what little she'd read of that book last night, these four didn't appear to be any immediate threat to her. If they decided to leave her stranded here, however, she had a feeling that her odds of survival might rapidly decrease.

"Alek is right." Aarae said brightly, "Mari, please, let us help you."

Velyna smiled hesitantly, "We'll do what we can to keep you safe until you can return home—for Eris."

Mari lowered the stick, feeling a weak sense of relief, "Eris?" She repeated.

All four faces turned to examine her, though it was Alek who spoke first.

"Yes, Eris. The Goddess of all Seelie folk and friend to all humankind. You know of her?"

"I think she is why I was sent here," she dropped the branch to the ground and reached for her cat.

Alek held out the purring ball of fur and smiled encouragingly, "It sounds like we have a lot to discuss. However, here, in the forest, may not be the best place for such a conversation."

When Hank was safely in her arms, she looked up at Alek, nodding, "Okay, I'll come with you."

ERISTALD

lek didn't live far, for which Mari was thankful. As the adrenaline from their encounter wore off, her knees began to wobble, and she was unsure just how much farther she could go.

They had all settled down in the tiny living area of his modest forest home. The space was filled with brightly colored pillows instead of furniture, and someone had brought Mari water in what looked like a small hollowed-out gourd.

"I didn't think it would actually work," she admitted to the group, "I thought the old lady at the shop was full of it and I just wanted to…" she trailed off; it wasn't easy to explain your plan when you hadn't thought it through very well in the first place.

"I was in a mushroom circle," she began again, slowly, "and I threw some gems on the ground; an offering, I guess. Suddenly there was a door, in the forest, and Hank jumped in, so…"

"But how did she see the door?" Fyodor asked no one in particular. "The king hid the doors from the humans."

"Well I only saw it when I used this," she pulled out the seer stone from her pocket.

"A hag stone." Aarae, the winged female, leaned in for a closer look. "Where did you get that?"

"I found it, in the sand."

"More like it found you," Velyna muttered.

"The stone alone shouldn't have given her the power to step through, though," Alek mused, "it would only allow you to see the door. Was there anything else new that you'd done? Or eaten?"

Her stomach growled at the mention of food. "I hadn't even had a chance to eat lunch yet, I only drank half a cup of tea..."

"Tea? What kind of tea?"

She described the blend of tea Serena had given her, "I don't know exactly what was in it," she admitted, "but it was light and floral and a bit citrusy. I put some honey in it to sweeten it up a bit, but that was all."

"That was it." Alek sounded pleased as if he'd solved a riddle, "The Faerie Ring, the gems, the hag stone, the tea... the perfect combination."

"No way all of those pieces came together by accident," Aarae said.

Velyna agreed, absently petting Hank's back, "Too many things had to fall perfectly into place for this to be a coincidence."

Alek turned toward her, his brow furrowed. "You're shaking like a leaf, Mari." He placed his hand on her shoulder gently, "You're not in danger here, with us."

His touch was warm and calming, though she couldn't seem to stop the shudders flowing through her. Mari sighed.

"It doesn't matter what you do. I'm in danger everywhere." She had their full attention now. Mari took a deep, shaky breath.

"The reason the old woman told me how to get here in the first place is because," she lowered her voice, "I'm cursed. My whole family is. And I was told I could find a Goddess to break it here."

They were silent, letting the information sink in.

"Eris," Alek whispered, understanding.

Mari nodded and sighed, relieved that Alek caught on so quickly. "Until I know for sure that my family curse is broken, I'll never feel safe."

Twenty-four hours ago, Mari would have said the words *family curse* and not truly believed that curses actually existed; she would have repeated the words she'd been fed from medical professionals about childhood trauma and the things we convince ourselves are real just to protect our fragile minds. Now, she knew that an entire magical realm existed and the concept of a curse wasn't so far-fetched anymore.

"How much do you know about Eris?" Fyodor asked.

"Pretty much nothing." Mari smiled sheepishly. "Do you think I'll be able to get in touch with her?" She mentally scoffed at the simplicity of her own question; as if a Faerie Goddess would be so readily available for everyone's beck and call.

Everyone was silent, confirming her suspicion.

Finally, Mari spoke up again, "If I can't find Eris, then you all can help me get back, right?"

Again, silence.

"Right?" She whispered again, meeting Alek's sad gaze.

"We can try." He said, looking at the group. "Can't we?"

The group didn't look optimistic but slowly nodded in agreement.

"The thing is..." Velyna started sadly, looking to Aarae who continued for her.

"Eris has been somewhat... absent lately." Aarae's expression was apologetic.

"But, I can read up on portals, to help you find a way home," Fyodor offered, trying to keep the conversation positive.

Mari looked at Fyodor. He wasn't very easy to look at, admittedly, but his smile was kind. He was the least human-looking out of all of them, and yet his mannerisms and reserved personality reminded her of a friend she used to have back in elementary school. A shy boy who sat alone playing with an action figure that he carried around everywhere with him. He shrank back when she approached him, but slowly he warmed up to her. She smiled at the memory and found it a bit easier to smile back at Fyodor.

"We'll help find you something to wear in the meantime," Velyna—who, after Mari got a closer look, resembled a white-tailed deer—glanced toward Aarae and then back to Mari, "you'll stick out like a selkie without her skin wearing that outfit."

Mari looked down at her oversized t-shirt that read "street cats" in glittery letters and featured a cartoon opossum, raccoon, and skunk. Her black leggings had ripped at the thigh at some point during her adventure, and her tennis shoes were coming untied.

"Not to mention your ears alone would give you away," Aarae added, not impolitely.

Of course, Mari had noticed Fyodor's excessively long, droopy ears instantly. And then there were Velyna's ears that were shorter than Fyodor's and yet still longer than a human's ears. They were rounded and constantly twitching, just like a horse or deer.

Until now, Mari hadn't looked very closely at Aarae or Alek's ears. She now noticed that both pairs came to triangular points at their ends. Aarae's stood straight up, about three inches in length, while Alek's were longer and angled backward, extending to the back of his head.

An odd feeling of embarrassment crept up on Mari as her fingers rolled over her short, blunt ears.

"I can wear my hair over them." She suggested.

"I don't think it would be enough to fool everyone forever," Alek sighed, "but I guess the hope is that you're not going to be here for very long, right? So, it could work for now."

Fyodor stood up. "No time to waste, I suppose. I'll get to the library."

Aarae and Velyna stood too, handing Hank back to Mari, "I'm sure we've got some clothes at our house that might work for you as well."

"I—" Mari spoke up as the three of them headed towards the door. "I just... Thank you. For your kindness."

They smiled sweetly back at her, a mixture of hesitance and pity in their eyes. Alek stood to get the door for them as they exited and Mari sank into the cushions, exhausted.

Fyodor stopped at the threshold, turning back to speak to Alek in a low voice, "Keep her hidden."

Alek nodded once, gently closing the wooden door and pulling down the bar to secure the door behind his friend. He turned back to Mari with a kind smile on his face.

"I bet you're ready to get some rest," Alek practically read her mind, "my room is right over here if you need anything." He stood and quietly exited, looking back over his shoulder once as if to see if she were really there.

When Mari was alone, she lay her head down and Hank came to snuggle closer. An unfamiliar mixture of emotions bubbled in her stomach and hung heavy in her heart. She didn't feel like crying, exactly, but a certain sadness tightened her throat and hitched in her chest.

"Oh, Hank," she whispered, pulling the little purring ball of gray fur close, "what have I done?"

———— ✦ ————

Alek sat in his room, unsure of what he should be doing in a situation like this. He found himself on the chair, staring at the wall, his thoughts racing. He knew he was still in shock; his leg was tapping and he could hear his heartbeat in his ears. Right now, in his living room, right beyond that thin wooden door, was a *human girl*. A human! In his house!

He'd never met a human before. They'd been banned for the majority of his life here in the city of Eristald, and for the years of his childhood in Thorne... well, humans didn't go to Thorne and, if they did, they didn't last long.

She was smaller than he imagined, and much less vivacious than he thought humans were. Alek had assumed most humans were strong, tall, and loud. He wasn't sure exactly why he had that vision in his mind, but either way, Mari was nothing like what he'd pictured. Yet, still, she practically oozed with humanity.

He cringed as he conjured the memory of the fear in her big brown eyes as she looked at him and his friends earlier. He might be from an Unseelie family, but he had always done his best to grow beyond the

Unseelie's narrow-minded beliefs that they were superior to everyone and that all creatures—especially humans—should fear them.

Instead, Alek made it a point to leave Thorne, his family, and the Unseelie lifestyle behind by moving to Eristald where Fae from all over the realm lived together in harmony.

Moving here was the best thing he'd ever done. It's where he learned how to be independent, where he met Velyna, Fyodor, and Aarae, and where the four of them founded their group. They called themselves The Adventurers and spent plenty of time searching the forests around Eristald with hopes that, one day, they'd continue to travel further and further until they were finally able to say they'd been all around the realm.

Perhaps though, if he had to pick between all of his new experiences while living on his own, he'd probably say that his favorite parts included all of the new food he'd gotten to try. One of many perks of having a diverse group of Fae all living in the same city, is also getting to experience a seemingly endless supply of interesting and new meals.

At this, his stomach growled. He placed his hand over his belly, suddenly worried that perhaps Mari was trying to rest and he was being too loud. He wasn't sure just how sensitive a human's hearing was, but he didn't want to be rude, regardless.

He stood from his chair, and tip-toed over to his bedroom door, slowly opening it and peeking out.

Mari was still there, stroking her cat absently, her eyes unfocused and far away. When the door creaked, her head whipped around, her gaze focusing on him.

"Alek?" She sounded tired.

He nervously pulled the door the rest of the way open and stepped into the room. He rubbed his neck with one hand, the other waving around as he tried to explain in a rush.

"I'm sorry, I just… well I'm hungry and it's about time for the last meal of the day and if you're hungry… that is if you aren't trying to rest… I thought maybe we could go get something to eat?" His voice hitched up at the end of his statement, making it sound more like a question.

"I thought it was dangerous for me out there." She noted, looking nervously towards the door.

"Well, you have to eat, do you not? I will keep you safe." He smiled as encouragingly as he could, "Come on, what do you say?"

He held his breath in anticipation of her answer, only letting it go when she smiled.

"I've never had Faerie food." She chuckled.

Alek smiled back, "You'll love it! I'll get you a cloak to wear over your clothes. And as long as you keep your hood up, you should be fine. I know the perfect place for your first meal in Eristald."

Mari left her sleeping cat on the cushion behind her and Alek found his smallest cloak, handing it to her. It was a dark blue velvet, trimmed with brown, a gift from his friends on his first birthday that they got to celebrate together. Even though the cloak was small on him, Mari was practically swimming in it. Nevertheless, it did hide most of the things that made her seem so human.

The walk into town was quiet at first; only the sound of their shoes on the gravel filled the space between them. Alek was trying to decide between discussing either the topic of human clothes or human food—both of which he was mildly curious about—when Mari broke the silence.

"Eristald? I heard you say it earlier. Is that where we are?"

Alek nodded, "Yes, the capital city of the Realm of Faerie. Fae Folk from all four kingdoms live here, together. Seelie, Unseelie, it doesn't matter in Eristald. All are welcome. Except," Alek added slowly, his face crumpling, "humans aren't exactly welcome, of course."

Mari's pace slowed at that. Alek rushed to reassure her, "But, please, don't worry. You're safe with me."

Alek knew he might not be the strongest, tallest, or even the most skilled of the Fae in Eristald, but he knew as he said the words that he would do whatever he could to keep Mari safe. After all, she needed him. He'd never turned away someone who needed him before, and he wouldn't start now.

Mari gasped as the lights from the city came into view. They sparkled and shone like diamonds against the black night sky. There were some colorful lights that she couldn't quite tell the source of and others that were just fire contained in a sconce.

There were no skyscrapers or concrete buildings like she would expect to see in human cities. Instead, this main street appeared to be something from a much older time, with a stone and dirt pathway and buildings that were made either of wood—mostly natural and misshapen pieces, but wood nonetheless—or stone or something akin to plaster that she couldn't quite make out. It felt as though she'd stepped right into a scene from a history book.

Something she wouldn't find in any history book, though, were the crowds of *creatures* making their way through the narrow streets and in and out of buildings. She took a step closer to Alek when she nearly bumped into an extremely tall alligator-skinned person. A shiver of fear ran through her body, threatening to freeze her legs in place. Thankfully, Alek appeared to be attentive enough to realize she needed a bit more support, and he held his arm out for her.

She gratefully linked her arm with his as they crossed a threshold into what Alek assured her was a restaurant of sorts, even if it smelled more like a gym full of sweaty bodybuilders.

They took a seat at a small wooden table in the corner and when a Fae waitress the size of a butterfly came to them, Alek ordered for himself and then for Mari. Mari pulled her hood a bit further over her head and pushed herself so close to the wall that it looked as though she were trying to melt into it. She hoped a few steady breaths would lessen the anxiety that came from being surrounded by seemingly dangerous Fae Folk with their sharp teeth, misshapen bodies, and oddly colored skin.

While they waited for their food, Mari looked over at Alek, focusing on his kind human-like smile and gentle black eyes. Her tension softened a bit, seeing him so calm.

"I bet you have a million questions," he kept his voice low, leaning over the table towards her.

It was true, she realized, tearing her eyes away from a lanky gray-skinned creature. It had been sloppily devouring its food that appeared to be covered in a substance much like blood. Mari told herself it was only strawberry syrup.

She cleared her throat as her stomach flipped, remembering the passage in Serena's book that said only certain varieties of Fae were friendly, "I think I just want to know what everyone is. Unless," she added quickly, "that's a rude question?"

For a moment Alek's brow furrowed. His eyes lit up when a second later the response came to him, "Ah, no, no, not rude at all. That makes complete sense! Well, to start, everyone here is considered Faerie Folk, or simply Fae will suffice. Of course, there are quite a few different races that make up the realm. There are two different sub-races of elf, and I am the Unseelie race." He looked around the room quickly, his head stopping once he'd spotted a thin, very human-looking girl. Her ears were pointed like Alek's but the tips looked like they had been dipped in golden paint. "She's a Seelie elf."

Mari nodded slowly, then inclined her head in the direction of the gray-skinned creature, "And him?"

"Goblin," Alek's face crumpled at the sight of the goblin's meal. "Sorry you had to see that. I didn't expect there would be any meat eaters here tonight—there usually aren't. Most Fae stick strictly to fruits and plants and the like."

"Why?"

"Nearly all Fae can take the form of any living thing they'd like and sometimes will choose to stay in the form of an animal for long periods. If we were to regularly hunt the animals of the realm, we would undoubtedly be accidentally eating our neighbors and family. Some Fae," his tone turned sour, "especially the Unseelie, don't really care about that."

"You said you're Unseelie, though." Mari pointed out.

Alek sighed, "Unfortunately. But, I don't live by their ways anymore. I haven't for a long time now."

Although logically she knew he could easily be lying to keep her from being afraid, Mari chose to believe him. Alek was easy to like and easy to trust. His eyes were kind and curious, his smile gentle and sincere.

"Your family," she wondered aloud, "did they choose to follow your path?"

Alek stared at her, deciding what to say. He settled on a simple, "No."

"You must miss them." She whispered.

Alek was spared from answering as their food arrived. Mari was shocked to see the tiny flying lady—whom Alek told her afterward was a pixie—effortlessly carrying two bowls that were easily five times her size.

The contents of the bowl looked to be variations of fruit like Alek had explained, but it was fruit unlike anything Mari had seen before. The colors alone were vibrant and shocking to the senses, and the smell was equally sweet and intoxicating.

Mari hesitantly took a bite of something that looked similar to a banana but was purple in color and much wetter in texture. Its uniquely sweet flavor filled her mouth, reminding her of honey. The flavor intensified as she continued to chew.

"What do you think?"

"Delicious!" She said, shocked at the truth of it.

"Aarae, or as we call her, Rae," Alek continued with his explanations, his eyes darting back to look at the waitress, "whom you met earlier, is a pixie also, though she chooses to remain full-sized."

"And is she Unseelie too?" The unfamiliar word felt even stranger on Mari's tongue than the blue sour fruit she'd just eaten.

"No," Alek drank the juice from the bottom of his bowl, "Rae and Velyna—Lyna, is what we call her—are Seelie. Lyna is a faun, by the way. And, Fyodor is also a goblin though if you ask me he is much more palatable than any other goblin I've met before."

"It will be important to know which are Seelie and Unseelie, right?" Mari wondered aloud, "I've heard both words and read a bit about them but I'm still unsure what they really mean."

"For you, yes, it makes a difference. Seelie will typically be more kind and accepting of humans while the Unseelie... not so much."

"But you're Unseelie, and you've been extremely kind to me."

"I'm..." Alek searched for the right word while poking at the fruit in his bowl, "Different. It's usually safe to assume a Fae's alignment by their race, but sometimes, like in my case, they choose to align themselves with the opposite side."

Mari had nearly finished her fruit and was beginning to feel a little dizzy. Was it the massive amount of sugar she just ingested or the exhaustion finally settling in? Suddenly she felt a bit sick.

Alek noticed the change in her demeanor right away. "Are you okay?"

"I think I'm about ready to sleep for the night," she admitted.

"I'll pay, and we can leave."

Mari watched as Alek took several polished stones out of his pocket and walked them up to the counter. He handed the cashier two black stones and a larger green one. In return, he received a small blue stone that he threw in his pocket.

As they slowly walked back to Alek's tiny forest home, Mari's head raced with more questions and ideas than she'd ever had at once. She'd taken in so much new information in such a short time; her head might actually burst if she asked even the simplest of questions. It would be impossible to remember it all. Though, if she woke up tomorrow and discovered this was all some very terrible dream, it wouldn't matter anyway.

"Alek," she said, snuggling into the pillows back at his home, "I think I'm going to need a journal or something. To start writing all of this down. I'll need proof that this actually happened," a yawn overtook her, "when I get home."

Alek smiled softly, heading for his bedroom. "We'll find you something. Sleep well."

BIZARRE BAZAAR

Mari startled awake the next morning, sending Hank—who had been peacefully sleeping on her chest—flying across the pillows.

Alek's front door had slammed open while Lyna, Rae, and Fyodor happily let themselves in.

"*Ilduy!* Good morning!" Lyna sang cheerily.

Mari managed to croak out a greeting as well, but couldn't seem to slow her panicked heart. "Alek's still sleeping I think."

"On it!" Fyodor ran into Alek's room. His departure was followed by a loud *thunk* that sounded like a large object being pushed to the floor. Mari chuckled picturing tiny Fyodor shoving a sleeping Alek out of bed.

Rae, who was carrying a large pile of what appeared to be clothing, sat down next to Mari. "You look to be about Lyna's size," she began, "but we brought plenty of options just in case!"

Mari looked at the pile and then back to Lyna and Rae who were both wearing variations of the same long, linen skirt complete with a white petticoat. Their matching white shirts were loose at the neck and sleeves but then were pulled closely to their chests by thicker leather vests—or were they a form of corset? Another look back at the clothes in the pile Rae had handed her confirmed Mari would be wearing much the same outfit.

Mari forced a smile onto her face, though she was already beginning to feel today's first dose of anxious sweat bead on her forehead.

"Thank you," she said, "but, where should I change?"

Alek's home was small. From the living space, she could only see the door to Alek's room and a small kitchen-like area. Surely they didn't expect her to strip down right here?

Alek emerged from his room then, Fyodor behind him. "You can use my room," he said, with a yawn.

With a nod, and another yawn of her own, Mari went to Alek's room and closed the door gently behind her.

This room was small too, and sparsely furnished. A wooden bed, with a lumpy mattress made from linen and filled with what Mari assumed to be hay or grass or some other natural material, sat against one wall. The blanket had been tossed to the floor beside it.

A wooden wardrobe was against the other wall and next to it sat a bookshelf, packed to the brim with books with titles written in a language Mari didn't know.

She laid out the clothes on the bed and stared at the unfamiliar cuts of the material. She wasn't typically the kind of person to wear long skirts and billowy shirts, but she'd especially never even touched a corset like this one; she wasn't even sure if this was considered a corset or something else. It looked more like a vest to her.

With a deep breath, Mari tugged on the skirt, which was linen dyed a pale, cheery yellow. The white shirt was a bit on the big side, and the sleeves only came down to about her elbows. Next, she put her arms through what she assumed were the appropriate holes in the leather vest. She breathed a sigh of relief when she saw that the vest had a button closure on the front instead of something like laces that she knew she'd get confused with.

There was no mirror to see how she looked, though she was thankful her skirt was long enough to hide her human tennis shoes because other than those, Mari was confident she would blend in well. She quickly ran her hands through her thin hair, remembering to leave it un-tucked from behind her ears to prevent anyone from noticing their lack of point on the end.

Slowly she made her entrance into the living room and Lyna clapped her hands together with a happy squeal.

"You look gorgeous!"

Rae, who was holding a loudly purring Hank, smiled brightly. "That's a good color on you!"

Only then did Fyodor and Alek look up from a piece of parchment they had been discussing.

Fyodor commented how Mari would blend in nicely but Alek's face seemed frozen in an expression of shock.

"You look beautiful." He said, quietly, then cleared his throat. "Fyodor here was just showing me an old map that he found showing the former locations of the portals."

Fyodor nodded, "I was thinking—well, hoping more like— that if the king missed the portal that you came through, perhaps he missed another portal somewhere along the way."

Mari made her way over to look at the brown paper on the table. It was curling at the ends, and bits of the corners seemed to have either been ripped away or were never there to begin with. The dark ink was thickly drawn on the page, showing an outline of the continent. The drawing wasn't detailed in any way except for little red dots scattered over the land.

"There are hundreds of them." Mari gasped in dismay. "How would we possibly be able to look for all of them?"

"We couldn't," Alek shook his head sadly, "that's what Fyodor and I were just discussing."

Fyodor sighed, "This was all I could find at the library, and I'm lucky that I did. Most references to portals were destroyed when the portals themselves were banned."

"Let's go to the bazaar," Lyna spoke up.

"Yeah," Rae added, finishing Lyna's thought, "the vendors travel to the human world all the time. Maybe we can get some information there."

Mari looked to Alek, waiting to see his reaction to the suggestion. He only shrugged and said, "Couldn't hurt. Let's go."

The five of them headed down the dirt path that led into Eristald. Lyna and Rae stood side by side, and Mari stayed near Alek while Fyodor brought up the rear.

Mari was excited to see the city in the daylight. Although the lack of magical fire that had lit the streets the night before made it seem a bit less foreign, the increased amount of unusual Fae prevented any possibility of Eristald being mistaken for a normal, human town.

Alek and the group stayed close to Mari, shielding her from view as much as they could. They expertly ushered her through the main street and into a few narrow alleyways, taking her deeper into the heart of the city.

Eventually, they emerged into a large open area, where the sounds of people haggling for goods filled the air. Some of the vendors of the bazaar had their wares laid out on tables made of wood or stone, but most just used dirty, old blankets to display their treasures.

A closer look at the supposed "treasures" and Mari was quickly disappointed. Most things were dirty or broken in one way or another. What was more, they were all easily recognizable items, which she didn't expect. Among the heaps of things for sale were a hairbrush, missing most of its bristles, a metal lunch box with a depiction of a rocket ship being piloted by a dog, and a child's doll.

Mari turned quietly to Alek, "Where did all of these human things come from?"

He drew his hand across the doll, brushing a hair out of her face, "When the portals were open, Fae of every kind traveled freely throughout the human world; every continent and country alike. It used to be that the bazaar was full of offerings and gifts from the humans."

He shook his head sadly, ushering her away from the stall, "When the portals closed, humans stopped telling stories of the Fae as fact and started telling them as mere folklore. Over time, they stopped believing in us and stopped leaving offerings. Now, the king still grants certain Fae passage to the human world, but they have to gather human's lost items now, or, in some cases, I'm sure they steal some of the things, too."

Mari silently wondered if the single socks being sold on one table were perhaps one of the matches to the countless pairs she'd lost over the years. Who was desperately looking for their set of keys that were currently being haggled over by a pair of gnomes? Did that bike wheel that an orc just purchased come from the garbage or did someone's bicycle just become a unicycle?

"You guys go on!" Rae called from behind them. She and Lyna were looking at a pile of old hair clips and hair ties that still had the previous owner's hair attached to them. By the looks on Rae and Lyna's faces though, you would think they'd just found a winning lottery ticket.

"We'll catch up later!" Lyna assured them.

Mari scanned the crowd for Fyodor and found him arguing over a ripped hoodie with a female who, with her soaked hair and clothes, appeared to have just emerged from the water.

The excitement in the air was electric. Raised voices, the hurried footsteps of others who didn't care if they bumped into you, and the smells that filled the air; it was a symphony for all of the senses.

As they walked, a table nestled in the shadow of a tree caught Mari's attention. The furry Fae male smiled with a mouth full of yellow teeth as she approached, but said nothing.

This table's items were in much better condition than others in the bazaar. Perhaps most shockingly, Mari found a tall wine glass, a glass angel figurine, and a colored light bulb, all of which somehow hadn't broken during the journey from the human world to this realm. Among the glass and other trinkets, Mari's eyes came across a leather-bound book, wrapped up with a piece of blue ribbon. She picked it up, surprised at how flimsy it was. She unwrapped the ribbon and opened the book.

"Alek," she gasped.

"What's wrong?" He appeared by her side in an instant.

"It's a journal," she smiled, thumbing through the pages. Most of them were blank, as the owner—whose name was Nina, according to the signature on the front—had only had the chance to fill in the first three pages before the journal had ended up here.

Alek asked the stall owner how much he wanted for it to which he replied, in a gravelly voice, "Five black."

"*Five black*?" Alek's voice shot up as he questioned the unreasonable price. He muttered in an annoyed sort of way, digging five polished black stones from his pocket and handing them over to the furry man who simply nodded in return.

Alek sighed, but smiled at Mari, "Now you can write down your adventures. But for that price, just make sure I sound good."

Mari smiled back, too happy to point out that she didn't have anything to write with. That could easily be sorted out later though. She also added a mental note to figure out a way to pay him back.

They continued along through the bazaar, looking at the items, and Mari held Nina's journal close to her chest. Most everyone was too enthralled by the objects to pay her any attention, which she was thankful for. After all, wearing the right clothes to fit in still didn't hide the tone of her pale skin or the fact that she didn't have ears poking out from underneath her hair.

One Fae stall owner—a tall, blue-skinned, and black-eyed female with shark-like teeth-had her gaze fixed on Mari as she walked past. Her cold eyes narrowed as she started to step out from behind her stall. Mari hid herself as much behind Alek as she could and they dove deeper into the crowd.

Alek grabbed her arm, sensing her fear, "Come on, let's get you off of the street for a while. I have something I want to show you."

Mari focused on keeping up with Alek's long-legged pace as he raced through the busy street. Finally, he stopped in front of a dark brick building with the word "ERISTALD THEATER" barely visible through flaking paint.

Without another word, the two of them walked in. With a shudder, Mari took in the disarray of the lobby. Cobwebs covered every inch of the ceiling and litter covered the floor. She was just about to ask Alek what they were doing here when he pushed open a creaky door and led her straight to a stage in the back of the building.

The theater area was taken care of a little bit better, but it still looked as though no one had been here in years. Mari's eyes took a moment to adjust to the dim light coming from sconces along the wall burning with blue flame.

The theater looked like it could've sat at least a hundred people if it were in better condition, though even in the dim light Mari could see she and Alek are the only ones there. Alek found the least ripped seats in the very front row and as they sat, the sconces flickered out cloaking them in complete darkness.

"Alek?" Mari's voice pitched higher with shock as she reached for his hand. He squeezed her hand reassuringly.

His warm breath tickled her ear as he leaned over, whispering, "The show is about to start."

On cue, the maroon patchwork curtains opened with a dense *swoosh*. Mari attempted in vain to shield herself from the cloud of dust that was released.

Lights, that Mari couldn't see the source of, flickered from above, casting a bluish glow on the stage as actors piled out. Music from a kind of string instrument filled the air, starting slowly, tentatively, then picking up pace.

Quickly, Mari began to realize they were not actors, but dancers. A tall, green-skinned female leaped into the air. She was caught by a stocky and very hairy male. The two spun around, smiles on their faces, as their movements continued to intertwine, their somewhat tattered costumes floating around them.

"The Unseelie God, Etaldin, seduced the Seelie Goddess, Eris," Alek narrated, leaning towards Mari as the female, Eris, stepped away from the male, Etaldin, and began to summon more dancers from offstage.

"One day, Eris created humans," Alek continued while Etaldin spun around throwing ribbons and confetti into the air, "while Etaldin created magic, trying to impress Eris and earn back her love and attention."

The music turned harsh and deep, booming throughout the room as Etaldin became enraged, stomping around, his sharp teeth bared.

"Eris adored the humans because they could grow, change, create art and music and love and laughter. Etaldin was jealous of her affection towards them."

Etaldin and Eris were dancing together now, gentle and sweet. Suddenly, Etaldin twirls Eris away and heads towards the humans. He shoots a few more strings of ribbon and handfuls of confetti at them and they fall to the ground.

"Did he kill them?" Mari gasped.

"No," Alek responded as the dancers rose, throwing confetti of their own, "he just imbued them with magic, thus creating Faeries."

"Oh," Mari's face crumpled, "then why does Eris look so sad?"

Eris fell to the ground, her face buried in her hands. The music fell quiet, playing sorrowfully with long, low tones.

"The magic changed the humans into creatures that could not create art or music without the help of magic. They could not grow old and die like humans were supposed to, and they no longer loved in the same way they did before. Etaldin took everything that Eris loved about the humans away, turning her beautiful creations into his twisted minions."

A few more human-looking dancers popped out onto the stage, their movements stiff and jolting, as if they were afraid. The music quickened and so did Alek's narration.

"The Goddess swept up the rest of the humans that hadn't been tainted by magic yet, and took them to another world—your world—where they could grow and thrive safely."

Eris and Etaldin danced individually on opposite sides of the stage. Eris's movements were rhythmic and beautiful like the waves of the ocean gently falling ashore. In contrast, Etaldin's movements were fast and strong, like a rock slide down a mountain.

"The angry God and mournful Goddess separated from each other, telling the Fae they would now have to choose sides, Seelie or Unseelie, and follow either Eris or Etaldin."

Half of the Fae dancers swept to one side of the stage and half to the other, their dances slowly matching either Etaldin's or Eris's to show their alliance. Poorly made cardboard stars dropped from the ceiling then, as Eris threw her hands up.

"Eris created *Indis*—starlight—as a gift to the Fae so that they could use the celestial energy to make magic, instead of using their own life energy. Many of us believe that she did this because, despite the creatures Etaldin had turned us into, we were still her creation and she still cared for us. If magic was the only way we could survive, and using too much of our life energy could kill us, then Eris wanted to give us a more sustainable source of energy."

After all Fae had chosen their sides, the dancers froze, and the curtain slowly fell, the music fading just as the light above went out.

The sconces on the wall lit and Mari jumped from her seat, clapping as hard as she could with a smile spreading across her mouth.

"They were amazing!" Mari turned to Alek, "How lucky are we that they just so happened to be performing this particular story tonight?"

"It had nothing to do with luck," Alek smiled, standing, "this is the only dance they ever do. They physically *can't* perform anything else."

Mari had stopped clapping. "What do you mean? Why not?"

"It has nothing to do with what they *want*." Alek explained, extending his arm for Mari to take as they made their way out of the theater, "You saw what happened when the Fae were born; their ability to create and make art without the help of magic was taken away."

"So, if the Fae can't create music and art, how did they develop that play in the first place?" Mari struggled to keep up.

"Just because we can't *create*, doesn't mean that we can't be *taught*." Alek sighed, "Humans weren't always banned from this world. When they came—or were brought here—" *against their will* was implied from his tone, "they would bring with them different art forms, like the theater, and teach us to be like them. They would help us build beautiful architecture, and paintings, and music and…" Alek stopped briefly, his eyes far away, "the thing about this theater is, they may have mastered this one show after the humans came and taught them, but there haven't been any new stories in years, since the humans stopped coming here."

"Why did the humans stop coming here?" Besides the dangers of the Unseelie, Mari was starting to see that the Realm of Faerie could be a beautiful place.

They had reached the front door again, and Alek lowered his voice, trying to keep their conversation between just the two of them.

"After a human killed our Seelie Queen, Elowyna, the Unseelie King, grieving, destroyed all of the portals and began to enforce the rule that no human is welcome in Faerie."

"Not all of the portals, apparently," Mari whispered back.

Alek smiled, putting his hand over Mari's where it rested in the crook of his elbow, "Thank the Goddess for that, hm?"

They were headed back to Alek's house, Mari noticed with relief. As wondrous as this afternoon had been, Mari's anxiety and worry were beginning to exhaust her and she couldn't imagine anything better than settling into her makeshift bed.

"What our much-feared King Iraforn," Alek's tone was sarcastic when he spoke of his monarch, "didn't realize is that after losing Elowyna and then banishing the humans, he'd also lost the Seelie's support. Now the Seelie and Unseelie are attempting to separate the two courts once again. We're all worried there will be a war among the kingdoms soon." Mari looked up at his grim expression as he opened his front door for her.

"Let's hope it doesn't come to that, though, for your sake; the realm is dangerous enough as it is for you, and a war starting while you were still here," he shook his head sadly, "would be deadly."

5

CAUTIOUS OPTIMISM

The Realm of Faerie was starting to feel more comfortable to Mari, despite the obvious fantastical elements. She'd spent nearly a whole week here so far, exploring the town with Alek and his friends, learning and taking in everything she could.

She was beginning to be able to recognize different races of Fae and was slowly memorizing which races were primarily Seelie and which were mostly Unseelie. It felt good to be able to focus her mind on learning and growing instead of the fear that still sat like a rock in the pit of her stomach. Still, she never stopped wishing that she had the book Serena had given her so she could learn more without having to ask her companions a million questions each day. At least she was writing everything down in her journal so that she wouldn't have to ask the same questions twice.

Today, Mari was getting ready to meet up with Lyna and Rae to walk around the market with them—an activity that was clearly a favorite pastime of theirs.

Surprisingly, on this cloudy afternoon, the bazaar was nearly empty. The stalls and their owners were still diligently posted in their places, but the crowd was much thinner than it had been the first time Mari was here.

Mari didn't mind though; she was finding it much easier to see what was for sale now that she wasn't dodging large Fae. She realized the increased space was a double-edged sword as she passed two palace guards. She tried to make herself smaller, less noticeable, by slouching and moving to the edge of the walking path as she pulled her hood up more.

She was toying with the polished rocks in her skirt pocket that Alek had kindly given her to buy something she liked. They'd quickly gone over the value of the different stones; the darker the stone the more value it held, with black onyx being the most valuable and the clear quartz being the least valuable. She was reciting the colors of the stones and their value in her mind when she saw what at first looked like a pile of mud on a table.

At a second glance, Mari saw that this was a lump of modeling clay. Mari had never been very crafty, but suddenly an idea popped into her head. Could she be able to fashion some ear tips from the clay to better blend in?

The shop owner wanted only two yellow stones for it, and Mari happily agreed, wrapping the clay in a few leaves before sticking it in her pocket.

She caught up with Lyna and Rae who had been filling their bags with random goods. They decided to grab some lunch on their way home—another mixture of grains and fruits and nuts and honey.

The buzz of voices in the distance was growing quickly. What at first seemed like the typical city noise was becoming more like a crowd of people yelling, and squealing excitedly. As they came into view of the crowd, Mari could see the Fae were all impatiently waiting for a turn to go up to the large stone water fountain in the middle of the square. Mari slowed her pace, clutching Lyna's arm.

"What's going on?" Mari asked nervously, never having seen such a large group of Fae so frenzied.

"The King's Ball." Lyna snorted, "Once every few months the king holds a ball—"

"— a poor attempt to bring harmony to the Realm," Rae added to Lyna's thought "The Seelie will never accept him."

"But still," Lyna nodded in agreement, "everyone in Eristald is dying to go. They are all rushing to get their names in before the drawing tomorrow," she shrugged, "too bad the guests are chosen at random."

Mari wondered what a Fae ball was like. Was the castle filled with valuable human items that the king claimed from the Fae that he sent to the human world? Were the people dressed extravagantly and served only the finest food?

"Hey," Mari grabbed Rae's small hand, looking between her two friends, "didn't Alek say the king has a portal that sends Fae to the human world to get items for the bazaar?"

"Yes, that's right," Lyna said hesitantly.

"How didn't I think of this sooner?" Mari exclaimed.

"Think of what?" Rae exchanged a worried glance with Lyna.

"Couldn't that same portal take me home?" Mari asked in a harsh whisper. She smiled her widest smile, trying to stop herself from becoming overly excited at the thought, "We have to get to that ball."

"Did you forget that the king would kill you on sight if he found you?" Lyna and Rae didn't seem convinced.

"What else am I supposed to do?" Mari watched as hopeful Fae threw their names, written on leaves and acorns and pieces of tree bark, into the water like throwing a penny into a wishing well. "This might be my only chance to get into that castle. I can either die hiding out here or I can die attempting to get to that portal and at least if I chose the latter, I can say I tried."

Lyna and Rae hesitated. Their eyes darted to the fountain and back to Mari. Rae began to flutter above the ground slightly, wringing her hands nervously in front of her.

"Mari, are you sure?"

Mari, in fact, was not sure. She found herself nodding anyway.

"Yes. I'd like to try."

Lyna leaned down to grab three leaves off of the ground. With a snap of her fingers, their names appeared on the leaves as if they'd been etched with fire.

"This doesn't mean we'll be chosen, you know."

Mari nodded again, unable to speak after witnessing magic for the first time. It was so quick, and simple. Alek had said that any magic the Fae used now that the stars were gone came directly from their life energy, and using too much could be dangerous or even fatal. Lyna however, seemed unfazed. Perhaps that was such a small amount of magic that it didn't affect her outwardly.

Rae smiled and sighed, watching Lyna take the leaves to the fountain.

"Well," she said as Lyna returned, "we'd better add dresses to our shopping list, just in case."

"Yeah, the dressmakers are about to be bombarded with orders. If we don't get ours now we'd be going in our nightgowns."

Mari's heart fluttered with cautious optimism, ignoring the massive amount of names that were going into the fountain. Mari didn't typically pray—a lifetime of losing people she loved had bittered her view of any possible deity—but she still took a moment to send up a silent wish to Eris, asking that their names would be some of the few chosen.

6

OPPOSING GOALS

"How do you know to move your fingers like that?"

Mari looked up from her work with the clay she'd bought the day before. Alek was studying her intently as she squeezed and pulled and smoothed the clay into something resembling Alek's ear tips. The others had told her that attempting to recreate an elf's ear would fit her the best, considering elves were the most human-looking of the Fae.

"Well, I just feel the way the clay moves and...move my fingers along with it?" Her explanation sounded more like a question. "I'm really not sure how to explain it." Mari stopped, pondering the clay in her hands. Fae might not be able to create things without magic, but they could learn if a human taught them first.

She handed him some clay. "Squish it."

Alek silently took the small ball of clay and pinched it between his thumb and forefinger. The sphere flattened into a small circle and Alek's mouth crumpled.

"Now what?"

"Well, just play with it. Squeeze it, pull it, see what shapes you can mold it into." She demonstrated the movements, and Alek quickly mimicked them. "There, you're getting it!"

The two of them smiled as Alek played with his portion of the clay and Mari continued sculpting her pieces into the best pointed ear-like shapes she could manage.

When she was satisfied with the shape, she held it up to her ears to make sure they were the proper size. It wasn't perfect, she knew, but it would be passable from a distance. The texture was a bit too smooth and shiny to look like skin, and the color was a bit darker than her skin tone. Without her makeup from back home, she wasn't sure she'd be able to get it to just the right shade but wondered if she might be able to find something in Alek's food storage that could help.

After rummaging through dried gourd pots filled with nothing but nuts and dried berries and other foraged foods, Mari was ready to give up and just hope the ears were good enough to keep her under the radar. The final container she opened was full to the brim with dried pieces of a pale mushroom. When the lid was removed, a few bits of the mushroom fell to the floor.

Mari took a step back, looking down a moment too late as she crushed the mushroom with her foot. She lifted her foot and found that the delicate mushroom had been crushed into a shimmering, golden powder. A smile crept onto her face as the idea came to her.

She took the lid off of a gourd and flipped it over, using its shallow and yet sturdy surface to hold a few of the mushroom pieces. Using one of the smaller acorn cups, Mari began to crush the pieces into a silky, fine powder.

Excitedly, Mari took her powder to the ear tips on the table, gently brushing it over the clay with her fingers until the dark tan clay, formerly the color of Lyna's beautiful doe-like fur, began to get closer to the golden ear tips of the Seelie elves she'd seen around town.

Mari looked up, still smiling and proud of herself. Her smile faltered for a moment upon seeing the intensity of the awe in Alek's eyes, as if she'd just performed life-saving surgery in front of him. He'd set his clay aside, which hadn't really taken shape of anything in particular, and was now staring at her, slack-jawed with a smile in his eyes as his head shook in wonder.

"You're amazing," Alek said softly.

She could feel herself start to blush, "I'd never done anything quite this crafty before," she admitted, holding the clay tip up to her ear and covering the seam where the clay met the skin with a few strands of her hair. "What do you think?"

"The most beautiful thing I've seen." The intensity in Alek's voice and gaze hadn't dissipated.

Mari looked away. She shrugged off the growing feeling of awkwardness with a smile, "You must be walking around with your eyes closed most of the time, then."

A knock on the door had Mari sighing with relief. She decided to ignore Alek's disappointed huff before he called his guests to come in.

Lyna, Rae, and Fyodor entered. Lyna carried three garment bags, her face alight with the biggest smile, her doe ears twitching with excitement.

"Mari!" Lyna rushed to her side, "We've been chosen!"

Rae handed Mari a thin roll of birch bark and straightened it out. Black script was scrawled on the inside. Although Mari couldn't read the Fae language, Rae explained that it stated Mari and Lyna were both invited to King Iraforn's ball, in three night's time.

"So soon?" Mari's heart leaped, her hand nervously reaching to pet Hank who had crawled onto her lap.

Alek had taken the invitation from her hand, "It's only addressed to two of you though."

"Yes," Lyna acknowledged, draping the garment bags over the table, "but each person is allowed to invite a guest. I'll be taking Rae, of course, and Mari can choose between you and Fyodor."

Fyodor quickly spoke up, "I'll pass. I have a lot of reading to do on breaking curses. Three days certainly isn't a lot of time... Mari," he turned to her, his long green ears flopping with the movement, "if I can't find anything for you, are you still going to try to find the portal?"

All four of them turned their eyes to her. Silence fell, awaiting her response. Hank's purr sounded more like a lawnmower, filling the quiet room. Mari took a breath.

"The way I've been thinking about it," she spoke slowly, "and, I *have* been thinking about this a lot over the past few days. I'm in more danger here, staying in hiding, hoping I won't be caught and killed, than I would be taking my chances with this supposed family curse back at home."

No one spoke right away. Mari smiled sadly. "you all have become really wonderful friends to me and, I don't even want to think about where I'd be if you hadn't been out in the forest that day. Please don't think I'm trying to leave you. I'm just trying to leave the dangers here."

The silence continued, so Mari reached for the garment bags in an attempt to change the subject, "I'm assuming these are our dresses?"

Lyna's excited smile began to return. "Yes! And, I must say, they are gorgeous."

Alek made his way across the room to where Fyodor stood. The girls were holding up their dresses, complimenting the colors and styles. The three of them had decided to help Mari try on her dress and they all rushed into his bedroom, shutting the door behind them.

"Thank you, for taking the lead on the research," Alek said to Fyodor.

Fyodor leaned against the wall, "of course. You know I love being in the library as it is."

Alek chuckled, nudging his friend gently with his elbow, "Is Yaslyn still working there?"

Fyodor's green skin darkened on his cheeks, "she is."

"And you still haven't talked to her, have you?"

"I talk to her every day!"

"Asking her to help you find books doesn't count."

Fyodor squirmed, "Alek, what am I supposed to say to her? She's the most beautiful goblin I've ever laid eyes on. And when she smiles, I can't breathe, let alone talk!"

Alek smiled slightly, then sighed, looking towards his bedroom door, "I understand."

Mari had consumed his days and dreams of her consumed his nights. Her deep brown eyes were full of endless curiosity when she took in his home, his city, his people. He wanted to tell and show her everything, just to see that light in her face when she learned a new thing, frantically scribbling about it in her notebook.

He could see the fear too, when they came a bit too close to some of the Unseelie in town. With that fear, though, came bravery and her passion to understand and learn about the things she was fearful of. His heart nearly burst with awe whenever he watched her interact with the world around her. Life through Mari's eyes must be extraordinary, he mused.

The thought of her leaving him in just a few short days pulled the air straight out of his chest. Maybe, once they found the portal, he could go through with her. Keep her safe in her world. His heart leaped at the idea. Yes, it was the perfect plan! He would tell her tonight after—

The bedroom door opened then, and she stepped into the room. Anything Alek had been thinking about before had been blown away, Mari filling every corner of his mind. He was sure his heart was about to break free of its cage at the sight of her.

Mari's dress fit perfectly, as far as Alek was concerned. He may not know much about dresses specifically, but anything that could make an already beautiful woman even more incredibly gorgeous had to be perfect itself.

It was floor length, and a shade of blue that Alek had only seen before in the setting night sky. A fairly see-through fabric, laid atop a solid, dark blue silk. The sleeves were cropped close to her shoulders while the neckline dipped below her collarbone in a generous V shape. It was pulled tight to her skin just below her bust with a band of fabric that then loosened, cascading like a waterfall to the floor.

Alek felt himself blush then, as his eyes desperately flowed across her frame, trying to memorize every detail.

"Well, guys?" Mari smiled shyly, the beauty of her features nearly stopping his heart altogether.

Alek couldn't breathe properly, let alone speak. What had he done to deserve the gift of Mari bestowed to him by the Goddess?

"Beautiful!" Fyodor clapped, "all of you!"

Alek had noticed then that both Lyna and Rae had also changed into their dresses, which were similarly made but were instead shades of pink and yellow, respectively.

He cleared his throat, "Yes, they fit quite well." He managed a smile.

The thought crossed his mind to perhaps prevent Mari from finding the portal in the castle at all; to keep her here a while longer. Alek knew, as soon as the thought flashed, that he could never do something so selfish. He'd just have to convince her to stay of her own free will. He had to.

7

LION'S DEN

Mari sunk into the pillows of Alek's home that had become so familiar in such a short time. She opened her journal, flipping gently past the few pages that the previous owner, Nina, had filled, and a few more that she had filled herself. At some point, she'd decided not to tear out the other woman's journal pages and instead chose to honor her by writing each entry in the form of a letter to Nina. Of course, Mari knew she'd never meet her, but it still felt like a form of human connection that she'd been missing.

Dear Nina, The last three days have passed so slowly, waiting for this ball. Waiting to go home. And Alek has been quite strange. He seems to be a constant source of energy, wanting to take me to all of his favorite restaurants, buying me odd little gifts from the bazaar at every chance he gets. It's not hard to see that he's starting to develop feelings for me, Nina. I just wish I knew how to break the crush without breaking his heart.

However, the longer I stay here, in his home, I know it will be harder to do. He's been so kind, and thoughtful; even if the motivation for his kindness is a misplaced infatuation. When he was explaining the Eris and Etaldin performance, he did tell me that Fae tend to feel love differently than humans do... does that mean that they can't feel anything deeply? Is that why, barely knowing me, he's seemed to have developed such a shallow and yet consuming feeling?

And sweet little Fyodor, who has been tirelessly researching in the library each day, is no closer to finding a way home for me. I'd help him in a heartbeat if I knew any of the languages that these books are written in. It seems that finding the portal in this castle might be the only chance I have. Sometimes the thought creeps in that perhaps I don't have to go home at all. But I quickly threw the romantic notion away; it's not realistic. I can't hide my humanity forever, and eventually, I'll be killed for sure. At least at home, I'm not being hunted for simply existing.

Well, I've got to start getting ready for the ball. I'll talk to you soon!

—Mari

———— ✦ ————

Mari felt as ready as she was going to feel. The only thing keeping her hands from shaking was clenching them into fists as she held up her dress from the ground. She focused on her breathing—in through her nose, out through her mouth— as their group headed out into the dark.

Tonight was a big night. The possibility that she could finally be going home was closer than ever before and yet, still impossibly far away.

This ball was their chance to get inside the castle but from there, they still had to find where this portal was located. Fyodor had done as much research on the castle as he could. Between reading, and talking to former guards and current merchants, he'd narrowed it down to just five possible rooms.

The four of them—Fyodor was staying behind, happy to be missing the action—were dressed in their best and headed into the heart of Eristald. Hank, who couldn't be left behind and would have to go through the portal with Mari, if they found it, was being cozily carried around in Lyna's satchel. He'd been given a harmless sleeping potion, to keep him calm and quiet.

Their plan—if you could even call it a plan—was to split up and check each room in pairs. Lyna would go with Rae to the two rooms on the uppermost floor. They suspected that there may be more guards higher up, and Rae's ability to shrink and fly around would be useful if Lyna could get no further.

The other three rooms were all on the ground floor and one they would have to walk directly past when entering the ballroom. If it wasn't there, Mari and Alek were going to slip away and find the final two rooms.

If they were all unsuccessful, they would meet by the main entry and head back to Alek's home. If they found the portal, and Mari was able to slip through, only three of them would be meeting outside.

The silence was nearly tangible as they continued down the cobblestones. Everyone was probably just as nervous as she was. Had she even properly thanked them for the risk they'd all decided to take by helping her over the past couple of weeks?

"Hey, guys," she cleared her throat and smiled at her new friends, "I don't know if I've said thank you enough, for doing this. I understand what you're all risking."

"No thanks necessary," Alek smiled at her, adjusting a maroon suspender that had slipped a bit down his shoulder.

"If the tables were turned," Lyna said, "you'd do the same for us."

"Of course," Rae agreed, supporting the cat-filled sack at her hip, "besides, this is the most fun I've had in years!"

They all chuckled at that. Mari's laugh ended in a sigh, and she did her best to brighten her tone, attempting to lighten the tense mood, "I know we have a goal here, but, we *are* going to get to dance a little, right? Have a little fun?"

"We'd better!" Lyna said, and the others nodded in agreement.

Mari no longer recognized any of the buildings they were walking past as she'd never been this far into Eristald. They rounded a corner, and Mari couldn't help but gasp at the sight in front of her.

A castle, covered in warm, yellow, magic-fire light, was carefully built into the city. It towered over the houses and shops that it surrounded, and yet, it seemed perfectly in place. Made of pure white stone, with several spires and turrets shooting out from the main portion of the building, the castle only seemed to grow in size as they approached.

"Beautiful, isn't it?" Rae's eyes sparkled.

"It's excessive." Alek was less awed.

Mari swallowed hard, a new wave of despair falling over her. It *was* huge. Gargantuan, in fact. It must take hours to walk its halls, and who knew how much time they would have to search?

The crowds of guests were thickening around them as everyone inched closer to the gate in the castle's outer wall. Before they were surrounded and in earshot of others, Mari stopped her friends, turning them all to face her.

"I've been trying to stay positive," she admitted, "but just now I've got this feeling that maybe we're setting out to do the impossible."

"How do you feel when you think about going home?" Lyna asked.

Mari blinked, "relieved and excited at the same time, I guess. Warm. Safe. Happy..."

"Hold on to that feeling, Mari." Rae smiled, putting her fragile hand on Mari's shoulder, "Anytime the fear threatens to take it away, hold on with all you've got."

Rae and Lyna linked arms and paraded forward into the crowd. Alek held his arm out for her.

"And if you can't hang on to that feeling, just hang on to me." He smiled down at her.

Mari smiled back and linked her arm in his, thankful for his warmth. They followed behind Lyna and Rae, merging in with the flow of the guests that steadily crossed the threshold into the palace. She paused at the entryway, a rabbit entering the lion's den, and took the final few steps forward.

They entered into a tall and massive hallway, lit by dim firelight for the first couple hundred feet then falling ever darker down the way. The guests were being ushered through a pair of tall doors on the right where the sound of string instruments spilled into the hall.

An arched doorway to the left, shortly before they were to turn into the ballroom, was the first room to check on their list of guesses of where the portal might be held. Without even looking, Mari was confident that the portal would not be there. Surely, they would not keep something so precious out in the open and so close to the entrance.

Alek left her side for just a moment to peer inside the room then turned back to her, shaking his head slightly. Mari nodded to show she understood and continued with the crowd into the ballroom.

Many guests flowed directly to the dance floor in the center of the room and began to twirl to the slow tempo of the music. Those with wings took to the sky, twirling and floating above. Others lined the far wall that was covered in windows and overlooked a fine garden illuminated by silver moonlight. Crystal chandeliers lit with magical firelight hung from the ceiling and gold embroidered tapestries were draped across the walls. To their left, a grand double staircase rose to a landing too tall to see onto, save for the shadows that danced along the walls cast by the guests that had made their way up there.

Between the stairs, refreshments and little cakes were waiting on a long table tended by elves all wearing the same black uniform complete with top hats and tight-fitting vests lined with golden buttons.

Mari and Alek had come to stand beside Rae and Lyna who had entered the ballroom just moments before.

"It's everything I ever dreamed it would be in here." Lyna's eyes darted around the room.

"If not a bit too crowded," Alek grumbled.

"Oh stop being such a negative nixie and do something kind instead like get us all drinks." Rae teasingly slapped Alek's shoulder.

He bowed dramatically, a hint of a smile on his lips, "Anything for you."

Alek was pouring three glasses of a suspicious purple liquid when the music quieted and the room became still. The guests cleared their way from the dance floor, crowding themselves along the walls of the room, and opened the path to the stairs. Mari stayed close to Lyna and Rae, shuffling alongside them.

When every head in the room turned to look at the grand staircase, Mari turned as well, finding a young elvish male beginning his descent. He held a tall glass in a white-gloved hand. His long, white coat with gold, vine-like embroidery hung open, though several round military-style buttons lined each side of the garment. A ruffled golden shirt peaked out from underneath the jacket and his tight black pants were covered from the knee down by tall black riding boots.

As he descended further, Mari saw his wavy black hair was neatly cut and styled, his skin a shade of tan that reminded her of coffee with a healthy amount of cream. These dark features contrasted greatly with his light outfit, drawing every eye in the room to him.

Certainly, he was a sight to behold; the most stunning Fae in the room. However, stunning as he may be, Mari could see by the all too confident tilt of his chin and smirk on his lips—not to mention the narrowed catlike eyes that looked down his nose at all of those that he passed by—this male was not only used to the attention and adoration of his guests, but he expected and thrived off of it, too.

"Is he...?" Mari whispered to Lyna.

"Prince Cylan." She confirmed.

"Next in line for the throne," Rae added quickly, before dropping into a curtsy as the prince stalked by.

Mari had never before curtsied to anyone, and although the movement felt foreign, she did her best to copy Lyna and Rae, bending at the knee, then at the waist, keeping herself steady with a foot extended slightly behind her. She was staring at the floor, unsure when to look up, when the prince's boots came into view and stopped, directly in front of her.

Her heart beat in her ears, her breathing kicked into high gear. She dared a glance upward, tilting her head just enough to peek through her lashes. Her eyes met the prince's and she froze.

"Rise," he told her in a silky, deep voice.

As if his words overcame her senses, forcing her muscles to move, Mari stood. At her full height, the top of her head came just to his chin, and she had to raise her face upward to see him.

Words evaded her and blood rushed to her cheeks as his eyes appraised her every inch. She fought the urge to break eye contact and instead focused on her breathing. This man... Fae... Elf... this *Unseelie Prince*, could be the end of it all. Their plans, their hopes of ever getting her back home. If he looked too closely, it could all be over.

"I would like you to be my first dance of the night." He finally tells her.

Mari felt her eyes bulge with shock. To be that close to him for the full length of a dance—not to mention she didn't know *how* to formally dance—would heighten the possibility of him realizing she was human. How could she back away now? The whole room was looking at her.

She risked a glance over to Lyna and Rae who both nodded vigorously in approval. Gathering any bravery that she might have left, Mari took a deep breath and met Prince Cylan's gaze once again.

"I'd be honored."

He held out a hand for her. She took it gently, noticing a large black ring on his finger. At the top of the ring was a carved gold symbol. Half of the sun, with straight lines jutting out to the left to resemble its rays, formed part of the symbol while the other half of the sun's curve was completed by a waning crescent moon. Together the sun and moon created a perfect circle.

She didn't stop staring at the ring as she let him lead her to the middle of the room. Their feet hit the center of the dance floor and the music started back up at a quicker pace.

Mari worried that she might be holding his hand too tightly, and surely she was about to leave creases in his perfect jacket where she was grabbing his shoulder with her other hand. To her slight relief, he didn't seem to notice.

Prince Cylan guided her around in circles, swirling with ease around the room. The scent of him filled her lungs, reminiscent of pine tar and something smoky yet sweet, like incense. By the time others began to fill the dance floor around them, Mari was beginning to feel a bit sick to her stomach. She took a breath and focused on Cylan's face instead, which helped a bit, even if his probing eyes made her heart flutter.

"I have not seen you before," he mused; his eyes—the same color as his golden embroidery—sparkled devilishly.

"This is my first time." Mari was grateful that her voice didn't sound as shaky as she felt.

"First time at the ball? First time dancing with royalty? Or perhaps this is your first time in public at all, judging by how incredibly terrified and unprepared you are."

Mari swallowed hard. His observation wasn't wrong, exactly, but his tone implied he was more annoyed than sympathetic.

"Yes." She simply replied.

He sighed impatiently, rolling his enchanting eyes, "And your name?"

"Marianne— um, Mari, preferably."

His eyes narrowed and his long, pointed ears perked up. He was scanning her face and looking over towards the side of her profile. She could feel the prosthetic ears were still attached but she also knew they wouldn't look very realistic this close up. Mari scrambled her mind for something to say to distract him.

"This is all very wonderful. The castle, I mean. I've never seen anything like it."

"Of course you haven't."

His arrogance and impolite manner of addressing her was beginning to stir up an annoyance in Mari that was almost stronger than her fear. She scoffed quietly, looking away from him for a heartbeat to notice Lyna and Rae slipping out into the hallway to execute their part of the plan. Had Alek taken his chance to slip away as well? She couldn't find his white hair and maroon outfit in the crowd.

The music began to slow and finally melted into another song. They stop dancing, and the prince releases her waist, but not her hand.

"Thank you for the dance, your highness," Mari attempts to step away but his grip is like a vice, "but I really must find my friends."

"Come to the garden with me." It wasn't a suggestion.

Mari nervously scanned the crowd once more for any sign of Alek as Cylan led her through the tall glass doors and out into the chilled night air.

They were alone. The only light in the garden came from the full moon above. The greenery was all perfectly pruned and shaped, while many flowers still bloomed when they should be wilted with the cold. Cylan kept her hand in his until they reached the center of the garden where a gently flowing fountain sat. They were far enough away from the ball now that the music was but a muffled blur, hardly indiscernible over the sound of the trickling water.

Cylan released her hand suddenly, spinning around to face her. His eyelids hung heavy—with annoyance or boredom, Mari couldn't tell.

"Can't decide if I should be offended that you thought this ruse would pass," he reached out toward her head. Mari flinched as he broke off one of her prosthetic ears, "or impressed that you'd be so brave to come here and dance with an Unseelie Prince. Or maybe," he smirked, returning the ear piece to its place where it hung, limply, "you're just stupid."

Indignation stirred in her chest at the insult but the panic of being discovered bubbled up with more intensity. Although she wanted to chide him for being so rude, all that Mari could manage were three words, her quiet voice barely escaping her lips.

"What happens now?"

"That depends." He crossed his arms, "why are you here?"

"It was an accident," she explained quickly, "I'm only trying to get home. If you could just take me to the castle portal, I could be gone tonight and you'd never have to worry about—"

He looked amused as he spoke over her frantic pleas. "Only one Faerie knew how to open a portal to the human world, and that was my mother, Queen Elowyna. Her portals have all been destroyed now, of course. Sadly for you, she *did* tell *one* other person before her passing."

Mari blinked, "Don't you mean, 'luckily'?"

"No," he smiled cruelly, "because the person she told was my father. But good luck getting him to open a portal for you; he'd kill you the second he saw you."

Mari only blinked again, unsure how to respond. She knew the chances of their plan succeeding tonight were slim, but Prince Cylan's words only further validated just how much of a long shot this attempt had been. Mari tried to swallow the anxiety that was growing more intense by the second, and failed, her lip quivering instead.

"Are you going to tell my secret?"

He paused, thinking with that smirk still plastered on his face. He held all the power here, and he knew it.

"I don't know yet." he said finally, chuckling lightly, "at least, not tonight, anyway." He turned to walk back toward the castle, calling over his shoulder, "Enjoy the party, little human, while you can."

———— ✦ ————

Alek downed the last of the drink and tossed the cup aside. His stomach churned nervously; not being able to find Mari in the crowd stirred up feelings of anxiety he didn't know if he'd ever felt. Had she gone to search the rooms without him? Surely not. His heart dropped at the thought of her jumping through a portal without saying goodbye.

He saw the prince, talking with some of his friends, and scowled at the male. After he'd demanded a dance with Mari, what had he done with her? The dance floor was too full to track their moves the whole time, and at some point, Alek had lost sight of them altogether. Worry was quickly overwhelmed by anger towards the arrogant prince. Alek found himself moving towards the royal ass to inquire about Mari when a flash of blue by the window caught his eye.

The relief he felt when Mari came through the garden doors was brief. He quickly saw the tears building in her eyes and the misshapen clay ear that hung at an unnatural angle. Without care for the other partygoers, Alek shoved through the crowd to be by Mari's side.

"What did he do to you?" Alek's hands gripped her shoulders, then cupped her cheeks, searching for any sign of injury. The rage was burning white hot behind his chest.

She gently pulled her chin away from his hands, "nothing," she sniffled, "not really. He danced with me, easily saw through my disguise." She scoffed, "I can't believe I thought we would get away with this."

"He knew you weren't Fae?" Alek's whisper was harsh as he struggled to hide his shock. "And you're still alive?"

"Yeah." She cleared her throat, "but when I asked him if he was going to tell anyone he said he hadn't decided yet."

Alek felt helpless. He could see she was distraught and wanted to put his arms around her, hold her close, though he suspected she wouldn't find comfort in the gesture. From what he'd learned about her so far, Mari seemed to be the kind of person to handle herself well without intervention. Even now she was furiously drying her tears and taking deep, calming breaths.

A moment later her crying had stopped, and her breathing returned to normal. She looked up at him, her eyes rimmed with red.

"What can I do?" His hand reached out to touch her face, but he hesitated, pulling back instead.

"I have to get out of here."

"But, the portal?"

She shook her head, grabbing his hand and tugging him along the perimeter of the room towards the exit.

"We'll find another way."

8

BETRAYAL

"**I** don't care if he's a prince, I'll kill him if he harms you."

Mari gritted her teeth, holding back the annoyance that she felt in response to Alek's overly intense bravado. Apparently, Fae males and human males were not so different when it came to certain aspects of their demeanor. And, here Mari had assumed elves would be demure and elegant creatures; she scoffed at the thought.

Mari rolled her eyes, "he didn't seem to want to harm me, at least not in that moment. Maybe he could help me."

He snorted. "Help you? The Unseelie help no one but themselves."

"It feels pointless to remind you that you are, in fact, Unseelie, and you've done nothing but help me since the moment you saw me. Fyodor too."

Alek only grumbled in response.

"All I'm saying," she continued, "you can't judge an entire group of people by a bad few."

"In this case," his tone was harsh, "you can."

A knock on his front door made Mari jump. Fyodor, Lyna, and Rae typically let themselves in.

"Expecting anyone?" She asks.

Alek shook his head, his expression thoughtful. Wordlessly, he motioned for Mari to get out of sight and hide in his bedroom. She unquestioningly did as she was told, leaving the door open only a crack to hear what was being said.

The interaction was short. Alek answered the door with a polite, "*Ilduy.*"

The sound of paper being shuffled around came before the visitor spoke, "A letter for you."

"Many thanks, *Ilmore!*" Alek replied, closing the door and breathing a sigh. "All clear!"

Mari met him back in the living room. He extended the folded parchment out to her, a hard expression on his face. "It's for you."

"Me?" Mari's eyebrows shot upward as she took the letter.

Alek was correct, her name was written in thick black ink across the top of the page. Her curiosity piqued, she broke the golden wax seal and read the contents. She wasn't surprised to find it was written in her language.

"It's Prince Cylan." She gulped, knowing if she looked up at Alek his face would surely be a mixture of annoyance and anger. "He wants me at the castle today... to spend an afternoon with him?" She risked a glance at Alek, who shocked her by only looking as confused as she felt, "but why?"

"Your guess is as good as mine." He crossed his arms and sighed. "Better to stay on his good side and do as he asks, now that he knows your secret. I don't like it, but I'm coming with you."

Under an hour later Mari was dressed in a simple orange linen skirt and white blouse belted with a brown leather under-bust corset. Her outfit still included her fake ears because while the prince might know she was human, everyone she'd inevitably pass by between Alek's home and the castle did not.

She and Alek made their way up to the castle gate and Mari flashed her invitation at the guards—two tall, broad-shouldered orcs in fitted metal armor—and they waved her in. Alek took a step forward. He collided with a guard's hand, stumbling backward.

"Only the she-elf was invited," the guard growled.

Alek bared his teeth in an animalistic gesture but only smoothed the lapels of his dark jacket, calling over to Mari, "I will be waiting right here for you. I won't move a muscle until you return."

Mari managed to smile sympathetically, nodding once at Alek before turning down the hall. Truthfully she was thankful to be free of him for a moment. He had become annoyingly overprotective and somewhat suffocating lately. So much so that she had been considering asking Lyna and Rae if she could stay with them instead until they were able to find a portal.

A tall, lizard-like Fae—Mari believed he would be called a salamander, someone from the southern Unseelie lands—led her to the end of the long hallway. They stepped through glass doors that led to a large open yard where a group of Fae were busy playing a sport-like game of some kind.

On the patio, under a cloth tent, sat a few Seelie elves in ornate dresses. They observed the others as they sipped dark liquid from tiny porcelain glasses. As Mari's feet tapped against the stone, one of the girls turned.

"We've saved you a seat!" She said, cheerily. "Do sit!"

Mari did as the lady suggested. Prince Cylan was out on the field, she noticed, as she took her seat. He looked at her, making eye contact for only a moment before continuing with his game.

She gently cleared her throat before addressing the delicate elf closest to her, "I came at the prince's request," she began, trying to stay as formal as she could to match the air of the ladies she sat with, "his letter sounded most urgent."

They chuckled quietly in unison, startling her. She maintained her composure enough to smile back at them.

"Everything is urgent with him." The elf with a bird-like face said.

"What Prince Cylan wants, Prince Cylan gets," the tallest of the elves perked up her chin, staring down her nose at Mari with disapproval.

"Well," Mari smoothed her plain skirt, feeling abundantly under-dressed compared to her companions, "what, exactly, was it that he wanted from me?"

"As if we know." Another female scoffed, inciting more laughs from the rest of the group.

Her company totaled four ladies, all impeccably dressed and radiating confidence. Their pale skin was like glass, reflecting light in all of the right places, and the golden tips of their ears sparkled like the jewels they adorned themselves in.

Their conversation consisted of very little that was interesting. Apparently, there was a party in some city called Thorne that one girl was excited about while the others weren't so sure. As they discussed their differences in opinion, Mari's eyes began to glaze with boredom. She blinked a few times, dragging her gaze across the yard to watch the males play a game that seemed to have one team using their feet, like soccer, and the other team using their hands, like basketball.

She couldn't quite understand the objective or the rules and sighed turning back to the ladies she sat with. She couldn't even understand everything they were saying either, their words muddling into a vapid mess. What Mari understood the least, was what she was even doing here.

Heat rose in her face, burning in her cheeks and the tips of her ears like they always did when she was angry. Perhaps she was a bit disappointed as well; a small part of her thought that maybe Prince Cylan had called her here to send her home. Clearly, that was not the case.

Mari decided she wasn't going to stick around any longer to find out what her real purpose was here.

"Well," she stood, speaking so loudly it startled the ladies, "I think it's time for me to go, it was... lovely, being with you today." She turned to leave.

She had made it only a few feet down the endless hallway before she heard the garden door slam open behind her.

"How dare you leave a prince's company before being dismissed?" Cylan's voice echoed in the hallway behind Mari, "especially after such a rare and undeserved invitation?"

She whirled on him, anger overpowering her already weak sense of propriety, "why are *you* angry right now?" She threw her hands in the air, gesturing towards the garden door, "I didn't know what to expect when

I came here but it certainly wasn't being ignored and sitting watching you fail at some poorly played game!"

Cylan's eyes widened, but his mouth stayed shut in a thin line, shocked into silence. She took her chance to turn and attempt to leave again, stopping only when he grabbed her arm.

"Most would find it a great privilege to be in the presence of the Crown Prince during his leisure." His eyes searched hers, "I do not understand how to please you."

Her mouth fell open when she met his gaze. She felt her face soften, the heat slowly dissipating from her cheeks. He wanted to please her? Maybe now was a good time to bring it up again.

Mari took a breath and whispered, holding his gaze, "I just want to go home. That would please me very much."

The prince snorted, reminding her of Alek earlier, "What is so important about your world?"

"Nothing," she half chuckled, "that's why I like it! It's simple, easy, safe..." *and there are no entitled, arrogant, annoying Fae Princes either,* she added internally.

At this he nearly smiled, his lips twitching at the corner before hardening into a frown. His eyes narrowed and he released her arm.

Cylan turned to head back towards the garden, calling over his shoulder with confidence, "You may leave."

"I was already leaving!" She yelled back at him, but he was through the doors and out of earshot.

✦

"You're sure you're okay? He really didn't want anything from you?" Alek asked for the third time since they had left the castle.

"Alek," Mari said, failing to keep the exasperation from her tone, "for the final time, I'm *fine*."

The moon had risen, its silver light obscured by rain clouds. Mari had spent all day trying to convince Alek to lay off the "I-hate-Prince-Cylan" topic and enjoy the final time they had left together.

Fyodor believed he was close to discovering the secrets of the portals and Mari was feeling more confident every day in her decision to go home. She was tired of Alek's well-meaning but overbearingly protective attitude; his home was beginning to feel more like a prison than the safe haven that it had felt like only two weeks ago.

Two whole weeks she'd explored the magical city of Eristald, made a few friends, avoided a few Unseelie that most certainly were *not* friends, attended a royal ball, and argued with a prince. She'd had more excitement here than she'd allowed herself over her whole life. Despite her belief in a family curse, she'd also been in more potential danger here than she'd been in her whole life.

From all of the exciting moments to the terrifying things and everything in between, she'd captured it all in her journal which was quickly becoming one of her most precious possessions.

Alek retreated to his bedroom, sulking, and Mari decided to take another opportunity to write a letter to her fictional friend, Nina.

Nina, It's been crazy, being here in Faerie. I've never regretted skipping over elementary school drawing lessons as much as

I do right now. There are so many exciting magical things I want to draw. The people alone are so intensely unique, that my stick figure portrayals of them could never do justice to their terrifying beauty.

Her mind wandered to a pair of golden eyes set in a sun-kissed face. Prince Cylan was certainly the most beautiful of them all, she could admit that. But his beauty was more than tainted by his attitude; it was overshadowed by it.

And that self-centered, rude, sorry excuse of a prince...

Her pencil dug into the paper a bit more intensely than she intended as she wrote, snapping her graphite. She sighed, standing to find the knife she'd been using to whittle the wood away and sharpen the tip.

Alek's door opened as she opened a cupboard, unsure where she'd last stored the knife.

"Alek," she called, "do you know where—"

She rose, her voice catching in her throat. Mari expected to be looking up toward her friend but he wasn't there. Exiting his doorway was a cloaked figure so tall that they had to duck down to fit through the door. The large Faerie threw their rain-soaked hood back, revealing dark red skin pulled tight into a sinister black-toothed smile.

Lightning flashed outside, quickly followed by a burst of thunder. Hank hissed from the pillow he had been napping on, burrowing further into the pile. Mari yelped as the Fae took another lazy step into the room. Her legs responded to the fear quicker than her brain did, and she found herself running towards the front door, throwing it open before she even knew she was moving.

She made it a few steps into the rain before realizing this intruder was not alone. Dread knotted tighter in her stomach as she skidded to a stop, falling to her backside.

"No!" She screamed. The green-scaled male in front of her lunged for her legs.

Her attempts to fight him off were quickly contained by his strong grip. The red-skinned male had come up behind her, carrying a bound and flailing Alek over his shoulder.

"Alek!" She called moments before her head was covered by a canvas bag. She felt them tying her arms and legs tightly with a rope, and soon she was fully immobilized.

"Mari!" Alek called back, his voice muffled by his hood. "Keep your hands off her!"

She'd been slung up over one of the male's shoulders, and they were walking. The crunch of their boots along with Mari and Alek's cries for help, were hidden by the roar of the storm.

"Where are you taking us?" Mari finally asked.

"Not far," his voice was nasally and bored, "we'll be there sooner if you would just stop thrashing."

Mari thrashed harder in response. Her head collided with her captor's. The pain that rattled through her skull was worth it to hear his hiss of pain in response.

Her throat was hoarse, and her clothes were soaked through to her skin. Water pooled in her hood. She tilted her head back, letting the puddle flow down her neck, giving her more room to breathe.

Light began to filter through the cloth, and the rain had stopped pelting her. Mari knew they had entered a building when she heard the sound of a door closing behind them and water dripping onto a solid floor.

They walked further into the building before their steps became more jostled. Were they climbing stairs? Mari lost track of the amount of stairs they'd climbed, doors they'd gone through and curves they'd gone around by the time they finally stopped.

Mari was set somewhat gently on a cold, hard floor. She gasped for precious breath as her hood was removed. She sat up, still bound, blinking furiously as her eyes adjusted to the light.

Alek had been placed to her right, his hood removed and ropes intact.

"Mari..." He took the sight of her in, making sure she was unharmed before taking in his surroundings. His black eyes widened as he looked beyond her.

"Fyodor?" He gasped.

Mari turned her head to see what Alek had seen. Three more tightly bound bodies sat next to them, fear and uncertainty on their faces.

"Lyna... Rae..." Mari whispered before whirling around to confront her captors, "What is going—" her voice broke, her eyes widening so far she thought she must look like a crazed goldfish.

In front of them rose a wide dais carpeted in purple velvet. Royal guards lined the length of the platform, and blue magic fire lit the room. Straight ahead, only a short thirty or so feet away, Price Cylan stood, solemn-faced at the side of a massive throne.

The broad-shouldered Fae that sat on the throne looked down at them, his tanned face grim. His black hair curled underneath a crown woven of precious metals, black and gold, that were curved perfectly to form the emblem of the crescent moon and sun that Mari had seen on Cylan's ring before.

He lifted his hand in the air and snapped his fingers only once.

As the sound echoed through the open room, their ropes fell from around their bodies and Mari fell forward, catching herself with her hands. Her friends all moved into a deep bow, their faces to the floor. She straightened up onto her knees, trembling but still defiant. He may be *their* king, but she held no such loyalty to this tyrant.

Still, she found it hard to look into the Unseelie King's black eyes and instead chose to glare at Cylan. It was already clear that they were all here tonight because he betrayed her secret. Now he got to stand proudly at his father's side and bask in the glory?

Mari gritted her teeth. Even if she were to die tonight, she'd find some way to make him pay for this.

9

DECISIONS

The king appraised her; she nearly felt his stare prickle over her skin. His robed chest swelled with his next breath as he turned to face her friends.

"It seems you all have been harboring this enemy for days now."

They did not move, but Mari could see them stiffen next to her.

Her stomach threatened to heave and her eyes threatened to spill over. Her body wanted to release the fear she felt for her friends in any way possible and yet she felt just as immobilized as she had when she was bound with the rope.

Mari found the will to take a deep, shaky breath. She prayed her voice would be steady, strong. She looked away from Cylan and dared to address the Unseelie King.

"I am not your enemy."

The king's eyes narrowed further and he rose from his seat, showing his full mountainous form.

"All humans are my enemies." His voice boomed throughout the space, vibrating in Mari's bones. "You are no exception."

He took a few paces forward, standing at the edge of the steps. With his hands clasped behind his back and his chest proudly raised in front of him, he spoke, almost sadly.

"Today would have been Queen Elowyna's celebration of birth. Each year I spend the day at her shrine, praying for her happiness in the Otherworld. Today, however," his tone darkened, "I am *here*. Staring down at an enemy surrounded by her traitorous companions." He paused, choosing his next words carefully.

When he spoke again, his words held a hint of annoyance, "In honor of my beloved queen, I will not be killing you today, human."

Mari's heart sank, and she couldn't stop the tears of relief that flowed freely from her eyes. She wanted to speak, to say thank you for his mercy, to say anything at all but her throat was tight.

"You will be sent back to your home world, never to return here again. For if you do, I will not be so merciful."

Mari bowed her head and closed her eyes tightly. This was it. Exactly what they'd all been searching for for days. She could finally go home. The bodies of her friends relaxed a bit beside her.

"Queen Elowyna held no such love for traitors." his voice boomed, "For these four, the only suitable punishment to ensure they will not make such a mistake again, is death."

Mari's eyes sprung open, her head shooting upwards to face the king. Her short-lived relief melted into terror. A heartbeat ago she was going home, safe and intact. Now, she may be going home, but her heart would be broken knowing what horrors she'd be leaving behind.

If she remained quiet, she could return home and try to forget all of this nightmare. If she chose to speak up, she could be risking it all, and would it even help? Her friends, the kind and brave Faeries that had given her so much with nothing expected in return. She couldn't let them give this, their lives, as well.

She cried out, "No! Please, spare them—take me instead!"

The prince stepped forward. "A proposal, father."

He approached the king, lifting his chin to speak into his father's ear too low for anyone else to hear. Whatever it was, it appeared to disappoint the king who frowned deeply. He nodded his head once before addressing the group again, his words holding every ounce of finality and authority possible.

"The girl will stay here as a ward of Prince Cylan. Her friends will be spared."

With no more to say, the king turned, exiting the room through large doors behind the throne. Two of the largest guards leave with him and the doors slam shut. The noise startled Mari so much that she fell back to the floor.

Alek was the first to rise, his eyes wild with emotion.

"Mari. You shouldn't have done that..."

Lyna spoke over him, "But, you were going to go home..."

"He was going to send you back." Rae's eyes were full of tears, and her wings trembled.

Fyodor only stood wide-eyed and silent.

"There was no way I was going to let him kill you for your kindness to me. And, I really didn't do anything." she narrowed her eyes at Prince Cylan's back as he turned to exit as well, "it was Prince Cylan who changed the king's mind."

She grabbed Alek and Lyna's hands in hers, sniffling away the tears, "Besides, maybe this is better this way. Maybe while I'm here," she lowered her voice, "I'll be able to find the portal and go home anyway." She smiled, "I'll be okay but, will you take care of my cat?" Her tears flowed freely at the thought of Hank, scared and alone at Alek's home.

Her friends nodded slowly. She rose as a pair of guards approached them.

"We'll take you to your room."

"We're seriously just going to let her go?" Alek's voice rose behind her. "This isn't right! Mari!"

Mari turned to see Alek lunge after her, but his friends each grabbed him to hold him back.

Fyodor finally spoke. "We've been given our lives, Alek. Don't throw yours away by doing something stupid."

Mari locked eyes with Alek's horrified gaze and forced a smile to her lips as the guards escorted her deeper into the castle.

The rain was a torrent, soaking Alek to the bone as he wandered away from the castle. His clothes nearly hung off of him, his shoes squelching in the puddles but he barely noticed. He wasn't sure where his feet were taking him, but he couldn't go back to his home where Mari's things were.

Alek had separated from his friends as they escaped the castle. He couldn't stand to be around them. The three of them went their separate ways, clearly feeling relieved while he felt like he might fall apart right there on the cobblestones.

They sickened him.

How could they feel relief when they'd just completely failed the only important mission they'd ever had? One could only imagine the horrible future that awaited Mari in that castle.

He had to save her.

"You look like a Fae that wants something."

A voice found his ears over the roar of the storm. He broke from his thoughts, realizing he was in a narrow alley deep within Eristald where he had never been before. He was too emotionally drained to display his shock and instead tried to do his best to dismiss the old crone hungrily staring at him.

"Don't we all?" He replied, turning to leave.

"Something you can't have." It wasn't a question.

He stopped and looked at the crone then, her dark gray robes hung heavily on her thin frame.

"Your point is?"

"It is only He who can help you get what you want." The way she said *He* made him shiver. Alek knew she meant *He* as in, the Unseelie God, Etaldin. Clearly, adorned in her cult robes and armed with her predatory smile, this woman was an Etaldin acolyte.

Alek knew these Unseelie extremist groups existed, but had never run into them before. He also knew that it was best to stay clear of people like this; nothing good ever came from getting involved with Etaldin.

"I doubt it." Alek sighed but, despite his better judgment, he didn't turn to leave again. Instead when she ushered him further into the alley, he followed, his curiosity getting the better of him.

She led him into a crack in the side of a tall brick building. It was narrow at the top but wide enough to squeeze through at the bottom. A pale purple light came from inside and he felt compelled to follow it, like a moth to a flame. Crouching down, Alek was able to stay close behind the old goblin lady as she crawled through the hole.

As his eyes adjusted, he saw they were in a small room in the back of an abandoned store. The front door had been boarded and sealed shut, though the main window was broken letting in the rain. Cobwebs and broken furniture cluttered the room. Along the perimeter of the space were carefully placed balls of purple magic fire. In front of three of the four flames stood more gray hooded figures with their heads down. The old goblin lady took her place at the fourth flame leaving Alek alone in the center of the room.

They were all facing forward, creating a circle around him and the altar—adorned with dead flowers and a tall, curved vase—that sat a few steps in front of him. His sudden jolt of fear broke him from his grief and helped him see clearly that he shouldn't be here.

Before he could make his way back out from where he came in, the four cultists raised their arms and began to chant, creating an unbreakable circle of magic around them all.

"From the *Enamir* in the north, we call you." The follower behind the altar said.

"Through *Niha* in the east," the follower to Alek's right called, "we call you."

"Out of the *Rinah* in the south," the male behind Alek shouted, "we call you!"

"Over the *Wyna* in the west," the old goblin lady to his left spoke, "we call you."

All four began speaking in unison. The vase on the altar shook.

"Oh feared and powerful Etaldin, giver of power, creator of the Fae, hear our calls!"

The lid on the vase shot upward, smashing into pieces as it hit the ceiling. Alek flinched, covering his head to protect himself from the falling shards. Purple smoke rose from the vase, slowly swirling in the air. As it swirled, propelled by a force Alek couldn't see, the smoke formed a loose figure of a male.

"I have heard your call." A weak voice called from the smoke.

"Master, we have found a dark elf for your appraisal."

"Appraisal?" Alek shuttered, taking a step back, "No, no, I've got to go..."

"Make a deal with me, boy, son of my blood," the voice in the smoke —Etaldin— addressed Alek directly, "and you will have what—or should I say, *whom*—it is that you desire."

Every inch of his body was telling him to run, and yet, the thought of getting Mari back was enough to defy his instincts. Making a deal with the ancient Unseelie God, known for his ruthless and selfish behavior had its risks, sure. However, Alek liked to think that the greater the risk, the greater the reward.

"What kind of a deal?"

An ominous laugh filled the air, rattling Alek to his bones.

"As you can see, my physical body is no more. I am nothing but the spirit of the all-powerful God that I once was. Son, I need your help to get back into the physical realm. For this, I'll need three items, and I need you to gather them."

Curious as he was about *why* Etaldin wanted to get back into a physical form, Alek knew he'd better keep his questions to a minimum.

"I don't want to hurt anyone to get what you want…"

"I'm sure you can find a way to acquire what I need while maintaining a clear conscience. After all, you never turn down a soul in need, right?"

As Etaldin spoke the final word, the smoke began to dissipate, falling gently back into the vase. Alek looked around, confused.

"Etaldin was too weak to stay for long," the old crone explained, "but do not worry. We can tell you what you need if you're ready for the honor of such a task."

Before Alek could reply, the tallest figure spoke in a hoarse voice, "A mermaid's scale, from the western waters."

The voice behind him was steady and strong, "The dust from a pixie's wing, the closest thing to stardust we will have in our lifetime."

"A page, from an ancient Unseelie text, is the last thing you'll need. Bring the items back here and you'll be rewarded, indeed." As the hooded figure to his right spoke, the four Etaldin loyalists stepped aside, clearing the path out of the building. Alek wasted no time finding his way back through the hole in the store wall, and out into the alleyway.

The cold night rain seemed warmer than it had earlier, though his body still shook. Alek stood before the old Unseelie God—the creator of the Fair Folk—and lived to tell the tale. Not only that, he thought as he rounded the corner that would lead him to the path toward his home, but now he had a real chance to save Mari. He wouldn't let it pass him by.

10

ATTENDANT & ALLY

Mari rolled over in the large bed she'd collapsed on the night before. Shortly after the guards had escorted her to her room—which, to her surprise, was *actually* a room and not a prison cell as she'd half-expected—Mari had thrown herself onto the bed and sobbed until she finally passed out.

A crackling sound had Mari peeling her eyes open to see that someone had come in at some point in the night and built a fire in the hearth across the room. Although grateful for its warmth, and the kindness it displayed, she still shuttered at the thought of some unknown Fae entering her room as she slept.

She made her way to the edge of the bed, a glint of metal catching her eye. Mari turned to see a golden object lying on the untouched pillow next to where she slept. Not only had the person who had started the fire come into her room, they'd come right up to her, close enough to touch her if they wanted to.

Shaking off the budding terror she felt at the thought, she reached over to inspect the object. It was a necklace with a pendant the size of a large grape. The pendant was a golden sphere carved to resemble a tangle of branches that reminded her of the king's crown that he'd worn last night. A note lay next to the necklace that had only one word written on it:

~CYLAN

With a scoff, Mari threw the necklace onto the nightstand. Was Cylan truly delusional enough to think he could win her over with jewelry the very next morning after he'd practically imprisoned her? Her stomach flipped anxiously thinking of the confrontation that she knew would ensue as soon as she saw him again.

The cold stone floor sent shivers up Mari's spine as she made her way to warm herself by the fire. She sat in a high-backed, red velvet chair and moved it closer to the hearth. Now that she wasn't crying and exhausted, she had a chance to take in her surroundings.

The square room was large with tall ceilings and one wall that was all window, overlooking the garden below. The furniture was old and practical including a tall wardrobe, the four post bed with a nightstand on each side, as well as the chairs by the fire, a settee in front of the window wall, and a writing desk in the corner next to a large, full-length standing mirror.

A knock on the door startled Mari. She stood from her chair as the tall door opened. A small, pink Fae walked in, her head down in a respectful bow.

"Ma'am," the cherry blossom-skinned female curtsied before lifting her head, "I'm Maelin, your personal attendant."

Mari blinked at the small female, unsure how to address her. She opted for a humble approach.

"I appreciate it, but I'm not sure what I'd need an attendant for. Aren't I... well, a prisoner here?"

Maelin's eyes widened, "oh goodness no. No, Prince Cylan said you were to be treated as well as any member of the royal family while you were with us."

Mari could feel her face crumple in confusion. Surely after last night's events, there was no mistaking that she was here as anything other than an enemy of the king.

"Ma'am," Maelin shuffled over to the wardrobe, throwing open the doors, "I'd be happy to assist you with dressing for the day. Perhaps you'd like to take a tour of your new home, or enjoy a walk in the garden."

Her confusion only worsened as Maelin spoke. Mari took a deep breath and walked over to her new attendant.

"Maelin, first, please just call me Mari." She smiled as sweetly as she could, though Maelin looked distressed, "and, I was hoping to speak with Prince Cylan today."

Maelin's breathing quickened, distress slowly morphing into panic. Her violet eyes darted around as if looking for a response in the room. Mari felt immediate sympathy for this fragile girl and went to sit back on the edge of the bed to give her space.

"Surely he didn't intend to hold me as his *ward*," she used the word loosely, "and never see me?"

"I do not assume to know what the prince's intentions are, ma'am," Maelin spoke, busying her shaking hands by pulling large amounts of clothing from the wardrobe.

Mari sighed, dropping the subject for now. Judging by the multiple layers of heavy fabric Maelin was preparing for her, Mari had another issue on her hands.

Maelin had led Mari around several of the castle's halls and corridors, cheerfully explaining the history behind every knickknack, painting, and decoration they came across. Of course, everything was either created by some poor captured human or stolen from a clueless one, and Mari was tired of the tour.

Maelin stopped in front of a giant tapestry, half green and half purple, with two figures battling in the middle. At the top, embroidered in gold, was the symbol Mari had seen on the prince's ring and the king's crown.

"What is that symbol?"

"The royal crest," Maelin explained, "this tapestry is one of the castle favorites," she continued, "the never-ending battle between Etaldin and Eris." Her eyes shone with wonder as she studied the design. "Eris, the green Goddess, bringer of starlight and keeper of humanity, is known for..."

Mari began to back away slowly. Maelin had been too attentive to stray away from all morning, and now that Mari saw an opportunity, she wasn't passing it up. Though she was having trouble moving in her heavy dress that was bustled in such a way as to make her backside seem impossibly large, Mari managed to step into a small corridor without Maelin noticing.

The corridor was short and consisted of only a handful of steps that led up to another level of the castle. Mari didn't know how long she'd have before Maelin caught up, but she was hoping she'd be lucky enough to find the castle portal quickly. She was nearly to the top and proud of herself for her successful escape when her feet became tangled in her obnoxious skirts and she fell out of the stairway and into the hall.

She sighed, lifting herself onto her knees as a pair of boots came to a stop in front of her. Hands reached down to steady her as she scrambled to her feet.

"You're not wearing your necklace." Cylan purred, releasing her.

"I'm not much for jewelry," she scowled and tossed her skirt with her hands, "or these horrible dresses. The Victorian Era ended over a century ago in my world."

Cylan looked down his nose at her, "What would you prefer?"

"Well, pants like yours, for starters."

A moment of confusion furrowed Cylan's brow, his nose scrunching as his eyes narrowed.

"I'll see to it that you have the clothes that you wish for." He spun on his heel and called over his shoulder, "You might as well stop sneaking around the castle; you won't be finding the portal anytime soon."

"Wait!" Mari called, her cheeks brightening with her anger as he turned the corner, "Cylan!"

The rage had spread its heat to Mari's ears by the time Maelin's head poked out of the corridor.

"Ma'am!" Maelin's purple eyes widened, "you gave me a fright when I turned to find you weren't still behind me!"

Mari sighed, the cold sting of failure washing over her. Not only had she only lasted a few minutes away from Maelin, she'd had Cylan in her grasp and all she'd managed to achieve was getting pants put in her wardrobe.

"I'm sorry."

Maelin gathered herself, offering Mari a polite smile. "Don't look so sad, ma'am. Perhaps a bit of fresh air would brighten your spirits?

The walk to the garden felt longer than Mari would have expected. How deep in the castle were they? It seemed that its hallways and rooms went on endlessly. Even if she did manage to escape from Maelin's kind but overly attentive gaze, would she ever be able to find the portal?

Maybe it was time to think up a new strategy. Maybe if Mari spent some time trying to befriend Maelin instead of escaping her, perhaps the little Fae could take her directly to the portal. After all, there wasn't an inch of this monstrous castle that Maelin didn't seem to know some obscure fact about.

The warm afternoon air filled Mari's lungs as they exited the stuffy hulk of a castle. While they strolled through the perfectly pruned bushes under the shade of tall trees, Maelin was quiet for the first time that day. Mari took her chance to start a conversation.

"Maelin, I wanted to thank you for showing me around today," she began, "despite the whole being-captured-by-the-king thing, everyone has been kind to me, for the most part."

Maelin smiled softly, "It is an honor to be the attendant to the first human to step foot in the Realm of Faerie for quite some time. My family has always befriended humans at their inn north of Eristald. I suppose you could say kindness to humans is in my blood."

"Your family owns an inn?"

"Oh yes," she smiled fondly as she thought about her home, "when I was little, traveling humans used to visit The Good Inn quite often. My parents found it to be a privilege to care for them while they provided knowledge and beauty to the realm. When King Iraforn banished all humans," her smile fell, "business at the inn dwindled and when I was old enough to find work, I came to Eristald."

"You must miss your family," Mari remembered saying something similar to Alek. It seemed so many of the Fae had been displaced by the mess King Iraforn had been making in the realm.

"I do."

They walked in silence for a moment, coming to the fountain that Mari recognized from the night Cylan had discovered her secret. They sat on the stone edge and Mari dipped her fingers in the water.

"I miss my family too. I lost them all a long time ago."

Mari looked up when Maelin grabbed her hand, squeezing it lightly.

"They are not lost, ma'am. Their souls are simply living in *Inohryil*. Some call it the Otherworld; the Final Realm. They are waiting for you under Eris' watchful eye. You will see them again."

Mari's eyes began to sting with tears. Although she wasn't sure that human souls from her world would follow the same rules as the souls of the departed here in Faerie, she still took Maelin's words for what they were; kindness and comfort. She squeezed Maelin's hand back, offering her a smile. Maybe making friends with Maelin wasn't a bad idea after all.

"So," Mari sniffed, wiping away her tears, "you seem to know a lot about the realm and its history. What about its present? I heard from my friends there were some... issues since the queen passed."

"Yes," Maelin sighed, "when our queen—may she live among the stars of the *Inohryil*—was taken from us, many of my fellow Seelie began to distrust the Unseelie King. Seelie and Unseelie alike began returning to their homelands, and the kingdoms in turn closed their borders. King Iraforn has been attempting to reunite the realm. I do not think it's been going in his favor."

"What has he done?" Mari wondered. She knew nothing about the intricate workings of a realm, but perhaps there was still something she could suggest to help.

"He's sent his children to govern each of the four kingdoms. Because the princes and princesses are half Seelie and half Unseelie, he thought they might win better favor with the kingdoms."

"Have they?"

"I'm not sure," Maelin said honestly, "but I don't think it's going as well as he'd hoped."

Mari stood and Maelin followed, making their way back through to the back of the garden. "So, Prince Cylan is not an only child?"

Maelin chuckled, "goodness, no. He's the second born of five children."

"Why didn't he go to a kingdom like his siblings?"

"I'm not sure but I'd guess that it's because the others have ties to the kingdoms," Maelin explained, "their magic manifests in elemental ways." Maelin saw Mari's confused expression and decided to elaborate,

"For example, young Thorsten went to Earth's Provence because he has an affinity for Earth magic."

"That makes sense. Cylan didn't have an affinity?"

"I do not know ma'am. If he does, it is something he's kept secret."

Mari decided to pause the questions for the moment. Any more and it might start to feel like an interrogation rather than a conversation. Nevertheless, the warmth she felt at the happiness she'd found speaking with Maelin was satiating enough.

"Perhaps you can ask him at dinner tonight."

Mari stopped walking. "Dinner? With Cylan?"

"He has told the staff that he will be dining with you as long as you stay here." Maelin's face crumpled, "surely you're not upset? You've been asking to speak with him all day."

"No, no," Mari picked up her pace, "I'm not upset, just surprised."

Now that she had a bit more information about what was going on in the realm, maybe dinner with Cylan would be a good thing. She found herself looking forward to surprising him with her knowledge. Maybe if he could see that she wasn't going to just sit quietly here in this castle like a bird in a cage, he'd start recognizing her as an equal and take her seriously.

The moon rose softly in the night sky, sending a silver light in through the windows of Mari's room. Mari sat at her writing desk, furiously scribbling down everything she'd learned today in a letter to her fictional friend, Nina.

Nina, A lot has happened since my last letter. I was captured by the king—but don't worry! I'm alive and safe. Well, as safe as I can be here in the castle. Prince Cylan has requested dinner with me each night while I am here. I don't know what to expect, but if he's hoping to win my friendship or something he's in for a bit of disappointment. Still, maybe going into this with an open mind could be a better approach. He might be more willing to send me home if he can find something to like about me. Dare I say there might even be a likable trait of his own that I could uncover?

A knock on her bedroom door had her pausing her letter. Maelin entered with a tray of food and an apologetic smile.

"Good evening, ma'am. Unfortunately, Prince Cylan had to cancel tonight's dinner plans so I've brought you some food."

Mari could feel the look of annoyance that fell onto her face but she only sighed and thanked Maelin for the food.

"I'll be back shortly to help you undress for the night."

Mari picked up her pencil.

Looks like I'm going to have to dig deep to find something to like, though.

11

TO BEG, BARTER, & BURGLE

A groan escaped Alek's lips as he woke the next afternoon. He'd fallen asleep in his rain-soaked clothes and his body was angry with him for it. He tried to stretch his stiff muscles and winced.

Etaldin's and his cultists' voices echoed through Alek's mind just as they had during his dreamless sleep. He tried to shake off the unsettling feeling, but it was no use.

A mermaid's scale, dust from a pixie's wing, a page from an ancient Unseelie text... and you will have what—or should I say, whom—it is that you desire.

It would certainly be a lot to do on his own. It was a good thing that Alek was never alone; his friends would always be there for him, he was sure. He knew, though, that it wouldn't be a good idea to tell them about the cultists or Etaldin. Working with an old and generally evil God was typically discouraged among everyday folk, like his friends. This was not a typical situation though, and atypical measures were necessary.

Alek changed clothes quickly and went on his way to find Lyna and Rae. The walk to their lofted apartment was quick and he climbed the stairs two at a time. He knew they may still be sleeping, as he was only a short while ago, but he banged on the door anyway.

A moment later Lyna opened the door, eyes half lidded and unfocused.

"Alek?" She mumbled, "Are you okay?"

"Lyna, love, who is it?" Rae's tired voice carried out into the hall.

"It's only me!" Alek called back, pushing his way past Lyna. "I need your help."

Rae sleepily emerged from the bedroom coming to stand by Lyna. "Better be important, waking us like this after the night we all had."

"Oh, it is," Alek couldn't hide the excitement from his voice, "I've found the way we'll be able to save Mari."

Rae sighed. Lyna's shoulders fell and her face crumpled.

"Alek, dear," Lyna began.

"No no," he cut her off, "hear me out. It's a simple spell! Only three ingredients."

"And where did you find this spell?" Rae asked, her arms crossed.

Alek easily lied, "Where we find all the good spells: in a book."

"What does the spell do?"

"And if it's so simple, why do you need our help?"

Alek sighed but kept a smile on his face. "Friends, would I ever lead you astray?"

Rae shot a dubious look towards Lyna, but Alek continued, "Please, help me save Mari. I couldn't live with myself if I didn't *try*. Together we can do this. I know."

The pair was silent for a moment. Alek could see they were faltering, and his smile widened when Rae spoke.

"Alek. We can do this for you but only on one condition."

"Anything," Alek leaned forward with anticipation.

"If this doesn't work..." Lyna began.

"...you have to accept that Mari is gone." Rae finished.

"And go back to living your life," Lyna added.

Alek winced at their words. They thought they were helping, but they didn't know what he truly needed. He needed Mari.

"I understand." He lied, again.

"So," Rae went in search of a drink in the kitchen, "what do you need from us?"

"Well, first, just a bit of your wing dust."

She stopped mid-reach into the cupboard. "Alek, you know that's a very... personal item."

"I know, I know, and I wouldn't ask if it wasn't important."

She sighed, turning to reach into the adjacent cupboard and grabbed an empty, corked jar. Lyna silently came up behind her to take the jar, removing the cork and holding it under Rae's bottom wing. Rae stood tall, fluttering her wings in quick, short bursts. A silver, metallic-looking dust falls into the jar, filling it a quarter of the way. Lyna corked the jar and took it to Alek.

She mumbled, "You're not getting any of my fur next, so don't ask."

"Rae," Alek stood to meet her gaze, "thank you."

Rae's smile was sad but she nodded. "I just hope you find what you're looking for, my friend."

"So," Lyna sat cross-legged on the couch, "what's next?"

"Do you two still keep in touch with Coralia?"

Lyna groaned. "Don't tell me you need a mermaid scale?"

Mermaid scales were common spell ingredients, so it would make sense that Lyna would quickly put it all together. Alek nodded sheepishly.

"Coralia won't leave us alone for weeks if we ask her for a favor," Lyna complained.

"That girl is always inviting us to some mermaid party or get-together and it always ends with me getting my wings wet." Rae shuddered, "I hate getting my wings wet."

Alek paused, the precious jar of wing dust tucked into his trouser pocket. He took in the worried and uncomfortable expressions of his friends, wondering if this had already gone too far. He was ready to rescind his request and tell them that he would find the scale by himself, that they'd already helped him enough, when Rae let out an exasperated sigh, heading for the door.

"Fine. If we head out now, I bet we can catch Coralia before she heads back to the Dominion."

Gratitude welled in his heart but he kept his mouth shut, worried that one wrong word and his friends would reconsider their assistance.

Alek seldom visited the taverns and had never stepped foot in a brothel, but Lyna and Rae had always had a more adventurous spark in them. When they were really in the mood to drink and dance and engage in the activities of Eristald's nightlife, they sought out their mermaid friend, Coralia. They'd stopped inviting Alek to tag along long ago since his answer was always a polite rejection.

They approached the Sultry Siren, the sound of drumbeats and laughter flowing from its open windows. Alek sighed, unexcited about entering but determined to get the scale he needed to save Mari.

Inside, the floor was slick with a mixture of ale, water, and Goddess knew what else. There were a few tables where the patrons with legs sat, but the rest of the room was filled with long troughs of water where the more aquatic guests splashed around.

Keeping close to Rae and Lyna, Alek stepped carefully, dreading the thought of falling into the murk at their feet. He heard Coralia before he saw her. Her voice grated against him. He cringed. She laughed, squealing like a pig, and splashed in her trough where she floated with two other mermaids.

"Rae Rae!" Coralia shrieked, "And little Lyn! What brings you,"—*hiccup*—"here?"

Rae's wings were tucked in close behind her. "Hello Coralia, you look... well."

Lyna stepped forward, a polite smile forced onto her lips. "We're actually here on business, not pleasure, my friend."

Coralia caught sight of Alek behind them and her eyes glittered. She lowered her chin, a smirk on her lips. She looked up through her thick pink lashes, her voice slurred and lazy.

"Who's this?"

Alek squirmed under her hungry gaze. *I can do this,* he told himself, *I can put on a show and play a role if that's what it takes to get what I need.*

"I'm Alek," he sauntered forward, leaning over the edge of her trough. He let his eyes graze up and down her body, stopping only when they ran over the sunset-colored scales that covered her lower half.

They were beautiful, shimmering swirls of orange, yellow, and pink. Though they were as small as a petal on a daisy, he still only needed one.

"Oh," Coralia sighed, her lower lip jutting out as she followed his stare, "and here I thought you might be interested in talking to me, but you're only interested in my scales, aren't you?"

"They *are* beautiful. So fitting on a gorgeous Fae like yourself." Alek tried to play it off, but being flirtatious was so foreign to him that his words fell flat.

Coralia hiccuped then took another gulp of ale. "Tell you what," she leaned in toward him, water splashing over the edge and onto his feet.

Alek resisted the urge to pull away as she stopped only an inch from his face. He did his best to remain in character, though he doubted he was playing a convincing part.

"What's that?" he said softly.

"I'll trade you a scale," her hot, ale-soaked breath coated his face, "for a kiss."

Alek couldn't contain the wince that came over him, but he quickly leaned forward, pecking her on her cheek.

He smiled at her, "satisfied?"

Coralia snorted, rolling her eyes. "Hardly."

Alek stood straighter, "well, allow me to try again." He tried to keep up his character of the seductive, confident male that he'd read about in books. However, he lost the concentration as he leaned in and Coralia wrapped her arms around his neck, pulling his face closer. She sloppily covered his mouth with hers and kissed him deeply.

He flailed his arms and legs to try to keep his balance as he felt his feet slipping out from under him. The next thing he knew Coralia had pulled him into her trough, and he was treading water.

Lyna and Rae guffawed behind him, sputtering and wheezing with amusement as Alek emerged looking like a wet cat.

Alek couldn't help but laugh as well when Coralia finally let him go. He scrambled backward and flung himself over the side, holding on to the edge of the trough as his feet slid around on the floor below.

Coralia was smiling innocently, "Oops. A swim usually costs extra, but since you're so handsome, "she plucked a scale from her lap and tossed it over to him, "it's on the house."

Lyna and Rae laughed the whole walk back to their apartment. Alek left them there and sloshed his way across town. He'd put the scale in the same jar that Rae's pixie dust was and re-sealed the lid.

Only one more item. And, thankfully, there would be no drunken merpeople at the library. He hoped.

Alek was mostly dry by the time he made his way across town. He found Fyodor sitting on the steps outside of the library, reading a thick, leather-bound book.

"Fyo, my friend!"

Fyodor looked up, a small smile spreading across his face, "Alek, how are you feeling?"

Alek brushed off his concern. "I'm fine. Great, really! Listen, I need your help."

Fyodor closed his book and stood. On the steps, he was nearly the same height as Alek.

"What can I do for you?"

"Will you help me find the oldest Unseelie text in this library?"

Fyodor blinked, "well, sure. I know of one but why the sudden interest?"

"I'll explain on the way in," Alek put his hand on his friend's shoulder and ushered him up the steps, filling him in on the same half-truths that he had told Lyna and Rae.

"And you've promised to give her up if the spell doesn't work?" Fyodor's kind eyes bored into Alek's, "Mari's a nice girl and all, but now that the king is involved, this has gotten a lot more serious than it was before. I don't want you getting hurt."

"Fyo," Alek whispered, telling the whole truth now, "I am hurt *now* knowing that I failed her. I don't think it can get worse than this."

Fyodor nodded. Without another word, the little goblin led Alek deep into the library. They passed the folk studying by magic firelight and made their way through narrow paths between overstocked shelves.

Along the back wall of the building, books sat in glass display cases. Their pages, yellow and thin, looked as though one small gust of wind would disintegrate them. The ink was fading though even if it weren't, Alek didn't know the ancient language that was scrawled along the parchment.

"How do we check these out if we can't get at them?" Alek places his hand on the glass, looking for a latch that might open the case.

Fyodor chuckled in disbelief, "Get them out? Aleksandr, no one has touched these books for hundreds of years."

Alek whirled on his friend, "Fyo, I need a page from this book. If you're not going to help me..."

Fyodor took a startled step backward. "Alek, you're not acting like yourself. Maybe we should grab some food and talk about—"

Alek wasn't listening. He was already trying to remember the magic spell he'd used when he was younger to steal extra sweets from his mother's locked cupboard. He closed his eyes and put his hand flat on the cold glass, then focused his energy through the center of his body. With a deep breath, he drew from his innermost life source and willed a spell into existence. Vibrations shook through his arm and into his hand, settling in his fingertips for a moment before transferring to the glass below. The glass began to shimmer, the once solid surface now rippled like a puddle of water.

"Alek!" Fyodor hissed, but it was too late.

Alek's hand sunk into the glass and landed directly on the open book below. He clasped his fingers around the edge of the page, giving a gentle tug to separate it from its binding.

Fyodor's eyes widened in clear horror as Alek raised his hand back through the glass which became solid once more.

"I didn't want to steal anything." Alek sighed, "But I had to do what I had to do."

"You didn't *have* to do anything!" Fyodor's voice rose.

"Fyo, keep your voice down, all is well! I have what I need now and—"

"Don't tell me to keep my voice down. *Nahil!* This is ridiculous! I can't—"

"Is everything alright?" A small voice came from behind them.

Alek and Fyodor spun to see the librarian, Yaslyn, standing with a cautious smile on her face. Alek smiled politely, nudging Fyodor forward.

"We're fine, ma'am. Just a slight...literary disagreement. You know how much Fyodor likes books."

The tiny silver goblin laughed quietly, "Oh yes, he's here every day for a new one."

Fyodor stammered but a smile crept onto his lips, "Well, you always have such great recommendations."

She chuckled again, "You know, I'm happy I found you, Fyodor. I'd been meaning to ask you..."

Alek took a step back and another. Only a few more feet until he was out of earshot and headed out towards the entrance. Folded neatly in his pocket next to the jar of Rae's wing dust, the page from the book was finally secure.

When he slammed the door to his home closed behind him, the exhaustion began to set in. He slid down the door, crumpling to a pile on the floor. His hand rested on his pocket where his three precious spell ingredients were stored.

Hank trotted over to where Alek lay and meowed plaintively. Alek reached out a shaky hand to pat the cat's head.

He succeeded in gathering the items and he could so easily be one step closer to rescuing Mari. So why wasn't he jumping for joy? Now that the adrenaline of the day was wearing off, and the muddled thoughts were slowly dissipating from his mind, Alek couldn't help but notice the apprehension that was still underneath his excitement.

Before he officially handed the items over and finalized the deal with Etaldin, he wanted to try one last thing on his own. Then he would truly be able to say he'd run out of options and wouldn't feel so guilty for making the deal.

"Come on Hank," he scooped up the lanky cat, "time to go."

12

GRASPING FOR STARLIGHT

Time at the castle was flowing like molasses. She'd only been here a few days, yet it could have been more like a week if she hadn't been tracking time in her journal. Tonight, Mari was eager to get to dinner with the hope that Cylan would finally be joining her.

Maelin had reluctantly dressed Mari in the new clothes that had been delivered to her room earlier that day. Mari immediately felt more comfortable upon seeing the several pairs of pants, button-down shirts, boots, and vests.

"Are you sure you want to wear these clothes, ma'am?" Maelin's voice held a hint of sadness as she examined the dark brown trousers that were cropped at the knee. "When you had such beautiful dresses before?"

"Where I come from, clothing isn't assigned to one gender." She took the pants, sliding them on, thankful for the perfect fit. The brass buttons on the high-waisted trousers matched the ones along the torso of her reddish-brown vest. The white shirt was loose and had a v-neck collar that poked out under the vest, and there were buttons on the end of her sleeves as well, by her elbows.

"I can wear what's considered a masculine outfit and no one would care. I prefer these clothes and, although you look beautiful in your dress," Mari gestured to Maelin's navy skirt and lighter blue, high-necked blouse, "you should try pants sometime. They're comfortable."

Maelin did not seem convinced. Her internal discontent presented itself as a shudder as Mari laced the black knee-high boots around her calves. Mari wondered if Cylan would have a similar reaction and smiled at the thought of upsetting him.

When Mari walked into the dining room, she was surprised to see Cylan already waiting for her. She took her seat, sending a polite smile in his direction. The staff, with their stoic expressions and graceful movements, began serving their food.

Her strategy tonight was killing him with kindness if she couldn't literally kill him with her dinner knife. Though, even if she had the opportunity to, she knew she'd probably never actually harm another living thing. Still, she'd never felt such white-hot rage towards one person before; it was disorienting.

She sighed at the fully vegetarian courses once again. She knew, as Alek had explained, that most Fae did not eat meat because some of the folk chose to present themselves as animals, and no one wanted to accidentally eat their cousin or something. Still, Mari was craving some red meat with a passion. A steak with sauteed mushrooms and onions and...

"What did you do today?"

Cylan's unexpected question made her jump. Her fork dropped, clinking against the plate.

"I'm sorry?" she said, shocked.

"Your day." He repeated, "What did you do with it?"

She took a sip of her wine and answered truthfully, "Maelin and I spent a lot of time exploring the castle, again."

"Hm." Cylan took another bite, nodding passively. "I see you found the clothes I had sent for you. Are they to your liking?"

"Oh yes, they fit perfectly, thank you."

Silence fell over them again for a moment. Mari was determined to make conversation and searched her brain for some topic that they would both have some knowledge of.

"I was wondering," Mari toyed nervously with her fork, "about your mother and father."

He set his fork down, looking up at her. "What about them?"

Mari took a breath. This was the most he'd been willing to converse with her since he'd brought her here and she didn't want to mess it up. She chose her words carefully.

"Well, they were... opposites. Your mother, Seelie, your father, Unseelie. I was just wondering...how that came to be?"

"I can see why that sounds odd." He went back to eating his dinner, speaking between bites, "but my mother and father were, somehow, made for each other. Some things can't be explained further than that." He thought for a moment and then added, "It wasn't love at first sight, of course. The two of them had led the Seelie and Unseelie separately for many years until my mother, who loved humans, got tired of how her human companions were being treated by my father's people. So, she married my father to unite their kingdoms in hopes that their union would protect the humans. The two didn't expect to fall in love, but they did."

"Wait, so, your mother *loved* humans?" Mari found this quite shocking, considering what Alek had told her about the Seelie Queen being murdered by humans. "But I thought..."

"That a human took her life?" Cylan seemed to read her thoughts. "That's what my father led the realm to believe. No," he corrected, "my mother and other Seelie Fae would..." he paused, seeming to look for the right word, settling on, "*invite* humans to our realm often, to learn more about their life, arts, and technology..." he trailed off, taking a drink of his wine.

"So it's not true that a human killed the queen?"

"It's a version of the truth." He looked like he wasn't going to say more. A moment later, he sighed. "My mother died trying to protect a group of humans from Unseelie Fae. My father still blamed humans in the end and banned them from the Realm. Ever since then, the stars began to fade."

Mari realized she hadn't been eating and her food was getting cold, but she didn't care. She was entranced by his voice, his words. The knowledge flowed through her ears like the sweetest music.

"The stars began to fade?" She repeated.

"When my parents reigned together, peace ensued. Starlight of every color filled the sky; a sign that the Goddess was pleased. Now, the night skies are black and we've been grasping for starlight ever since. One day," his chin rose and his tone was determined, "I'll bring the stars back. As king. But a king cannot have a land that does not fully accept him. For then he's not a king, but a tyrant."

There were no stars here? Surely she would have noticed over the nights she'd been here that they were missing. She tried to remember back to the fleeting moments she'd looked up at the moon and its silver halo in the dark skies. Had she been so blind as to not notice their absence? She remembered Alek mentioning stars at some point, but the memory was thin and dissipated as she mentally reached for it.

"Why are stars so important to you?" Mari asked, gently.

Cylan was silent for a moment, deciding how much to say. "You're certainly full of questions tonight." He raised an eyebrow at her and smirked. His smile was dazzling. Mari silently cursed herself for blushing in response.

He didn't seem to notice her internal struggle as he continued, "Stars are the main source of our magic. We can use magic without the stars but it consumes our life energy. Without our magic, we're even lesser to humans than we are with it."

With Cylan's words, it all came back to her. Mari remembered the theater that Alek had taken her to and his explanation of the stars' power. She knew what the introduction of magic took away from the Fae and how their Goddess wept for the loss of their humanity. Still, Mari found it hard to see the Fae as lesser than humans. Not only could they use various forms of beautiful magic—less now, without the stars of course—but they would not die of old age or disease. They could travel the world and immerse themselves in every culture imaginable. At the very least those things would be pretty interesting to a human.

"What's more," his tone darkened, "folk from all across the realm have been dying. Without magic, without what makes us *us*... my people are suffering."

Mari looked down at her hands, taking in this information. Their culture, their happiness, and their *lives*, all depended on starlight. Between the courts wanting to separate, their people dying, and no sign of magic returning, the realm was in more trouble than she'd realized.

Mari knew she was pushing her luck with her constant flow of questions, but she couldn't resist one more.

"How do you bring the stars back?"

He shrugged, dabbing his mouth with a napkin. "Please the Goddess? Bring peace to the kingdoms, maybe. I do not know for certain. No one does. The better question is, how do I get the kingdoms to accept me?"

"Surely the Unseelie accept you, as your father's blood child," Mari noted.

Cylan snorted. "The Unseelie know of my mother's Seelie blood and that is enough reason for them to shun me. And, likewise, the Seelie know of my Unseelie father and..." he shrugged noncommittally, but Mari could see the frustration behind his eyes.

The rest of their dinner was silent, save the sound of metal forks against porcelain plates. Without Mari asking more questions, Cylan seemed unwilling to keep the conversation going. Either way, Mari felt as though she'd just won first prize in a marathon; getting Cylan to give her so much information throughout one dinner was more than she'd ever expected.

When the meal was over, Cylan stood, bowing respectfully before wishing her a good night. She made her way back to her room with Cylan's question, and her own, burning a hole in her mind.

How do I get the kingdoms to accept me? How do you bring back the starlight?

She couldn't get it out of her head, even as she dutifully recorded the night's conversation on the parchment in her room. It was one of the first times Cylan had spoken to her with sincerity. As arrogant and unfeeling as he seemed to be most of the time, perhaps he was serious about wanting to be a good king to the realm. That, she could respect.

With a groan of disgust, Mari dropped her pen, leaning back in her chair. She hated to think of Cylan as anything other than the bad guy. He was an unfeeling, entitled prince, she reminded herself. He held her against her will, initially attempted to dress her up like a doll, and continued to keep his distance from her. Still, she couldn't deny that he had opened up to her tonight, and maybe that was a start. Her thoughts raced around the idea; maybe that was the answer: opening himself up to the kingdoms!

They might not know exactly why the Goddess was displeased or why she had taken away their starlight, but performing an act of goodwill with a peaceful intention had to be a decent place to start.

"Maelin?" Mari called and the tiny pink female appeared in the doorway. She was always there, just a step away. Did the girl ever sleep? "I'd like to get a little air before bed. I need to clear my mind."

Their boots crunched on the gravel path through the gardens. Maelin was silent, respecting Mari's need to think. It was true, she noticed, that the stars were gone. She stared up where the crescent moon shone all alone, with no stars to keep it company.

They were by the outer wall now, the glow of the city's lights shining just overhead. The bushes that grew closest to the wall began to rustle, stopping the girls in their tracks.

A hooded figure, all in black, emerged. Mari gasped, fear trapping her scream in her throat, though Maelin was loud enough for the both of them. The intruder lowered his hood and Mari's fear fell away with it.

She quickly wrapped her hands around Maelin's mouth to muffle the Fae's shrill scream.

"Alek!" Mari jumped into his outstretched arms.

"I've brought you a couple of things," he handed her a pack that was heavy and squirming.

A little gray head popped out of the opening and meowed grumpily.

"Oh, Hank!" Tears filled her eyes as she lifted her old tomcat from the bag. Below him were her other few belongings; her journal and her clothes that she came here in.

"I figured you'd like them for our journey."

"Journey?"

"I'm getting you out. We can run away. I've been offered the help I need to save you and there's a weak spot in the wall..."

"I can't leave," Mari blurted.

Alek stopped, his eyes narrowing. "What do you mean?"

"I've got a plan," which wasn't entirely a lie, though she had just thought of the idea an hour ago, "I'm hoping Cylan will help me if I..."

"Prince Cylan? You're going to trust the devil that sold you out to the king and then imprisoned you in his castle?" His voice dripped with hate, "Mari, you can't be serious."

"I've got to get back where I belong, Alek." She tried to keep her voice calm and understanding; after all, he had just risked his life to be here tonight.

"What has he done?" Alek turned to Maelin who shrank away. "What Unseelie magic has he used to make her want to stay?"

"Alek, calm down! There's no magic I just..."

"Mari!" He grabbed and shook her shoulders, "Come with me. Stay with me. I love—"

"Don't say it, Alek," Mari raises her voice over his, her anger heating her face, "please. You can't love me, you barely know me."

He backed away, hurt in his eyes, shaking his head.

"I'll save you, Mari," his tone was resolute, "even if I have to save you against your will." He turned, disappearing into the shadows by the wall.

Mari turned to Maelin, "Are you okay?"

Maelin was shaking, but she nodded her head. "I think we should go inside now, ma'am."

Mari nodded, snuggling Hank close. Alek didn't seem himself. What did he mean about an offer to help save her? She worried for her friend and wished there was something she could do to help him but until he gave up on the notion that she needed saving, he was on his own.

13

PLANS & PUPPETS

Frustration morphed into hot anger that bubbled into icy rage as Alek ran from the castle wall.

She said *no?*

He followed his vague memory deeper into the heart of the city, passing the newer, more well-kept buildings until he began to see boarded-up windows and crumbling rooftops.

Cylan must have done something to her, he reasoned, *poisoned her mind with dark magic.* Surely there was no other possible reason she'd want to stay with that egotistical prince that had just imprisoned her.

The spell ingredients tousled in his pocket as he ran. He'd tried to get Mari out on his own but clearly, he was no match for the Unseelie trap she was in. The only way to fight dark magic was with stronger dark magic.

He knew what he had to do.

"You've returned."

Alek spun as he heard the old crone's voice beckoning him from behind. His chest rose and fell rapidly as he caught his breath.

"I've got what you asked for."

She smiled wickedly, her chin tilting downward though her eyes stayed locked on his. The old goblin turned into the alley and Alek followed her through the hole in the wall. Inside, everyone was just as he'd left them; the goblin joined the others in the circle.

"Put the items in the vase," one of them—he wasn't sure which—instructed.

He reached into his pocket and did as he was told. First, he dropped in the crumpled page then the scale. A faint purple smoke wafted out from the vase. Alek held his breath, though he wasn't sure why, as he uncorked the jar and dumped out the silvery pixie dust. As he did, a sizzling sound rose from the vase, and he took a step back.

The cultists began chanting. Two of them stepped forward, grabbing Alek's arms and forcing him to his knees.

"What are you doing?" He protested and struggled but made no progress; their grips were like vices. The old goblin stepped in front of him, producing a dark and twisted blade from her robes.

"It is almost over," she croaked, "you've done well."

Her blade slashed across his chest and he cried out. The cold sting of the blade was quickly replaced by hot blood that soaked his white shirt.

"Help!" He screamed, hoping anyone out on the street might hear him. The cultists only chanted louder.

The goblin grabbed the sizzling, smoking vase, holding it under Alek's wound and allowing a bit of blood to drip inside.

The chanting stopped. Silence fell over the room; Alek could only whimper in pain and fear. He was an animal in a trap, and the hunter was coming.

"Please," he begged, "don't kill me."

The female chuckled but didn't respond. She set the vase on the ground in front of Alek and backed away.

He couldn't take his eyes off the vase as smoke billowed thickly from inside. As though a gust of wind suddenly appeared behind the fog, it rushed towards him, entering his mouth and nose against his will. He fought for breath as it choked him. He couldn't expel the purple mist, his body jerking wildly as he tried.

As the last of it entered his lungs, Alek gasped in a deep lungful of air, coughing with a panicked exhale. The cultists dropped his arms, and he fell forward, barely catching himself before hitting the floor.

"Do not squander this privilege you've been given, boy," the deep-voiced one said, "now that you've given the old God a body, he'll reward you with power beyond that of the starlight that the Goddess provided."

Given the old God a body? Alek thought as he shook on the ground. *No, no, this isn't right.*

It is exactly right. Another voice entered his mind, and he instantly recognized it from the conversation he had with Etaldin the night before. The Unseelie God chuckled, *Now you can—no, we—can do anything we so desire.*

"What is this plan you've thought of, ma'am?"

Maelin sat on the edge of Mari's bed, Hank curled up beside her. Mari could see from her nervous hand twitching that the little Fae was still upset that Mari wasn't allowing her to help get her dressed. Now that she had somewhat normal clothes, even if they were all multiples of the same outfit, she didn't need assistance.

"I'll tell you," Mari zipped up her boot, stepping out from behind the privacy screen, "if Cylan accepts it."

"You intend to tell him on your ride today?"

The glint of metal caught her eye and she turned to see the necklace Cylan had gifted her on her first night here. She sighed, reaching down to grab hold of the chain. Might as well wear it to butter him up at the very least. It was beautiful too, in a simple way. Maelin stood, taking the necklace and clasping it behind Mari's neck. The pendant sat gently in the hollow of her collarbone.

"Yeah, if I don't fall off the horse first."

Cylan had requested—more like, *demanded*—that Mari join him on a horseback ride through the forest outside of the city. She'd never ridden a horse before and, here in the Realm of Faerie where every animal could potentially be a Fae in disguise, she was even less fond of the idea.

Nevertheless, half an hour later she'd found her way to the stables on the north side of the castle and had successfully mounted a chestnut mare—after only four slightly humiliating failed attempts.

She'd held the reins with a white-knuckled grip as she bounced along with the horse's trot. Cylan sat atop a black horse next to her, a few royal guards on their mounts kept a safe distance behind them. They were making their way through the forest along a clear trail that went on as far as Mari could see.

"Mari," Cylan spoke for the first time once the castle was out of view behind them, "I'm interested in learning from you and your human abilities. What talents do you have?"

Mari blinked, surprised at his forward and blunt question.

"I don't really have any talents." She admitted.

Living her life so afraid of being injured or killed by the Dawson Family Curse also kept her from many opportunities. She never enrolled in sports or extracurricular activities and she only barely passed any semi-creative school courses like theater, band, and art. Sure, she might enjoy singing and painting and writing but she wouldn't say she was particularly *good* at any of those things and certainly wouldn't consider herself talented by anyone's standards.

When it came to all of the things she never let herself participate in, Mari preferred supporting her friends from the sidelines. She was always observing and analyzing instead of getting involved. She learned to find contentment and even some enjoyment in living her life that way.

"Every human has something they are skilled at." Cylan snorted, "That's why we kept bringing you all here: so that you could teach us."

Mari chuckled, "I hate to break it to you, Cylan, but if the only reason you captured me is to try and soak up some of my humanly talents, you're about to be sadly mistaken. I'm utterly ordinary."

Cylan didn't respond, his jaw set in a hard line. They rode on over hills and through small thickets for a while in silence until the horses stopped for water at a nearby stream.

Mari's bottom ached from the bouncing and her legs were beginning to feel like jelly. She hoped they would turn around soon, though she still needed to propose her idea to Cylan.

"Cylan, I think you and I could help each other."

Cylan snorted again and Mari bristled at the sound. "What could you help me with? As you said yourself, you're 'utterly ordinary'."

Mari bit back the angry and unkind things she wanted to spit in response and forced a smile on her face, "That may be so but I'm still the only human in the realm, so you're stuck with me." Mari felt a slight satisfaction at the eye roll she received from Cylan. She continued, "My thought was that maybe we could make a deal. We both need the help of the Goddess, so let's help each other get to her."

This caught Cylan's full attention. He locked eyes with her, "What do you need Eris' help with?"

Mari resisted glaring at him but decided honesty was the best policy in this scenario. Perhaps if she opened up to him, he might be more open to hearing her out.

"Long story short, I believe I'm cursed. I want Eris' help to free me from it. That's how I ended up in this mess in the first place."

Cylan looked away, processing this information. The horses had begun to move forward, slowly nibbling grass. Mari couldn't take her eyes off of him, trying to read his expression for any clue on what he might be thinking.

"And you have a plan on how exactly we will please the Goddess?" Cylan stared straight ahead, incredulity in his voice.

"Well, no," she admitted, quickly adding, "but, we could travel together around the realm and help the kingdoms where we can, and when the Goddess sees our good deeds and efforts, she could reward us, possibly even bring back the starlight for you." Cylan's mouth twitched as Mari mentioned the starlight but she didn't give him a chance to object as she continued, "In the meantime, by taking a tour around the realm you could get to know your subjects and they would get to know you making it much more likely that they'll accept you when you take the throne."

Cylan was silent again but this time for much longer. Mari wasn't sure what else to say and sank back into her saddle, thoughts of hopelessness and defeat beginning to fill her mind. She opened and closed her mouth several times, wanting to say anything to get Cylan to respond, but no words came to her.

"The journey will be dangerous," Cylan said finally.

Mari perked up, urging her horse forward so that she was directly next to Cylan. "I'm sure it will."

"And there are no guarantees that any of this will work."

"For either of us, I know."

"You could die."

Mari swallowed and took a breath. "Yes."

Cylan slowed his horse and Mari's horse followed suit. He looked her in the eye, and she fought her inner voice that squirmed and urged her to look away.

"We'll leave in two days. I'll send word to my siblings to prepare for our visits. Inform your maid that she'll be coming with us. Oh and," he began to trot away, calling back, "if you meet with your friend tonight, as you did last night, it might be best to inform him as well. No need to have him creeping about the castle walls if you're not going to be here."

Cylan urged his horse into a run, leaving Mari stunned in silence behind him. One of the guards followed after him, the other staying behind with Mari.

Did he know about her meeting with Alek? And, he hadn't said anything? More importantly, he'd just agreed to her idea. This was her first step in going home. A chuckle escaped her lips and she turned her horse around, riding as hard as she could without falling off, back to the castle to tell Maelin of her success as she'd promised.

As she entered the castle courtyard, she found Maelin loyally waiting for her. She was perched on the short stone ledge of the horse stables, gently stroking a white horse on its nose. Her head rose with a smile on her face as Mari approached. The smile fell as Mari got closer.

"Ma'am, you don't look so well." Maelin's tiny pink face was scrunched up with worry as she reached for Mari's hand.

Her legs felt weak as she hit the ground, her knees buckling under her. The strain of holding on to a horse for a couple of hours was more intense than she'd expected it to be.

"I'm fine, really. I just need to sit."

Maelin supported her, walking to a wooden bench nearby. When Mari sat, she began to chirp excitedly to Maelin, detailing her plan and proudly informing her that Cylan had agreed to the journey. A few sentences into the story she paused, realizing what she'd just signed herself up for.

You could die, Cylan had said.

The whole while that she'd been here she'd been so careful to stay hidden, even at the expense of staring at Alek's four walls to the point where she felt she might just melt into the pillows. Was that honestly all that this journey had in store for her? Secrecy and fear? She knew the fear would always stick around—it was here even now, in the shake of her hands and trembling of her lower lip.

She'd heard once that courage wasn't the absence of fear, but the act of pushing onwards despite it. Now, she had a chance to start actively working towards what she came here to do.

Break her family's curse.

Of course, she had no real ideas on how to do that, but staying trapped here in this castle wasn't going to help, she knew that much. Once her curse was broken she could go home, and live a real—normal—life where she wasn't afraid of her death waiting around every corner.

"Ma'am?" Maelin repeated, giving her hand a quick squeeze.

"I need your help." Mari begged, "I can't go into this journey blindly."

"Blindly? What do you mean?"

"I know next to nothing about the realm or its people," she admitted, taking a deep breath, "I don't know how to keep myself safe or what to expect to see outside of Eristald. I need to learn more and I have two days to do it."

Maelin smiled. "Well, then we will spend the day in the castle's library tomorrow. I don't know that I'll be able to teach you *everything* about the realm in only two days, but we will find as much knowledge as we can. For now," she stood, pulling Mari to her feet, "we will go on a much smaller quest to the dining hall to get you some food before you faint."

14

CONFIDENCE ANEW

Early morning light shone through the trees in the castle's courtyard and into Mari's window. She'd left the curtains open while staring at the rising moon last night and now she was able to watch it set as well, its translucent silhouette fading away as the sky lightened.

There were many similarities, Mari was learning, between the realm and her world and it brought her comfort in finding them. The most recently discovered similarity was the sunrise; it was just as beautiful here as it was at home.

Fluffy clouds, dyed pink and orange from the sunlight, streaked across the pale blue sky. Birds chirped in the trees, welcoming the dawn. Fair folk from all across Eristald stretched in their beds, fresh smoke billowing up from their chimneys as they built fires to cut away the last of the night's chill. Beyond the buildings tucked safely within the walls of the city, a few more plumes of smoke rose in the trees from the houses of those who lived in the forest, but that was as far as Mari could see.

What else was out there?

She dressed quickly, finishing up the latch on her necklace and tucking her journal under her arm when Maelin knocked on her door. For the first time since the day of the King's Ball, Mari was excited about what the day had in store.

The library was not far from her room, she discovered when Maelin took her through its tall double doors that were just down the hall.

The air in the library was stiff and Mari wrinkled her nose. She looked for a window to open and found that there were none on any of the walls. The door they had just emerged through was the only entrance and exit to the library.

Although the library was very cave-like, especially with the rounded stone walls, the light was plentiful from the magic fire. Countless flames burned at intervals along the curves of the stone and atop the bookshelves. Magic fire was so interesting, Mari thought as she realized the wood of the shelves was entirely unaffected by the flame atop it.

A few attendants were walking through the aisles, straightening the books and inspecting them for damage. Mari noted that there were only a handful of Fae working here and, considering the length and height of the room, it must take them several days to make a full round.

Three stories high the walls rose, balconies with golden railings lined each floor, and each floor was lined with full bookshelves. In front of them sat a wide space with a row of desks. Upon the third table in the row sat a pile of books stacked neatly with a few rolls of parchment lying beside them.

Maelin took a seat at the table, "I had the attendants pull a few books for us last night so that we didn't have to waste time searching for them today."

Mari sat next to her, "You're so thoughtful. Thank you."

Maelin smiled, reaching for one of the scrolls. "I suppose we should start with a map of the realm, hm?"

She unrolled the dark parchment, holding the edges down with her hands. Mari vaguely recognized the outline of the continent from the map she'd looked at with Fyodor when he was still searching for portals. This map, though, had more than just portal locations on it. Perhaps most interestingly this map appeared to be hand-drawn and there was what looked suspiciously like a coffee mug stain on the bottom right corner of the page.

Mari ran her fingers over the stain, imagining one of the previous humans that had possibly adventured through here. Maybe he'd been one of the lucky ones who'd come willingly. He could've come through the portal one morning, a mug of fresh coffee in his hand, and had accepted a warm welcome from the Fae who must have been excited to finally have a map drawn of their realm. Maybe he'd even drawn a few copies during his time here. Mari couldn't help but wonder if they'd let him go home after they'd made use of his artistic talents.

Maelin pulled a book over to hold the edge of the map down so that she could use one hand to point to a few places.

"Here's Eristald," she said, pointing to the near center of the main continent. With a strong, confident tone she continued to explain.

She started by showing Mari where the other kingdoms were settled. To the east of Eristald rose a long mountain chain labeled as the Airy Reach. The mountains of the Airy Reach curved southwest down the edge of the continent and into an area marked as Fire's Territory where a large volcano was depicted. She followed the map counterclockwise into the expansive ocean which didn't need the label of Water's Dominion for Mari to be able to guess that one. They came back around to the top of the map—passing a small island chain labeled the Indigo Isles—to the north of Eristald where the largest of the kingdoms was; the Earth Provence.

Mari could have studied the details of the map for hours, noting each delicate river or tiny inn along the paths, but still, she'd never be able to accurately memorize every detail. She'd be taking the map with her, she decided, turning to a fresh page of her journal to make notes as Maelin continued to teach.

They'd only stopped flipping through books and scrolls a couple hours later when Mari's stomach begged to be fed and she reluctantly tore herself away from the knowledge in search of food. Mari couldn't stop smiling on the way to the kitchen, her confidence was quickly growing with each bit of information she equipped herself with.

———·✴·———

He'd crawled home, fear and shame overwhelming him. Alek had slept for a full two days and nights, ignoring the frantic knocking from his concerned friends. On the third morning, his eyes opened.

You're awake.

Alek inhaled a sharp gasp, "So it wasn't just a bad dream?"

Afraid not. Etaldin's chuckle echoed through Alek's mind. *Now, we don't have much time to prepare, but our human is setting out on a journey today with the prince. We shouldn't waste this opportunity to capture her.*

Alek shook his head. "Her name is Mari, and we aren't capturing her, we're rescuing her."

Etaldin was silent. Alek stood, a wave of dizziness washing over him.

"How do you know that anyway?"

I know all; my magic is powerful.

Alek rolled his eyes and stretched, pain erupting in his torso. Fresh blood began to ooze from the wound on his chest.

"If you're so powerful, fix this," he gestured to his shirt.

You must wield the magic for me, I am not strong enough yet to wield it on my own. The more you use my magic, the more power I will build, and soon we can be rid of each other.

A twinge of relief blossomed in Alek's stomach. He wouldn't be like this forever; he could use Etaldin's magic to rescue Mari and maybe even open a portal for them to go through and then Etaldin would leave him.

Yes, Etaldin crooned, *we will both have what we want soon enough. Though we must be away now, my son, or we will miss our chance to get ahead of the girl and prince. Now, use my power to heal your wounds.*

"How?" Alek asked. Etaldin didn't answer.

His stomach bubbled, the tingling feeling spreading from his abdomen up through his arms and into his hands. The sensation was similar to when he used his own magic, but instead of drawing from his life energy, he was able to tap into something deeper. Something stronger.

Etaldin's power.

A faint purple glow emanated from his gray hands and he placed them over his wound. He pulled them back and wasn't shocked to see that his skin had knitted itself together again.

A smile crept onto his lips, his fingers tracing over the blood-stained skin feeling only a slightly raised scar where the gaping wound had been only a moment before.

"This is amazing."

This is only a small fraction of what my power can accomplish. Well done. Alek felt as though he could hear the smile in Etaldin's voice. *Now, away with you. We must make it to the forest before they do.*

He jumped out of bed; confidence and newfound hope vibrated through to his core. He could almost feel his doubts fading away.

All his life he'd run from his Unseelie heritage, fearing the dark magic of his blood. He'd left his family behind in Thorne, throwing aside all ties to his Unseelie life, afraid to be consumed by the Unseelie ways and lose himself in the process. Had he made the wrong choice? Was this what he'd been running from all along? The power bubbling through his veins was intoxicating; it was as if a layer of magic was there just beneath his skin at all times, waiting to be released.

He'd changed his clothes, not bothering to clean the dried blood from his body. He didn't want to waste a second of precious time.

"Where to?" He asked Etaldin.

They'll be heading out through the northern city gate.

Without another word, he burst through his door and made his way through Eristald. The town was busy, as it normally was, but this time, Alek could gently move people out of his way with a touch of Etaldin's magic. He even fixed a few loose cobblestones in his path. He felt Etaldin grumble and shrugged.

"What?" Alek whispered to himself, "You said the more I used it the better. Why not do some good?"

"Alek!" Lyna's voice called from behind him. He turned, smiling at his friend.

"Thank Eris you're alright. What happened to you?" Rae added as they stepped closer to him.

Alek tried to speak but nothing came out. Etaldin's voice filled his head, with a growl.

These two Seelie *do not need to know anything about us. Send them away.*

The magic beneath his skin began to rise from a simmer to a boil, begging to be let free, but he resisted. His head throbbed as he fought the God's command. His hands gripped his temples as he grunted with pain, shaking his head.

"Alek?" Lyna's tone grew more concerned.

"What's going on?" Rae took another step forward.

Alek's head shot upward and he screamed, his once black irises now a glowing purple. He heard the fear in his friends' resulting gasps as they backed away.

"Run!" Alek choked out the words, "I can't control him!"

He gasped as the magic boiled over. Any false sense of control he thought he'd had now vanished.

His vision began to cloud with purple smoke. Through the thickening smog, he caught a glimpse of his friends running toward the castle before he was completely enveloped in Etaldin's magic.

15

EARTH'S PROVINCE

Cylan had been absent from the moment he had agreed to Mari's plan of a tour around the realm. Mari didn't mind. She'd been too busy reading up on what she could learn about the four kingdoms and what she might encounter there.

The morning of the trip she'd rolled over in her bed and gave Hank a snuggle.

"You've been through a lot, you old tomcat." She whispered into his fur, "I wouldn't be here if it wasn't for you leading me through the door. This time," she kissed him and rolled out of bed, "I've got to go alone. I'm sure you'll be fine here until I get back."

If I get back, she mentally added.

Packing was easy as she didn't have many belongings. Everything she needed—a couple of sets of clothes, the map, her notebook, and her pencils—fit neatly in a small brown backpack that sat comfortably between her shoulders.

Part of her worried that Cylan had been elusive because he was intending to back out. If he did, she was sure she'd be stuck here forever. Her stomach flopped at the thought.

When she and Maelin rounded the corner and entered the courtyard, Mari hated the smile that crept onto her lips at the sight of him. He was standing by a large, grand, horse-drawn carriage with his personal knight— who, Mari had recently learned, had a very long and difficult name and was instead called Leo by those around him—standing only an arm's length away.

Over his loose white shirt, a black pinstripe vest—with brass buttons to match her own—was perfectly fitted to his body, accenting the angles of his torso. His dark hair was unruly and yet somehow perfectly gathered atop his head; short loose curls charmingly fell every which way above his pointed ears.

She looked away and quickly gathered herself before walking over to him.

"So, is this our ride?"

He angled his head toward her but didn't move from his spot, his golden eyes sparkling, "No. This is my ride. You and your maid will be in that one." He waved his hand lazily towards a smaller carriage behind them.

Mari nodded once slowly, smacking her lips before speaking. "Got it. Silly of me to assume we'd be traveling together on this trip."

"Yes," Cylan ignored her sarcasm, adjusting his black tie, "silly of you."

After allowing herself one eye roll of annoyance, Mari brushed off Cylan's dismissal. Today was a big day—an exciting day! Even his moody-prince attitude couldn't phase her now.

Their small two-carriage convoy was surrounded by upwards of ten royal guards on horseback. Cylan certainly wasn't risking anything when it came to protection. In a way the guards made Mari feel a bit more unsafe than they were supposed to; it was almost like they were expecting the people of the realm to be launching an attack on the prince at any moment.

She tried to distract herself by looking past the guards and out at the scenery. They were still making their way through the lush, verdant forest. Besides the unusual flowers and fungi that sprung up here and there, everything was eerily similar to the forest surrounding her cabin back in Eastport—right down to the birdsong and smell of the warm breeze.

Despite the beauty around her, she felt a discomfort gnawing at her heart. She didn't need to think long to realize that she still couldn't get Alek's love profession out of her head.

It made her stomach hurt, knowing such a kind and well-intentioned soul could be so confused and hurting so much. Still, there was no way it was love; they'd known each other all of a couple of weeks. Curiosity and intrigue? That was more than likely. Simple infatuation? She wasn't ruling it out.

Mari was pondering the differences between love and infatuation when a memory came back to her. She recalled Alek's narration of the play that he'd taken her to see. He'd said, *The magic changed the humans...and they no longer loved in the same way they did before.*

"Maelin? I've heard that the Fair Folk don't love in the same way that humans do. What do you think about that?"

Maelin paused, trying to find a thoughtful explanation, "For some Fae, it's hard to understand the difference between love and friendship."

Mari smiled, "That's no different than humans. What do *you* think love is?"

Maelin's already cherry blossom pink skin reddened and she toyed with a lock of her hair that had escaped its pins.

"It's not something I've ever thought about before. I've never felt love... I don't think."

"What about your parents?" Mari offered.

Maelin shrugged delicately, "I worry and pray that they will be alright without me helping them with the tavern, and I miss their warmth. I think of their smiles often. I smile too, when I think of how proud of me they were when I received this job at the castle."

"That's love." Mari smiled brighter. "Not the romantic kind of love, of course, but a human kind of love nonetheless."

If a Fae's sense of familial love appeared to be the same as a human's, maybe it was only romantic love that had been tampered with by magic. Maybe the Fae weren't as different as they led themselves to believe.

As they moved further away from the city the forest thickened. The trees here were taller and more mature, creating a dense blanket of shadows with their canopies. At some points, they grew so close together that Mari couldn't see more than a couple of feet past the treeline.

Eventually, Mari was able to make out a river winding through the forest to her right. Their party was following the flow of the water as they continued up the path. Curious, Mari pulled out her map to see how much further they had to go.

Maelin scooted closer, peering at the map. "Briar's Burrow is our first stop," she pointed at the page.

They'd have to cross the river at some point and then travel further east to reach the town. The map only showed trees in the Northeast corner of the map; no buildings or indication that there was a town there at all besides the name written there.

"Which of Cylan's siblings is here again?" Mari recalled their recent studies, "Thor..."

"Prince Thorsten," Maelin confirmed. "Fourth born prince of the realm."

Cylan's younger brother. Mari wondered if he would be a miniature of Cylan, arrogance and all. She hoped not. One Cylan was enough. Hopefully he followed the path of his Seelie mother more so than his Unseelie father and turned out to be gentle and kind.

Did Cylan get along with his brother? Mari wondered if perhaps a fondness for his younger sibling was why he chose Briar's Burrow as their first stop. It could also be that it was simply the closest to Eristald.

The carriage slammed forward and the horses whinnied outside. Mari looked out the window to see with satisfaction that they had entered the narrow river and were attempting to cross where it was shallow. Ahead of them, Cylan's horse was putting up a fight. She chuckled at the thought of him being tossed around his fancy carriage and pictured the annoyance on his face.

A moment later they were all across and she settled back down into her seat. The sun outside had moved higher in the sky and their carriage was heating up quickly. She fiddled with a latch on the window nearest her. As it came free, the window pane not only slid open but also slid off altogether, shattering on the ground outside.

"I see Cylan gave us a quality carriage." She sighed. At least the breeze was flowing nicely.

She and Maelin rode in silence for a while until the carriage stopped with a jolt, sending Mari's bag and its contents around the floor. With a groan, she gathered the items and shoved them inside just before the door opened. Cylan stood in front of her.

"Are all humans as slow as you?"

"Only when they know you're on the other side of the door."

He stepped aside to let them out. As her feet hit the rocky ground, she saw they had stopped in front of the wide mouth of a stone cave. Magic fire light lit the interior where two shadowy figures stood. A third slowly emerged from further in.

Cylan offered her his arm and Mari respectfully, if not still a bit reluctantly, took it. A few of the guards dismounted their horses and followed them as they walked forward, while a few more stayed behind.

"They aren't coming with us?" Mari questioned as they rode away.

"They're meeting us where we will re-emerge."

"Re-emerge?" Mari looked back at Maelin who was walking with her head down to avoid tripping on the uneven ground.

Cylan ignored Mari's alarmed tone and smiled as they stepped inside the cave.

"Thorsten!" He called, "You've grown!"

Mari's eyes quickly adjusted to the dim light of the cave and saw that the two closest figures were Fae males. They were short, the tops of their heads only reaching Mari's waist, and their long hair grew right into their long beards that brushed along the ground. Between their abundance of hair, bulbous noses, and overall stoic appearance, most of their facial features were hidden.

Her eyes didn't stay on them for long as the third figure approached, catching the firelight and all of her attention.

He was tall, like Cylan, with the same deep skin tone and black hair. He was clothed in dark linen and his feet were bare. The smile on his lips was bright and extended up to his eyes. The golden colored irises not only matched Cylan's but they also matched the speckles of color on his most striking feature; his wings.

Behind him unfurled a pair of wings that resembled a monarch butterfly, if monarchs were golden instead of orange. They fluttered gently as he walked, propelling him forward. His feet never touched the ground.

"Yes, that is what happens over time," Thorsten replied with a chuckle. "Welcome to the Earth Province!" He clasped his hands together and stopped in front of them.

The family genetics were strong; Thorsten could have easily been a copy of Cylan. His features, though extremely similar to Cylan's, were more boyish and rounded. Perhaps the biggest difference was the genuine and carefree smile poised on his lips.

"This is Mari." Cylan gently removed her hand from his arm and offered it to Thorsten who brought it to his lips for a kiss. "She's here to help bring the Goddess's favor back to the realm."

"An honor, Mari, to have you here in Briar's Burrow. Now," He clapped and the walls of the cave began to shiver. A few stones fell from the roof of the cave, piece by piece, until all at once the entrance to the cave collapsed creating a solid wall of stone, sealing them inside with a thunderous boom.

Mari gasped and jumped backward, dust swirling around the space. Thorsten caught her, supporting her with his hands. His wings beat a bit faster, clearing the dust from around them.

"Sorry to startle you," he apologized, standing her upright, "you must still be very new to the sight of magic."

Mari blinked in the dimmer light and nodded her head. That must be why there was no entrance to Briar Burrow on the map; the entrance was opened and closed at will. The actual city itself must be...

"We're going underground?" Mari felt stupid for asking as soon as the words left her lips. She was thankful when nobody laughed.

"Oh yes," Thorsten fluttered further into the cave and everyone followed. "While many Earth Provence subjects live above ground in the undeveloped forest, many more live below in the cave system they, and the humans, built long ago."

"Was that the only entrance?" She wondered aloud, sparing a glance behind her.

"Any Fae from the Earth Province can reveal an opening to the city wherever they would like. Though, usually, the Uppers and the Lowers stay put and don't often move from one place to another."

She hadn't seen the terms "Uppers" and "Lowers" in the books. However, she had enough context to understand that the Fae staying above ground—like the fauns, pixies, and woodwoses she'd read about—were the Uppers. Lowers must include the gnomes, trolls, and dwarven Fae, like the two walking beside them.

As they walked, the whole way lit by magic fire light, the walls of the cave started to become smoother, more polished. The ground evened out to the point where it was clear that the floor below them had been crafted by hand.

They were moving deeper into the earth, their path sloping downward. The temperature was dropping, raising bumps on Mari's skin. The sounds of their footsteps and voices were muffled by the dense rock adding to the unnatural feeling of being underground.

With every step, a rhythmic *woosh, woosh,* sound began to grow in Mari's ears. It reminded her of the rush of a bath faucet you might hear if you had turned the water on and left the room. As their path wound to the left and they rounded the corner, it was as though Mari had opened a door and the sound burst to life. The constant flow of water before them echoed throughout the immense cavern it coursed through.

The city of Briar's Burrow, so expertly carved into the cave system with a subterranean river flowing directly through it, was alive and bustling.

Dwarves and gnomes alike roamed the fire-lit streets while some peered down from the windows and balconies of homes carved into the rocky walls.

Over the sounds of the river, Mari could hear their voices as they engaged in everyday conversation. The sounds of metal slamming into rock rang through the air. Teams of the larger dwarves—who were still smaller than Mari but nonetheless incredibly strong—swung pickaxes and carried boulders, moving them from one location to another in a section of the city that seemed to be under construction.

Above, a few fissures and cracks let in rays of golden sunlight that sparkled in the river below. Further down the river the city darkened until all Mari could see was blackness and large silhouettes roaming within the shadows. She shivered again, but not because of the cold.

"Truly a sight to behold," Cylan's eyes were alight, "it's like I see it anew each time I visit."

"Which is not nearly often enough," Thorsten teased.

"How have things been since I last was here?"

In front of them a massive metal bridge connected both sides of the city. They crossed it slowly, admiring the metalwork as they moved.

"Well as you can see we were able to import more metal to fix the bridge; thank Eris that the same dwarf who had built it with his human companion ages ago was able to repair the damage. And the boulders from the last tiny collapse are being removed from the city… But really, brother, it's not the issues in the Lowers that I've been worried about."

Thorsten led them to a carved-out storefront with a few stone tables and benches outside of it. Inside, gnomes no bigger than Mari's forearm dashed about, jumping from ledge to ledge. The closer she looked, Mari could see that they were brewing and pouring steaming cups of tea. Her mouth watered as the scent filled her nose.

The three of them, Mari, Cylan, and Thorsten, took a seat while the royal guards stood watch. Maelin made her way to the counter to purchase a few cups for everyone and Mari was grateful to hold the warm clay mug in her hand.

"What problems are there above?" Cylan asked, sipping his drink.

Thorsten leaned in, "There have been signs that…" He paused, his brow creased and his lips pursed.

"Signs?" Mari encouraged, leaning closer across the table. This close to Thorsten, Mari was able to notice the pendant that hung from his neck. Engraved into the black metal was the royal family half-moon and sun crest.

Thorsten sighed, "I don't want to say it if it's not true, but there have been certain indications that have led me to believe that," his voice lowered even further, "Etaldin might be returning."

Although Cylan didn't immediately dismiss the claim, he didn't seem convinced. "Eris destroyed his body by cursing him to burn forever in the sun back at the creation of time itself." He leaned back, throwing an arm over the back of the bench, "There may be those that still follow him and his ways but the days of Gods and Goddesses roaming the realm are done."

Thorsten waved his hand dismissively, "Yes, Cylan, we all know the story. After Eris used the last of her power to banish Etaldin his weakened soul roamed free and hers went to become one with the moon and stars so she could continue to watch over us all." He set his drink down, tea sloshing over the sides and onto the table. His voice raised into a harsh whisper, "however you and I also know that the starlight has been gone for quite some time now, and when the moon wanes the folk of The Province suffer."

"What happens to them?" Mari asked in a small voice.

Thorsten looked up at her, a sadness in his eyes, "many of them have disappeared completely. Trees have died because their dryads have gone missing, forest spirits have been moving deeper to the woods, neglecting the outer edges leaving us susceptible to potential attacks and—"

"Mari!"

Mari whirled at the sound of her name and Thorsten's gaze followed hers. Cylan didn't flinch as the guards jumped into a line, weapons drawn. The slap of footsteps on the stone came to a stop in front of them.

"Lyna? Rae?" Mari stood with a confused smile blooming on her face. She turned to Cylan, "Tell your guards to let them by."

Cylan ignored her, still lazily leaning back in his seat. He raised his voice to her friends, "Bold of you to return to her side when you once were nearly executed because of her."

Mari glared at him and looked between two of the guards' shoulders to see Lyna and Rae's faces inches from their blades.

"We went to the castle first but they told us you'd already left for the Earth's Province," Lyna said in a rush, her eyes wide and focused on the sword in front of her.

Rae's voice held a bit of relief in the tone, despite being threatened by four armed guards, "I'm so happy we caught you before he did."

Mari's stomach flopped nervously.

"Before who did?" She asked, though somehow she felt deep down that she already knew the answer. Her fear was confirmed as Rae spoke.

"Alek. There's... something wrong with him."

"There was this spell or something," Lyna continued, "and he said he was doing it to get to you but—"

Cylan cut her off, annoyance dripping on his words, "I have a full royal guard surrounding us. An abundance of security, really. There's no threat to Mari while she's in my care."

"Care?" Mari echoed, annoyed at his rudeness towards her friends, "more like captivity."

Cylan sat up, his eyes narrowed on her. "This 'captivity' has consisted of a warm bed and a full stomach for you each day, has it not?"

"Those things don't make me any less captive!" The heat of her anger had risen to her cheeks, "You know, you—"

Thorsten stood, directing his voice loudly towards Lyna and Rae, "Thank you for your warnings, friends from above. We will heed them with care." He turned to his brother, "Maybe you two need a minute apart. You and I can finish our conversation another time. Let me watch her for a short while, Cylan. Perhaps fresh air and a walk through the grove will lower tensions."

Mari looked back to her friends, but the guards were already shuffling Lyna and Rae away.

"Be safe!" Lyna called, her brown ears twitching nervously.

"Good luck!" Rae smiled, using her wings to flutter over the guards, waving her arm wildly in the air.

Mari waved back at them, shouting her thanks, wishing she'd been allowed to have a real conversation with them. More so than the annoyance and frustration she'd felt with Cylan, worry began to grow within her.

She had seen with her own eyes that Alek had been *off* that night he'd tried to take her from the garden. However, after not hearing from him again, she had hoped he would have given up. The fact that Lyna and Rae risked their safety to come to warn her meant he must really be in trouble. By extension, was she now in trouble, too?

Mari, Maelin, and the guards followed Thorsten up a winding path to the surface. The other guards stayed with Cylan who was still lounging on the bench.

Mari didn't have the emotional capacity to wonder what he was up to. Only one thought was holding her focus right now. An anxious knot twisted in her gut as the question replayed in her mind.

What had Alek gotten himself into?

16

KINDNESS & SELFLESSNESS

"Cylan might seem like a bit of an insufferable old boggart," Thorsten raised his hands, shaking the ground below them and throwing it open as if it were a garage door, blinding Mari with midday sunlight, "but I think being here is just especially difficult for him."

Mari didn't want to insult his brother, but if she wanted to be truthful, she'd say she hadn't met any other side of Cylan besides the grumpy one.

"It's not just here," she admitted, "he's been pretty much exactly like this ever since we met."

They walked silently through the mature hardwood trees. Tall, thick tree trunks rose, their emerald leaves fluttering in the cooling breeze. The ground was clear of any debris—not even fallen leaves from the past autumn covered the ground. Perhaps they didn't have autumn here. Mari added that to her mental list of questions to ask Maelin.

Dust motes and tiny bugs caught the light like falling glitter, drawing Mari's attention further into the forest. It only took a moment to realize some of the sparkles were *actually* glitter, falling from tiny pixie wings as they made their way between the trunks and low-hanging branches. A sound like a cacophony of wind chimes filled the air as they flew.

"He'll probably kill me for telling you this," Thorsten rubbed the back of his neck, "but Cylan never really got over our mother's death. They were close. He's a lot like her in so many ways," he chuckled at Mari's dubious expression, "believe it or not! I think that's why Father was so hard on him to be more Unseelie and why Cylan was bitter that the rest of us got to leave home." Thorsten sighed, "It's also why he hasn't visited the Earth Province since Mother passed on. Her memorial is here, just beyond the temple to the south."

Mari blinked, uncomfortable with the stirring feelings inside of her. Part of her felt a bit guilty that she hadn't taken the time to inspect Cylan in any light other than the one she'd seen him in initially. To her, he'd always been some version of "the bad guy".

In many ways he still was, but Thorsten's words made some of the pieces of the puzzle fall into place. It made sense that his attitude was a front for his pain. Mari hadn't considered the personal trials Cylan had gone through in the last few years; losing his mother, being separated from his siblings, losing his connection to his Goddess when the starlight disappeared... Although none of it was a good excuse for making those around him miserable, perhaps it was the explanation.

Several of the pixies continued to buzz about, coming from every direction. It was clear to see they were all headed towards the same destination.

"Thorsten?" Mari stopped, turning to look in the pixie's direction, "what do you think they're doing?"

Thorsten turned his attention to her, following her line of sight. "I'm not sure," his contemplative expression lightened into a mischievous smile, "but we can find out."

He strayed from the path, following the trail of gold and silver dust through the trees. Mari smiled, excited to discover what had the pixies in such a hurry.

She stopped shortly after Thorsten at the top of a small hill. Maelin squealed, nearly running into her.

"Shh." Mari looked over her shoulder to Maelin briefly before taking in the scene in front of them.

Down in the little gully rose a gray, leafless oak tree. The pixies had perched themselves in the dead branches, clustering together like a flock of birds. Despite sitting still, their wings kept fluttering behind them, pixie dust raining down around the tree trunk.

"What are they doing?" Mari whispered.

"I'm not sure," Maelin looked on with interest, "maybe they are attempting to revive the tree?"

"I'd say you're right." Thorsten's tone saddened. "This is exactly what I had been talking about with Cylan. Dryads are going missing, and their trees are suffering for it."

The beauty of the shimmering dust falling onto the tree quickly became a vision of sadness. Mari's hands wrung anxiously in front of her, wishing she knew how to help. Her eyes scanned the area around them in hopes she'd see something that could be of any use.

From her vantage point atop the hill, Mari could see that the gully extended further south, the ground darkening and becoming muddier the further she looked.

She darted towards the mud, confirming her suspicions when she saw a blockage of leaves and other debris at the bottom of the gully with a small creek backing up behind it.

"Ma'am!" Maelin called.

The guards began to run towards Mari as she slid down the hill. Thorsten held out a hand to stop them.

"Let us see what the human can accomplish."

Mari went to work with a large stick, scooping the leaves and mud aside until finally, the creek burst through. With the floodgates opened, the water's speed increased, barreling towards the tree.

Mari scaled the opposite side of the gully and ran back towards the tree, following the flow of the creek. On this side of the ravine, a tall section of half-dead bushes rose just a few inches too high, blocking the last rays of sunlight from the tree. Mari made quick work of the dry stems, pulling them away until the sun was able to shine through, falling gently upon the little tree in the gully.

Mari slid down, coming to a stop at the base of the tree where the water was seeping into the soil. The pixies startled, the frantic jingle of bells rang as they flew away.

"Wait!" Mari huffed, catching her breath, "come back!"

"There is no need," a voice, gentle as the breeze itself, brushed over Mari's skin.

She looked around and up to Maelin, Thorsten, and the guards. Their eyes were wide and focused on the top of the tree. Mari followed their gaze, gasping at the buds that were forming on the ends of the branches.

Within seconds, the tree blossomed to life. Leaves burst from the buds, flapping open with a gentle *woosh*. The gray bark began to darken as water flowed up from the roots, bringing life back to the tree that had been rotting only moments ago.

"Ma'am!" Maelin might have been obscured now by the tree's full canopy, but Mari could hear the smile in her voice, "You've done it, ma'am!"

Mari was about to call back to her when a tall, thin Fae stepped out from behind the tree. Her arms and legs resembled the tree's branches, separating into three finger-like tendrils at the ends. Hair made of ivy hung gently down her back. Small black eyes were staring straight at Mari, and pale green lips curled up in a kind smile.

"A little bit of water did all of this?" Mari chuckled nervously, gesturing to the tree.

"Kindness and selflessness did this." The Fae's breezy voice filled the air, "I am Nysyll, the dryad who lives for this tree. As the tree began to weaken, so did I. You have restored us both."

Nysyll took a step forward, reaching up her long arm to pluck a single leaf from the tree. She cupped it in between her hands for a short moment before opening them in a great flourish, revealing that the leaf had changed.

Where the thick, green leaf had been just a moment ago, a delicate flower now unfurled. It resembled a Lilly in many ways, although the petals were so thin they were nearly translucent. They were a dark shade of green, with golden flecks speckled around them. The center of the flower and its spindles were glittering gold. With one more flourish of the dryad's hand, the flower became encapsulated within a transparent sphere. She offered the preserved flower to Mari.

"A gift," the dryad breathed the words, "for our savior."

"I don't know what to say," Mari smiled, accepting the gift, "thank—" she started to say, but when she raised her head the dryad was gone.

Thorsten floated down to her, a wide, thrilled smile on his face. "I knew that if anyone could help, it would be a human."

Mari held out the flower in the sphere, "she gave me this."

"Ah," Thorsten's eyebrows shot upward, "she's given you an Erisinium—the Goddess Flower. These haven't grown here in some time. This is a gift that should be treasured." He handed her the flower back then bent at the waist in a respectful bow, "Thank you for helping one of my people. I am in your debt."

Mari blushed but was spared from responding as Thorsten straightened up, offering her his hand.

"May I help you up the hill?"

Mari nodded, taking his hand. He stepped closer, wrapping his other arm behind her back before taking flight. Mari gasped, the feeling of gently floating upward sent her stomach flopping nervously.

They were only in the air for a matter of seconds. Maelin reached out to support Mari as they touched down.

Their group made their way back to the pathway, Maelin happily chattering about how amazing Mari was and how beautiful her Erisinium was. Mari turned the sphere around in her hand, examining it from all angles.

Kindness and selflessness, the dryad's words fluttered around her mind. What a beautiful way to start this journey. She tucked her gift safely into her backpack, her heart full.

Wasn't that what this journey was all about, anyway? Earning the Goddess's favor through kindness and selflessness to the kingdoms.

Perhaps, instead of solely focusing on what she was going to gain from completing their quest—like breaking her curse or going home—the real feeling of success would come from remaining selfless and focusing on what she could give to the Fae of the realm while she was here.

The thought renewed Mari with a warmth of optimism and happiness that she hadn't felt in a very long time.

17

DAGGERS & DEMANDS

As they continued on their walk through the grove, Mari wondered how she'd ever be able to accurately describe the beauty of the forest when she went to capture this moment in her journal later. Words like, lush, flourishing, and vivacious came to mind, and they still weren't enough. She closed her eyes trying to seal the memory of the dryad's features and the smell of the mud in her mind.

She glanced down, noticing a small bug munching on the petals of an orange tulip. Her mind roamed as she took in the sight of the creatures around her, knowing that the tiny garden slug moving across a leaf or the skittish deer nibbling on grass could either be a typical animal or a shapeshifting Fae.

As a hawk flew overhead, Mari wondered how the Fae decided on what animal they wanted to shift into. Maybe it was just what called to their souls; the swiftness and cunning of a fox or the intimidating and powerful presence of a bear. Maybe each individual felt more connected to the animalistic side of themselves and chose to present themselves in the way that felt most authentic.

She pulled off her backpack and took out her journal, jotting down incoherent ramblings of her thoughts that she would organize later. The map she'd taken from the library caught her eye. She plucked it from its place in the bag, unraveling it.

Turning to Thorsten she asked, "Where are we, exactly?"

"Beryl's Grove." He replied.

Mari's eyes widened as she took in the distance between the Burrow and the Grove, "how did we travel so far, so quickly? It took half a day to ride from Eristald to Briar's Burrow but somehow we've emerged this far west in only a handful of minutes?"

Thorsten smiled politely, explaining slowly the way one might talk to a small child learning a new concept, "when I am in the Burrow, I and those with me can emerge anywhere in the Earth Province that I choose." He shrugged, "perks of being the guardian there. I wanted to spare you from walking too far; I'm sure enduring my brother is tiring enough."

"Enduring?" Cylan's voice carried to them from behind. He rounded the corner, twirling a fallen leaf in his fingers, "I prefer to think of it as *enjoying* or at least *experiencing*."

He stopped inches from Mari. She held her breath, shocked by his sudden closeness. Her eyes tracked his hand as he reached up, plucking a twig from her hair. She blinked up at him. Without comment, he turned to address Thorsten.

"Brother," he placed a hand on Thorsten's shoulder, "I'll give your problems some thought as we continue to Maborough town. If it's true what you say about Etaldin returning..." Cylan took a deep breath. "Let us hope Eris has decided to return as well."

The carriages they'd left behind at the entrance to Briar's Burrow were heard approaching then, signaling the end of their visit with Thorsten. The youngest prince fluttered over to Mari, taking her hand and kissing it once before saying goodbye.

"*Ilmor.* Until we meet again, Mari. May *Indis* shine upon you."

She smiled politely, feeling awkward. She hadn't heard that farewell or those Fae words before and didn't know what to say. She hesitantly settled for "thank you, you too," which, judging by Cylan's snort of amusement, wasn't the proper response. She decided she'd ask Maelin what the proper response would have been.

A few minutes later, their party of guards and two carriages were back together. Mari settled in her seat and Maelin shuffled in beside her. The ride wasn't as smooth and slow as it had been on the way to Briar's Burrow. Mari grunted as her head jostled too far to the side, knocking against the window.

"Why are they in such a hurry?" Mari complained, rubbing her head.

Maelin braced herself with one hand on the ceiling and one on the wall, "I'd expect they want to get to town before the sun sets. Eris may be the Goddess of the moon, but these woods become dangerous at night."

Mari consulted her map, "are we headed west?"

Maelin peered over, "South first, through the Goddess Pinery. Then after we turn westward, it's a short and easy road to Maborough town."

Worried that the next large bump might cause her to accidentally rip the map, Mari carefully put it away. She turned to Maelin.

"Did you hear what Thorsten had said to me before we left?"

Maelin nodded, "Yes, ma'am. A traditional Fae farewell. He said *Ilmor,* which means goodbye, and then may the *Indis,* or, starlight, shine upon you.'"

"Is there a...proper way to respond to that?"

Maelin shrugged, "Some just offer thanks but most say 'may the moon watch over you' as Eris is said to reside within the moon."

"May the moon watch over you," Mari repeated, committing the phrase to memory. She couldn't be expected to know all of the customs here, of course. Still, she hated to look ignorant in front of judgmental Cylan.

Another large bump sent Mari to her knees on the floor. The carriage tilted at an odd angle and the horses cried out, halting instantly. Mari let out a grumbled complaint as Maelin leaned forward to help her up.

After throwing her backpack over her shoulder, Mari thrust open the carriage door, stepping outside to find Cylan walking her way.

"What's going on?" Her eyes scanned the scene, catching sight of the issue just as Cylan began to speak.

"Wheel broke." He sighed. "You two alright?"

She stared at him with one eyebrow raised. She kept her tone incredulous, "Like you care?"

His eyes raked up and down her. She squirmed under his confident and unwavering gaze.

"You seem to be fine." He turned to walk back to his carriage. "Feel free to stretch your legs while they fix the wheel if you'd like, though don't wander too far, the sun is nearly set."

Resplendent twilight covered the forest like a blanket. The shadows deepened and everywhere the last rays of light hit seemed to sparkle.

This part of the forest—The Goddess Pinery, she assumed—was full of dense evergreens. Their footsteps crunched over brown, dried needles and the sharp, sweet smell of the pines filled her nose. For a moment she remembered dancing with Cylan at the ball; the scent of him had a hint of this exact pine-sap undertone.

Her head swiveled, taking in the beauty when a large white object, contrasting greatly with the dark green pines, caught her eye a short way off the path. She started towards it.

She motioned for Maelin to follow her. The nervous little Fae agreed, gingerly picking up her skirt and biting her lip.

"I don't want to go far, but I just want to see what that is out there." She knew she'd be able to keep the carriages in her sight from such a short distance away, and the thought of having so many armed guards nearby was giving her confidence.

"Ma'am!" Maelin's voice shook as she stumbled over the uneven forest floor, "this is not the dress I would have worn for such a trek through the pines!"

Mari rolled her eyes, "I'm telling you, Maelin, you've gotta try these pants one day."

On the horizon, a white stone building began to take shape. As they came closer, Mari saw that this structure had four windowed walls, three simple steps to the entrance, and no roof. Moss had grown across some of the stones and vines had crept their way up and over the walls.

They approached the front archway of the temple. A full moon and stars were carved into stone above the door; the symbol of Eris and half of the symbol on the royal family crest.

"What is this place?" Mari touched the cold stone.

"The Goddess's Temple," Maelin spoke softly. "Ma'am, I know you're not from our world and you may not share our beliefs but I think despite that, our carriage must have broken down this close to the temple for a reason. Eris calls to you."

Mari swallowed, the weight of Maelin's words sending a shiver up her spine. She looked back at her friend, who smiled encouragingly.

"I'll wait out here," Maelin said.

Mari managed a small nod and took her first step into the temple.

It was smaller than she would have expected a temple to be—not as though she'd been in many temples before—and standing in the doorway she could see straight to the back where a small, rounded statue sat atop an altar. Along the walls, large vases stood in lines. They were filled to the brim with polished stones in nearly every shade of green.

Stained glass covered the three windows on either side of the room, also mostly in shades of green and gold. The shapes depicted a beautiful woman, with white hair longer than she was, floating among the stars. In some, she wore no clothing at all and in others, she wore a flowing green dress.

Mari hadn't been in many religious buildings in her lifetime but the few times she had she'd felt an overwhelming need to be as small and quiet as possible. It was as if there was a sense that being too loud or appearing as anything other than tiny and humble might be disrespectful to any God or Goddess watching.

She slowly made her way forward, careful to keep her arms close to her sides and to not click her boots on the floor. She knelt in front of the altar where a golden pillow rested.

The statue in front of her was of the full moon and Eris, bigger than the base itself, sat atop the moon. Her long hair wrapped around her and a serene expression rested on her face. Her knees were raised and she rested her head on them, looking down towards Mari.

Surrounding the statue on the altar were tiny candles, lit with green magic fire. More of the green stones from the vases and a variety of fresh and dried flowers were scattered along the surface.

"I'm not good at praying," Mari whispered up to the statue, "but I was told you could help me."

She paused, trying to find the right words. Her gaze drifted down to her hands, picking nervously at the nail on her thumb.

"As much as I would appreciate for you to break my curse, what I want just as much would be for you to come back to this world and help your people; especially my friend, Alek. Your starlight is very missed..." she trailed off, worried she might have sounded like she was scolding a Goddess.

She took a deep breath, "I don't know why you went away. But I know what it's like for those that are important to you to just disappear one day and suddenly you've never felt more alone." Tears stung her eyes and she wiped them with the back of her hand, "If you can't come back, please give me the opportunity to help your people in any way that I can. I'll show you that I'm worthy of having my curse broken."

Mari lifted her head and gasped. On the ground in front of her, a dagger sat. It hadn't been there when she'd knelt down, she was sure, and yet here it was. She reached out to grab it, the silver metal of its hilt cold on her palm. Embedded in the pommel was a large emerald stone that gave off a glow of its own. Smaller green gems and flecks of gold were set in the sheath to look like the phases of the moon, where the full moon in the middle was symbolized by a round white stone. She admired the handle where various sizes of carved golden stars swirled around in a spiral.

She pulled the blade out of its cover and kept her hand wrapped perfectly below the cross guard that protected her from the simple, yet sharp, nine-inch blade. Along the dull edge, words were etched into the metal, though the language was nothing Mari had seen before.

Behind her, a clay pot scraped across the floor. She gasped, whipping around, her heart beating fast, with the dagger held awkwardly out in front of her.

"Who's there?"

A frail, blue-skinned pixie emerged from behind a vase. Her hands were raised, palms outward, and her wings fluttered in a blur behind her.

"I'm sorry." She stepped out into the aisle speaking in a rush, "I'm a caretaker for the temple and I hid when you came in. I studied humans in class but hadn't ever seen one in front of me and I just wanted a closer look, I didn't mean to frighten you."

"What do you want?" Mari's shock was still palpable, her heart beating too fast. She considered calling for Maelin.

"Nothing, truly. Only to observe you," she took a step closer and Mari stood, taking a step back, "but, if I may... It looks like you've been given a gift from the Goddess herself. May I take a closer look?"

Mari hesitated. After a moment of looking the female up and down, Mari decided she could take on this small Faerie in a fight if she needed to, though something told her it wasn't going to come to that. She nodded and the girl stepped closer. Mari held tight to the grip but displayed the blade to the pixie.

"What does this writing say?"

The pixie smiled, her sharp teeth sending a fresh wave of fear through Mari's spine, though she remained non-threatening as she translated, "A blade that will leave only one. Defeat my greatest enemy, o' wielder of Eris's Fury, no matter the cost." The girl looked up, locking her purple eyes with Mari's, "The Goddess has entrusted you with a grand responsibility." She lowered herself to the ground, bowing at Mari's feet. "May the starlight be with you on your journey."

Mari slid the dagger into its cover and put it in her bag as the pixie moved past her to pray at the altar.

Even though the growing weight of the responsibility laid out before her was beginning to manifest itself in intense nausea, she managed to thank the pixie before heading back out to reconvene with Maelin. Perhaps this was a gift that, unlike the dryad's Goddess Flower, Mari would keep to herself for a while.

The dried pine needles of the forest floor were cold on Alek's cheek as he regained consciousness. He sat up, breathing heavily. The air was starting to get colder and the smell of burnt pine filled his nostrils. He wasn't near the city anymore; the rustling of tiny forest Fae came to him before his eyes adjusted to the faint setting sunlight.

"Etaldin." His voice was hoarse but he needed to say this, "Listen to me, Etaldin. This is *my body*. You will not take it over ever again. I will not hesitate to kill this body before I let you have it again."

Etaldin sounded weak as he responded, as if taking total control of Alek had used up a large amount of his energy. Even so, he was still characteristically stubborn.

Don't do anything to make me have to take it over again.

Alek grabbed a knife from his belt and held it to his neck. He hoped he wouldn't have to resort to taking such tragic and terrible measures, but he couldn't let Etaldin take complete control. He needed Etaldin to know he had the power here. He was serious as he spoke again.

"I'll do it."

There was a rustling inside of him, an uneasiness. Etaldin growled.

I will not take over your body again so long as you always do as I say.

Alek pulled the knife closer to his skin. His heartbeat quickened in his chest. He hoped Etaldin could feel the real possibility behind the threat.

Stop! Etaldin's growl burst into a roar. *Your body will remain yours, but so long as you want to use* my *powers, you will have to continue my bidding.*

Alek held the knife steady, "and if I choose *not* to do your bidding?"

Then I will withhold all magic from you. We will see how far you get in saving that girl without my help.

Alek knew the truth in Etaldin's words. He also knew that was probably as good of a deal as he was going to get. He lowered the knife, the relief within him was both his own and Etaldin's.

"Deal. Now, why have you brought me to this pinery?"

We're here to cast a spell.

"What will this spell do, exactly?" Alek spoke aloud, though he was speaking only to the God within him.

You will use my power to summon Unseelie spirits. If they lie in wait here, they can help you separate the girl from her companions and she will be all yours.

Alek took a deep, shaky breath, "*the girl* has a name, you know."

He noticed the spell ingredients and the pentagram scorched in the ground below him. "You've been busy."

Etaldin ignored his comment. Instead, he relayed the instruction. Alek obediently performed the spell.

As he spoke the ancient words, shadows around them began to move. Alek felt the power inside of him once again, a simmer growing to a roaring boil.

"Will this hurt anyone?" Alek asked, nervously looking at the lethal grin on the shadow demon that had appeared before him. He shivered at the excitement in Etaldin's response.

Of course.

18

MONSTERS IN THE FOREST

"Mari!" Cylan's scream caught her attention moments before the harsh ring of metal against metal filled the air.

"Ma'am! Hurry!"

Mari's heart thumped, beating hard and fast. She scrambled down the temple's steps taking Maelin's outstretched hand for support.

"What's going on?" Mari's voice rose with her panic as they ran towards Cylan and Leo who were headed their way through the pines.

"Ambush," Leo said, sword at the ready.

Mari looked back towards the road where the chaos ensued.

The royal guards were fighting, their swords swinging through the air, though at first Mari couldn't see what they were aiming for. They were surrounded by purplish-black smoke that didn't seem to be affected by the breeze that rustled the leaves.

At second glance, the smoke wasn't just a collection of random clouds; within the shadows of each cloud, the smoke curled and twisted, forming the silhouette of a large body with arms that came to sharp points on the end. As the soldier's swords collided with their enemies' arms, the metal-on-metal sound reverberated through the forest.

"Head south, stay off the trail! I'll catch up." Leo handed Cylan a short sword before running into the heart of the brawl.

Mari felt so vulnerable that she might as well have been standing there naked with a big target on her back. *So much for keeping this a secret,* she thought as she reached around for the dagger in her backpack. She may have never used any kind of weapon before, but in that moment she decided the curse wouldn't take her without a fight. If this damned curse that took her mother and father had finally come for her, she would face it with as much bravery as she could muster.

Mari followed Cylan with Maelin close behind. They darted through the pines away from the sounds of the fighting. They had only made it a few yards when Mari felt the strain of her breathing and the beat of her frantic heart. She risked a glance behind her, immediately regretting it.

A massive cloud of purple and black smoke sifted through the trees, right on their tail. Everything the smoke touched withered, turning black. They could keep running, but for how long? It was gaining on them. Fast.

"Cylan!" Mari shouted.

Cylan turned his head, his teeth bared and eyes blazing as he saw the monstrous form only a yard away. He grabbed Mari's wrist with his free hand, changing his direction and heading for the trail.

"Leo said to stay off the trail!" Mari protested, grabbing Maelin's arm to keep her close.

"We'll be faster without the uneven ground and trees in our way! We've got to outrun this thing."

Mari couldn't argue with that. The three of them ran, dodging holes and rocks in their path. Just as Cylan crossed onto the trail, a rogue tree root caught Mari's foot. She went down, her backpack falling aside and Maelin tumbling atop her.

Cylan released her hand, stumbling forward. The girls tried to scramble to their feet, but the momentary delay was enough for their pursuer to close the distance between them.

The smoke cloud hovered for a moment, the purple and black inky wisps swirling around until they formed a faceless being that stood nearly seven feet tall. The arms formed next, spreading out with a massive span; it would only need to take one step before being able to reach them.

Mari unsheathed the dagger. This was the end. Nowhere left to run. She tried to stand only to fall to the ground again, shooting pain radiating up from her ankle. She groaned, wishing she could die on her feet.

The being's legs were formed now. Mari closed her eyes, holding the dagger out in front of her. The only thing that made this bearable was knowing she would see her parents soon.

Mari was startled at the shrill and unexpected sound of horses crying out nearby. Her eyes shot open just in time to see a long sword cutting the shadow monster in half. As the smoke dissipated, two horses took shape. Atop one, Leo sat, pulling his sword back from where the smoke had just been.

He hopped down, rushing to them. Maelin took his extended hand, pulling herself to her feet. Cylan was at Mari's side in a second, lifting her in his arms. He carried her to the horse nearest them as Maelin and Leo mounted the other. Mari winced as she lifted herself, trying to keep all weight off her injured ankle. Once she was in place by the horse's shoulders, Cylan grabbed her backpack and jumped up behind her, taking the reins and signaling for the horse to go.

"What were those things?" Mari called back to him as their horse galloped down the path.

"Demons." His teeth were gritted, his voice tight. "That's what happens to the souls of the Fae that are called back from the Otherworld against their will."

"Who called them back?" She couldn't help the question though she knew Cylan only had the same amount of information that she did. To her surprise, he answered.

"Etaldin. What Thorsten said must be true. He's back."

As the moon peaked in the starless night sky, the horses came to a stop in front of a tavern in Maborough town.

"We'll rest here for the night," Leo said, helping Maelin down from their horse.

"I'll go secure us a couple of rooms." Maelin headed towards the door. Mari could see she was trying to keep herself composed but her unsteady breath gave away her fear.

"What about the others?" Mari asked, letting Cylan support her as she slipped down off of her seat.

Cylan gave Leo a knowing look. Leo lowered his head. That answered her question.

"If anyone survived," Leo said gently, "they will know to come here and we will meet with them tomorrow."

Mari nodded to Leo as he took the horses' reins, leading them to their stalls for the night.

Cylan was still supporting her weight on her right side, her arm draped over his shoulders. A day ago, being this close to him would have been something she avoided like the plague. Now, she appreciated the warmth of his body against hers in the chilled night air.

"Let's get you inside and take care of your injury." He said softly, guiding her through the tavern door.

Inside warm firelight filled the space, casting shadows on the thick stone walls. A few patrons sat at wooden tables, eating and drinking. The only sounds were of light chatter and crackling firewood.

Maelin approached them with two small keys, "Our rooms are up the stairs," she reached towards Mari, "let me help you up there, ma'am."

Cylan didn't move from her side, "I can take her. I've got to see to her leg anyway."

Maelin curtsied and led the way up the stairs. Cylan supported most of Mari's weight the whole way as she kept her injured leg lifted. The upper level of the tavern only had a handful of doors and Maelin led them to one on the right. Inside, two lumpy beds sat on either wall. Moonlight filtered in through the one small window. Maelin went to the hearth on the far wall to start a fire.

Mari limped over to one of the beds, falling onto it. Slowly, she removed her shoes and examined her ankle. The skin was covered in various shades of blacks, blues, and purples, spreading down her foot in a bruise that made her cringe. The ankle was swollen and she could feel her heartbeat as the blood forced its way through her veins.

"A solid injury." Cylan sat next to her, a tone of taunting approval in his words, "Good job."

Mari rolled her eyes, "how am I supposed to travel the whole realm like this? I can barely walk."

Cylan lifted her injured ankle onto his lap. He hovered his hand over the bruise. A yellow glow began to shine from the center of his palm, slowly spreading to his fingertips. Mari felt a soothing heat from the magical light and braced herself in anticipation of pain when he lowered his hand gently down to rest on her ankle.

The pain didn't come. In fact, his touch was more than soothing, it was relieving.

"Thorsten may have gotten the gift of earth travel, which is useful when you're stationed in the largest kingdom in the realm," Cylan explained, his eyes focused on his work, "but yours truly got the mostly useless and overrated gift of healing."

Mari looked over at him and scoffed, "Useless? My pain is almost entirely gone and you've been working on it for all of a minute? Cylan, that's amazing."

His head rose, his eyes locking on hers. "If the king didn't despise humans, I'd ask you to tell him that; might make him look at me differently." He sighed, shaking his head back as one of his curls fell into his eyesight, "My father believes such a gift is pointless because the Fae do not die of sickness and everyone's personal magic allows them to self-heal most minor physical injuries. My gifts have only ever been useful to myself or animals that cannot heal themselves. And, you now, apparently."

He lifted his hand and Mari gasped. The bruise had faded to an almost undetectable yellow shade and the swelling was non-existent. Hesitantly,

Mari moved her ankle in a circular motion, happy to find that there was no pain.

"You're amazing. Thank you, Cylan." She smiled warmly at him.

He stood, ready to leave, when a thought popped into Mari's mind, "So, when do you assume the throne? How do you decide, if you all live forever and never get sick or die, does your father just choose to quit or…?"

"Usually, yes, Fae can choose when they are ready to move on to the Otherworld— but it's a journey they cannot come back from unless they want to become those things in the forest. The Fae can die from other things besides sickness or old age. Murder, of course—our immortality cannot withstand that; there are some wounds that even magic can't fix. Most former Unseelie Kings have assumed the throne by killing their predecessors."

"You're not…"

"No," Cylan scoffed, "I'm not going to do that."

Cylan stared into the fire. "We can also die from drawing our magic off of our life force, instead of starlight for too long." Cylan sighed, "My father is stubborn and refuses to quit using magic, although each time he does, it drains him and he's struggling to recover. Truthfully, I think he's ready to be back with my mother, Elowyna. Though, he'd never admit it." Cylan looked at her then, his tone certain. "He will die, one day not too long from now. That's why our journey must succeed."

———— ·✦· ————

Mari must have fallen asleep though she didn't remember doing so. One moment she was lying there, writing in her journal about the events of the day and the next her eyes fluttered open to warm afternoon light blanketed across the room.

Maelin's bed was empty and the fire had gone out leaving only ashes in the hearth. With a yawn, Mari sat up. She stood, testing her ankle. It was perfect; Cylan truly had an amazing gift. She felt a twinge of empathy for him, remembering the way he talked about his father's disappointment in his abilities.

She opened her door and headed down to the tavern, hoping to find Cylan and the others there. The murmur of multiple voices rose in volume the further she made it down the stairs. Sounds of haughty laughter melted in with a stringed instrument that someone was playing a lively tune on.

Mari rounded the corner, sighing in relief when she saw her three companions sitting at the bar, drinking from large mugs. While her eyes were focused on her friends, she noticed that many of the other tavern patrons, who ranged from kelpies to elves and everything in between, were staring at her. A few whispered to their friends next to them, not even attempting to hide that they were talking about her.

With a deep breath and her chin held high, she took a seat by Maelin who looked up cheerily at her arrival.

"Ma'am," she said, passing Mari a mug full of brown liquid, "glad to see you're awake. You were sleeping like the dead!"

Mari chuckled, accepting the drink and giving it a sniff before taking a small sip. It was sweet, like honeyed water, with the zesty undertone of something fermented. She wrinkled her nose and pushed the drink away.

"I've never felt more rested, that's for sure." She looked around the room where most of the other patrons had gone back to minding their own business. She lowered her voice, leaning in closer, "Did anyone else show up after... yesterday?"

They all silently shook their heads.

Cylan met her gaze briefly before burying his face back into his mug. He hadn't worn his pinstripe vest today and his loose white top hung open at the collar. His hair fell in his face and he looked like he hadn't slept. It was the most disheveled that she'd seen him so far, and the most relatable. In fact, each of the four of them—all that was left of their original company —looked like they'd seen better days.

Mari returned to slowly nursing her drink. The music slowed and then stopped; the faun that was playing headed towards a table for a break. With the music gone, the conversations around the room were much clearer. Mari closed her eyes, listening to a group of females—she tried to recall the name for these Fae from her books; perhaps they were undines?—chatting excitedly.

"It's true," one said, "I saw something too, out by the lake, but it wasn't a monster as you say, it's a white bird; a beautiful lake spirit."

Another scoffed, "I know what I saw and it was *not* a beautiful lake spirit. I barely escaped with my life! It was drinking at the edge of the water, and it had the sharpest teeth and claws that—"

A slouched and time-weathered goblin approached the table, slamming his drink down and startling the undines. He belched loudly, tipping back his torn captain's hat.

"Pardon me, but you're both wrong," he said, his voice gravely, "the being is most certainly a spirit of some kind but it's neither bird nor does it have claws and teeth. The creature has tentacled arms, countless arms, and it's been keeping my crew and me off the water for some time now."

Mari sighed as she listened to them argue over what they saw, each of them sure that the other was wrong. She was tired of hearing and thinking about undefinable monsters in the forest.

"I'm going to get some air."

Leo and Maelin nod. Cylan stood with her.

"I'll join you," he said casually, "just to be safe." He rested his hand on the hilt of the sword in his belt, the same place that Mari had her Goddess dagger secured.

Mari couldn't think of a good reason to object and let him lead the way. The sun had finally settled below the horizon and the twilight had cooled into the blue cover of dusk.

Mari and Cylan walked side by side along the dirt path that twisted through town and around the lake. They were silent, the only sound came from their feet rhythmically patting across the dirt.

Mari cleared her throat. "My ankle feels perfect. Thanks again."

"Of course it does," Cylan smirked, "and you're welcome."

Mari couldn't hold in the eye roll or the smile that followed. The reaction was quickly becoming a reflex response to Cylan's confident attitude. It was easier to be near him without feeling the rage she had before.

With this realization came the moment that Mari was very aware of the little gold necklace that bounced against her collarbone with every step she took. Each time the metal touched her skin, she was reminded of the night Cylan had her kidnapped and gave her the impossible choice of going home at her friend's expense or staying with him to save them. She could see now that he'd known there had never been a choice to be made. Cylan had already known what the outcome of that night was going to be before it even began.

She picked up her head to look over at him, his golden eyes shimmering in the faded light. He smiled softly at her.

Despite his wrongdoings, she couldn't help but see a sad and frightened boy who'd lost his mother, been separated from his family and had been consistently degraded by his father. He was a boy who had too much on his shoulders and not enough support to carry it all. Still, was that enough of an excuse to make everyone around you feel miserable as well?

They followed the path as it rounded the edge of the lake. The reflection of the rising moon shimmered in the dark water. To their right, a rustling in the bushes had Mari and Cylan reaching for their weapons.

Cylan grabbed Mari's arm, pulling her backward into the cover of the trees behind them. Mari relaxed from her defensive position as a woman emerged from the bushes. Her fear for herself quickly turned into fear for the woman as she dove into the water, swimming gently toward the middle of the lake.

"What if there really is a monster in the water?" Mari whispered to Cylan, "We've got to tell her."

Cylan pulled her back down when she started to stand, "just watch."

Mari sighed, her face crumpled in confusion. She looked back at the girl who had reached the center of the lake. The Fae leapt upward, sending water spraying through the air only for it to turn to mist as it fell.

Mari gasped, watching as the woman did not fall back to the water, but stayed elevated above the swirling mist, and began to dance along the surface of the water. She smiled as bright as the moonlight she twirled in. The whole lake was her dance floor, the mist her silent partner.

"She's a vile," Cylan whispered, "a shapeshifter. It's rare to see them in their true forms like this. Usually, they only appear as—"

"Let me guess," Mari said, "wolves, swans, sea creatures?"

Cylan chuckled, "Sea creatures are not a typical shape for them but I suppose anything is possible."

"She's beautiful. Definitely not the monster that the townspeople thought she was."

"Viles are harmless," Cylan agrees, "just tricksters that find a lake and claim it as their own and don't want to share it."

"So, should we tell the locals there's not really a monster out here?"

Cylan shrugged, "maybe one day. If they were able to resume fishing here it would certainly help the local economy..." Cylan mused, "But, let's let the vile have a bit more peace, just for a while."

Mari smiled at him as they backed out of the trees and onto the path toward town. Maybe he was finally softening up a bit.

"After all," he continued, "if the villagers are too dense to figure it out themselves, who are we to intervene?"

Mari chuckled, amused that he instantly contradicted her thoughts, but didn't say anything further on the subject.

"Where did you get that dagger?" Cylan asked.

Mari blinked at the suddenness of his question, her hand instinctively reaching to touch the hilt at her hips. There was no point in lying, especially now that he knew of its presence.

"Um," she cleared her throat, "when I was at the temple, back in the Pinery, I was praying with my eyes closed and when I opened them, the dagger was in front of me."

He pursed his lips, staring ahead. "A gift from Eris then."

"Yeah, I suppose so." Her voice was barely a whisper.

Cylan didn't respond until they had reached the doors of the tavern. When he spoke, his voice was low enough that he had to lean in close for her to hear him.

"Keep it close. If Etaldin is back—and I really believe he is—then you'll need a bit of the Goddess's magic at your side."

19

FEAR & FLOWERS

"Ah, good." Leo said as Mari and Cylan approached, "I was just telling Maelin to pack up so that we may leave shortly."

"Now?" Mari couldn't hide her shock, "but, what happened to it being dangerous to travel at night?"

"It is not ideal, you're right," Leo explained, "but now that we are all rested, I'd like to get off of the mainland, quickly. Likely, the creatures from the forest won't be able to follow us across the water."

Mari's heart dropped farther into her stomach. *Across the water?* Mari had spent her life deliberately staying away from open bodies of water, afraid the curse would take the opportunity to drown her. She never learned to swim and wasn't fond of the idea of learning now.

"Ma'am?" Maelin came to stand by Mari's side, "You look ill. Are you alright?"

"I'm fine," she lied, swallowing hard, "let's get our things from upstairs."

With the door of their room closed securely behind them, Mari let her fear show fully. Her breathing became shallow and rapid as she paced the room.

"Maelin," she said, "I can't go in the water. I'll die, I know it."

Maelin's eyebrows rose, shock plain on her delicate face.

"Die? Ma'am surely that isn't true!"

"I can't swim, I'll drown for sure." Panic rose in her throat, tears brimming in her eyes.

Maelin reached out to grab her shoulders, effectively stopping Mari's pacing, "Mari, you must calm down. All is well, I assure you."

At the sound of Maelin using her name, Mari was shocked into focusing. She took a deep breath, hoping to steady herself.

"I'm sorry. I'm just afraid."

Maelin reached into the pockets of her dress, pulling out several tiny bottles filled with blue liquid, "While you were sleeping I purchased several Potions of Breathing. It allows those of us who breathe air to breathe underwater for a short time, and there are plenty here to last us for our whole trip in Water's Dominion."

Mari took a small rounded bottle, examining it, "you're sure they work?"

"Of course," Maelin looked confused, "I've used them myself, several times before."

Mari took another deep breath. She was still shaking, but nodded, forcing a weak smile on her lips.

"Good." Maelin smiled back, leading her towards one of the beds, "Now, you sit here and keep breathing while I pack up our few belongings. You'll see, ma'am, all will be well."

——— ·✦· ———

"Surely you didn't think we'd be avoiding going in *wyna* when the entirety of the Water's Dominion is, in fact, water?"

Mari had finally stopped shaking from her fear of going out into the ocean, but the rock-like dread still hung heavy in her stomach. Cylan was chuckling at her now as she hopped up onto their horse.

"I'm not stupid." She replied, indignant. "Of course, I didn't think we were going to skip one whole kingdom. I guess the reality of it just didn't sink in until now." She gulped, realizing her poor choice of words a second too late. The thought of anything sinking—boats, perhaps— sent her heart rate skyrocketing all over again.

Cylan was behind her now, Leo and Maelin on the other horse, and they were headed west. Maborough town was not more than half an hour away from the shoreline where they would then take a rowboat over to the Indigo Isles and stay at the inn there.

"Don't they have oceans in your world?" Cylan's tone was still teasing.

"Of course." She tried to stay calm and not give him the satisfaction of getting under her skin, "I live by one."

"And you've never learned to swim?"

Mari's voice lowered in embarrassment, "I was afraid. Of the curse."

Cylan scoffed, "Why are you so sure that you're cursed, anyway?"

Mari inhaled deeply. Somehow, after all of these years, it was still hard for her to say aloud the terrors that haunted her dreams. Perhaps showing Cylan a bit of vulnerability would help him find some of his own. She decided to keep the story as short as possible.

"Everyone that's had Dawson as their last name has died. All in some tragic, unexpected way. My grandparents couldn't get out of their home when it caught fire. My mother didn't make it through giving birth to me." She felt Cylan wince behind her, but continued, "My father and I were safe for a while until our car crashed on the icy roads and I was the only one who walked away. He had two brothers, one of them had passed a long time before I was even born and the other, Jacob, became my legal guardian for a while until he got really sick." She let out a shaky breath, "it only makes sense that I'm next."

The ocean ahead of them was coming into focus. Mari breathed in and out, focusing on the pattern. In. Out. In. Out.

"The *wyna* is so shallow here, ma'am," Maelin's soft, kind voice rose over the sound of crashing waves in the distance, "you'll be able to see the bottom the whole time you're in the boat."

"I can assure you I won't be looking over the side."

The horses' hoof beats quieted as the ground transitioned from hard-packed dirt to loose, fine sand. Waves lapped up against a long wooden dock where multiple rowboats were tied, bobbing in the water. The four of them dismounted their horses and started towards the dock.

"People just leave their boats here? Seems like they'd be easy to steal." Mari noted.

"You steal one of these and you'll drown for sure." Cylan chuckled darkly.

"These boats are for rent by the nixies that live here," Maelin explained, "no one would be naive enough to steal one of these and think that the nixies wouldn't pull them under before they made it ten feet."

"Where are they?"

Although she didn't know what a nixie looked like, she still didn't see signs of anyone lurking about.

"Wait just a moment and you'll find out," Cylan said, stepping onto the dock.

He went to the end and knelt down. Just as he did, the water there began to bubble and a figure slowly emerged from beneath the waves.

The waves did not move the nixie; the creature was still and steady in the water. Frog-like skin covered the nixie's face. It was slick and olive green, with darker green splotches along the sides. Adding to the eerie features, its kelp-like hair hung over totally black eyes. It blinked with two sets of eyelids that closed in opposite directions. It didn't speak, but lifted a webbed-fingered hand out of the water, waiting for payment.

Cylan reached into his pocket, pulling out three onyx stones. He was careful not to touch the nixie's hand as he dropped the stones into it. The nixie's hand closed over the stones and it silently sank below the water, instantly disappearing.

Leo untied the boat nearest him, pulling it closer to the shore. Cylan jumped in first. Maelin started over that way, stopping when Mari grabbed her by the wrist.

"You said you had water-breathing potions?" Mari asked nervously.

"Yes ma'am, but you won't need them for such a short journey. The Indigo Isles are just—"

"Please." Mari interrupted her, "It will make me feel a lot safer, knowing that if something happens I won't immediately drown."

Mari hated the pitiful look that Maelin wore on her face, the one that planted a seed of shame and doubt in Mari's belly and made her question her capabilities. Even so, when Maelin pulled out the small round bottle, Mari was relieved.

"What's the hold-up?" Cylan called impatiently.

"We are on our way, your highness!" Maelin started towards the boat again. "Quickly, ma'am."

Mari uncorked the bottle and, without question, poured the liquid down her throat. Surprisingly, it held a hint of the familiar taste of seaweed, though the slimy texture made her grimace and wish she had something to wash it all down with.

Tucking the empty bottle in her pocket, Mari jogged over towards the boat. Leo offered his hand to assist her over the edge and into her seat. She took a deep breath and grasped it, allowing him to steady her as she climbed in next to Maelin.

Leo pushed the boat into the water before jumping in, jostling the boat before picking up the oars and starting to row. Mari stifled a startled noise, knowing Cylan would have something snide to say about her weakness if she let it out. Maelin noticed, reaching out a hand to place over Mari's in silent support, smiling kindly.

"You see, ma'am," Maelin's voice was soft as she pointed out in front of them, "the isle is just on the horizon. We'll be there in no time at all."

Mari nodded silently, acknowledging the dark blob on the horizon that she assumed was the isle. Instead of trying to make out details of the island from this far away, she continued to focus on her breathing. *In through your nose, out through your mouth*, she repeated in her mind.

Her eyes darted to the waves that surrounded them, wondering what horrible creatures lived below. With another deep breath, she tore her eyes away, attempting to find something less terrifying to focus on.

Her gaze settled on Cylan, his black curls swept up by the wind. He was staring out over the water, lost in thought. His golden eyes nearly glowed in the white light of the full moon while his long lashes cast shadows over his tan cheeks. The muscle in his jaw tensed as if whatever he was thinking about was beginning to stress him.

Cylan blinked a few times, coming back to the present, straightening his tie and smoothing his vest. It was no secret that Cylan valued outward appearances, as he worked to get the sand off his boots, not satisfied until each grain was gone. Although Mari could admit it was odd to see him dressed in a style that was arguably a bit too formal for their situation, she couldn't deny that he still looked damn good in it.

His eyes flickered up to hers.

"See something you like?" He purred.

Mari blinked, the embarrassment of being caught sending heat through her cheeks and trapping the air in her throat. She looked past him; the isle was close enough now to see the waves falling onto the beach.

"Yes," Mari cleared her throat, "land."

A few moments later their boat settled on shore. Mari jumped onto the sand, her knees weak. She let out a sigh of relief, taking in her surroundings.

The isle was longer than it was wide—from where she stood, Mari could make out the shore on the other side—and hosted only one large, stone building with a thatched roof. A sign hung over the door, the words etched onto it were in a language she didn't know. The sea breeze carried the tune of a simple song played on a wind instrument from the open windows where a warm yellow light shone.

Under her feet, the sandy shore quickly dissipated as she went further inland where a thick clover-like plant covered the ground. Between the clover, taller green stalks popped up every few inches, with closed buds on top that looked ready to bloom at any moment. As they approached the front door of the building, a bud on one of the flowers popped open, its petals unfurling gently. Deep, rich indigo color saturated each petal as they pointed in each direction, like the rays of a star.

Mari left the beautiful flower behind and made her way inside behind the rest of her group. The smell of a savory meal washed over Mari like a wave once she stepped over the threshold. Her stomach growled in anticipation.

Cylan, Leo, and Maelin had all taken a seat at a table near the large hearth on the far wall. Mari hurried to join them. She inhaled deeply, savoring the scent coming from the thick cauldron that hung suspended above the roaring fire, steam billowing from the top.

"Good evening," a silky female voice drifted from behind Mari, "and welcome to The Big Narwhal."

A Fae with pale skin and bright eyes stood beside them. She wore a translucent white dress that clung tight to her skin. It was easy to see every detail of her body. So much so that Mari had to avert her eyes for a moment to gather her thoughts. She was gorgeous, and the sultry smirk that paired perfectly with her piercing gaze made her even more intoxicating to behold.

"Help yourself to our famous Seaweed Stew." Her voice was low, smooth, and seductive. "It is sure to be the best thing you've ever let pass your lips." The female held four wooden bowls, setting them on the table, her long blonde hair draping around her. As her hair fell in perfect waves, the tips of her ears were revealed. Mari was startled—they were blunt and rounded, like her own!

The moment of shock brought Mari back around to the present, where she noticed the rest of the table had become infatuated with the waitress as well. Maelin was doing her best to keep her staring respectful, only taking little glances, while Leo was outright staring so intensely he looked like he might forget to breathe.

Cylan's gaze was more confident. A quick appraisal of the woman from head to toe, stopping somewhere in the middle for a moment, before turning his stare on Mari, and giving her a wink.

Mari rolled her eyes, gathering her bowl and heading towards the cauldron to ladle herself some stew. The others lined up behind her and when their bowls were full, they tucked in at their table.

"Is she..." Mari spoke between mouthfuls of the delectable soup, "human?"

"Selkie," Maelin said simply. No time for full sentences when the food was delicious and everyone was starved.

Cylan, who had taken his last bite, explained further. "They can look exactly like a human if they shed their coat. I'm sure she's keeping it behind the bar for after her shift when she returns to the Dominion."

In the corner, a satyr skillfully played a small wind instrument. He wore very little—just enough to cover his hips and groin—leaving his double-jointed legs bare. His red hair curled around two goat-like horns and covered his body in thick patches around his chest, arms, and legs.

He took a breath before changing the tempo of his song to something more upbeat. A few of the patrons laughed and jumped up to start dancing. Mari was surprised to see Cylan tapping his foot to the rhythm as well, a small smile on his lips.

"Lady Maelin," Leo stood, offering his hand to her, "would you care to dance with me?"

Maelin's pink skin reddened even more, but she smiled and accepted. The two of them joined the other dancing partners in the middle of the room where squeals of laughter and excitement grew.

Soon, Mari was clapping along with the music, laughing as well. The rest of the tavern joined in, and soon the entire room was on their feet, sloshing their drinks around and adding to the joyful noise.

"Would you like to join them?" Cylan stood, holding his hand out to Mari.

"You want to dance with me?" She smiled at him, exaggerating a look of shock.

He rolled his eyes but couldn't hide his own smile, "don't make me change my mind."

Mari giggled and took his hand, following him out to the dance floor. They flowed into the group of dancers where they began to bounce to the beat, round and round in circles. It was impossible to contain her laughter and joy. Cylan held her hands tightly, ensuring the two of them never collided with another pair of dancers. To her surprise, he even broke into laughter of his own a few times.

The song came to an end and the dancers retreated to their tables. Mari stood for a moment to catch her breath, smiling up at Cylan.

"I think maybe it's a good time to head to bed," she sighed, "between the excitement, the belly full of stew, and the warm fire, I'm ready to sleep for days."

Cylan appraised her for a moment. His eyes studied her face so intently, that she began to feel self-conscious.

"What?" She asked, "Is there something on my face?"

"Did I tell you why we call this the Indigo Isle?"

Mari blinked, "I don't think you did, no."

Cylan smiled his catlike grin, "I'll show you."

Mari turned to see Leo and Maelin enjoying a drink by the bar, engaged in conversation. They wouldn't miss her or Cylan, it seemed. Mari hurried after Cylan, stopping behind him where he stood in the doorway.

He took a step behind her, leaning in close enough that his hot breath tickled the back of her neck.

"Close your eyes," he instructed, placing his hands over her eyes and guiding her through the door.

They walked a couple dozen feet forward before Cylan stopped them, his voice right at her ear.

"Ready?"

Mari nodded, unsure what exactly she was ready for. She blinked her eyes when Cylan removed his hands and gasped at the sight before her.

Hundreds of flowers covered the island from shore to shore, their purplish-blue petals shimmering in the bright, silver moonlight. The rest of the flower buds had opened while they had been in the tavern, enveloping the island in an indigo blanket.

"Not every moment of this journey has to be business you know," Cylan said, guiding them to sit on a large piece of driftwood by the water, "we can enjoy the beauty of the realm, too."

"These are some of the most beautiful flowers I've seen." Mari reached down, gently running her fingers along the satin petals of a flower nearest her. "What are they called?

"The Indigo Star. One of my favorites. They only grow on the isles and only bloom in moonlight. No part of the plant has any use in alchemy, so they don't get picked really, they just... exist to be adored."

Mari was silent for a moment, taking in the bluish glow around them. The dark water was calm. She tried to not think about what was lurking beneath. Mari took a few deep breaths of the salty air and stared up at the moon.

"It seems so lonely," she mused.

"What does?"

"The moon. All alone up there in the dark. Back at home, it's got at least a few stars nearby."

"I can relate," Cylan muttered.

Mari turned and inclined her head towards him. "It must have been nice, seeing Thorsten. I'm sure you don't often see your siblings, now that they are all across the realm."

For once, Cylan didn't taunt or make a sarcastic comment. He sat, picking at a stray thread in his clothing for a moment before sighing deeply.

"Thorsten and I were never close, really. Tomorrow though, you'll get to meet Brynn, my favorite sister. I haven't seen her since she went to the Sunken Palace."

"It will be nice to meet her then." Mari attempted a cautious but encouraging smile.

Cylan scoffed, his lips hinting at a smile, "No, it won't be. Not for you, anyway."

Mari couldn't help but chuckle in response, "Why not?"

"You may have liked Thorsten, but that would be no surprise because he aligns himself with Seelie ideals. Brynn, on the other hand, is probably one of the most Unseelie Fae I know."

Mari swallowed the jolt of anxiety that his words sent through her, but she decided to keep the mood light.

"She can't be any worse than you," she teased, nudging his shoulder.

He laughed, and smiled over at her, "We'll see how you feel about that tomorrow."

They were quiet for a moment when another question fell from Mari's lips.

"And you? What side do you align with more?"

Cylan's smile fell and his gaze diverted out over the black water.

"I don't know."

"Is it a choice?" She wondered, "Or just the way you were born?"

"Partly both, but..." he paused, his eyes studying her face.

Perhaps he could see the honest curiosity behind her eyes, or maybe he was waiting to see judgment and disapproval, but something in Mari's expression seemed to encourage him to continue.

"The Realm of Faerie is very polarized. For the longest time, Fae consistently and wholeheartedly aligned with either one side or the other and their future generations went along with it, unquestioning. It wasn't until about a century ago, in your time measurements, when my mother and father decided to form an alliance and bring Unseelie and Seelie together in Eristald, that some depolarization began to happen. Some

Fae that had always been traditionally Unseelie chose to adopt a more Seelie lifestyle, and vice versa."

His face crumpled and he shook his head lightly, "It's complicated things, to say the least. When myself and my siblings were born, we were some of the first who were born with ties to both sides. Hanli and Thorsten felt called more towards the Seelie ways, while Brynn and Xerxes fell into the Unseelie habits."

Cylan smiled over at her again, his golden eyes sincere. "All of this to say, I can't decide. I feel called to both, in a way. My father would ask me to throw away all Seelie ties and take his place as the Unseelie ruler, but that doesn't feel right to me. My Seelie blood—my mother's blood—sings within me. I can't ignore it."

"Maybe you don't have to choose," Mari said softly. "It sounds to me that what your realm needs is someone to rule who understands all aspects of all of the Fae that live here."

"I hope you're right, Mari."

At this moment, Mari could feel the wall between them start to lower. Cylan was starting to appear to her in a new light, one where she could plainly see that his attitude was largely a facade for his pain and confusion. There was so much more to this Cylan-iceberg than one might see on the surface. He was so torn, so worried about making the wrong choice for his people.

Although Mari wanted to help him make the best decision as much as she was able to, there was really only one choice of his that she had a personal interest in. A final question burned in her mind.

"Cylan?" She began but hesitated. Was now the right time? Maybe not, but she wasn't sure she'd be getting another chance. When his gentle face peered over at her inquisitively, she decided to ask him the question she'd been itching to have an answer for.

"Will you help me get home, when all of this is over?"

Cylan's smile melted and instantly the mask of the cold prince was back on his face. His whole body visibly stiffened, and his voice held a clear disdain, "What's so special about that boring place?"

"Well for one, I'm not in danger around every corner."

"You're not in danger here either."

Mari couldn't help but scoff. "Seriously? Did you forget about the demons we just escaped? We've only been away from the castle for a few days and we've lost the majority of our party!"

"*Nahil!*" He bared his teeth, "You know what your problem is? You're selfish and ungrateful."

Mari recoiled, her mouth falling open, "Ungrateful? I'm supposed to be grateful that you kidnapped me? And who is calling who selfish? You're the one using me to try to win your kingdom over." She knew that wasn't exactly true, but logic had left the conversation.

"Using *you*? Darling, don't forget whose idea this whole thing was. Do I need to remind you whose funds and supplies we have been using as well?"

"This was pointless." She said softly, turning to head back to the inn, "To think I was starting to believe you were a good person. You'll always just be cold and unkind."

He grabbed her arm, stopping her in her tracks. She whipped her head around, pouring as much venom into her scowl as she could when she met his gaze.

Cylan stepped closer, eyes blazing. The muscle in his jaw clenched. He looked as though he wanted to say something, his lips twitching. Mari tugged her arm out of his grasp, taking a defiant step back. Wordlessly, Cylan stalked off towards the inn, leaving her alone on the shore.

She waited until he was a few feet ahead to start walking back toward her room. Her thoughts were an incoherent mix of anger and despondence. She had to hold on to the hope that one day she'd be able to convince him to let her go home. Today, however, was certainly not that day.

20

WOES & WAVES

From this far away on the northernmost point of the Indigo Isles, Alek couldn't hear Mari's voice but it was clear that she was in distress. Through the lens of his spyglass, he could see their heated expressions. They leaned in towards one another as if the words they spat could do more damage at a closer proximity.

Mari turned away from Cylan who was standing nearest the large ship that had come to take them to the Sunken Palace. She crossed her arms and held her chin upward in defiance.

"That's my girl," Alek whispered to himself, "stand up to him."

Cylan threw his arms up in exasperation. Alek savored the annoyance that radiated off of him. He wished he were closer, wished he could help Mari get away from that selfish prince.

The wanting ache in his stomach only reinforced how badly he wanted to be by her side. That wanting was quickly overwhelmed by anger when Cylan took a step nearer to Mari. He ducked down, wrapping his arms around Mari's waist, and hoisted her up over his shoulder. She flailed angrily, to no avail. Cylan carried her onto the ship and the ramp went up as the vessel started its path to the open sea.

"We should strike now," Alek said through gritted teeth, "before he hurts her."

We must stay ahead of them, Etaldin's tone left no room for objections. *The only way to leave the Dominion alive is through a portal ball in the south. We must make way immediately if we are to get there before them.*

Alek looked back at the rowboat that lay submerged a few feet offshore. He shuttered remembering the nixie's teeth as they tried to pull the boat he'd stolen underwater. Etaldin's magic was able to fend them off long enough for him to scramble ashore, but now he was stuck on the island.

He sighed, remembering the deal they made, knowing that if he wanted to keep control of his body, he must obey the God's commands. Their deal didn't forbid him from having an attitude, however.

"I don't suppose, in your infinite wisdom, that you know how I'm going to procure a ship, do you?"

———— ·✦· ————

Mari had drunk three breathing potions once the ship set sail. It made her feel a bit less anxious, even if Maelin had mentioned that taking multiple doses didn't do anything different than if she had just taken one.

The wind filled the large cloth sails, stretching them until they were taut against the ropes that secured them. Mari refused to get anywhere near the edge to look at the water, but she could still tell the ship was moving at a high speed, as the last bit of land that she could see became a blur in the distance.

Cylan and Leo were talking with the captain of the ship—a tall, lizard-skinned man with golden teeth—who had kindly offered Mari access to his quarters in case she would feel more comfortable tucked away. Maelin was perched near the edge on the upper level of the deck, looking out over the ocean with wide eyes and an awestruck smile.

"Ma'am!" She called, her neatly pinned hair coming loose in the wind, "Are you quite sure you do not want to see this view? The water, it looks like it's made of pixie dust from up here!"

"I'll take your word for it!" Mari called back, feeling nauseous.

She looked towards the double doors of the captain's cabin and decided to take a short rest before they reached their destination, although she didn't know exactly how long that would be.

Inside the small room, the captain's desk sat in front of a large set of windows that looked out behind the boat. Along either side of that window, shelves were filled with books, scrolls, and other treasures that the captain had acquired. The hammock bed was situated along the eastern wall, near another set of windows.

Mari gently lowered herself into the hammock and peered hesitantly out the window to her right. From inside a solid room, Mari was feeling a bit more brave. She was able to take a few deep breaths and before she knew it, she'd dozed off to the white noise of the wind and water.

The sun had moved in the sky enough for the shadow from her hammock to be coming from a slightly different angle when she woke. Sitting up, she could see that the ship had slowed; they were nearly at a full stop. She looked out the surrounding windows, seeing nothing but endless open water.

Mari stood and smoothed her clothes, intending to find Cylan and ask how much longer they had to go. She didn't get more than a step towards the door when movement beyond the window caught her eye.

She turned, wondering what it was she could have possibly seen this far away from land—perhaps a bird had flown overhead, casting a shadow over the water. Gentle waves moved across the ocean's surface, rocking their ship back and forth. Then, as she was about to turn away, the movement came again.

A bubble rose from somewhere below the waves. Curious, Mari watched as a series of smaller bubbles danced along the surface. With no explanation of where they could be coming from, Mari could only look on, staring as they multiplied until the once gentle waves began to churn, reminding her of simmering water on a stove.

A nervous feeling began to bubble up inside her belly before her stomach finally dropped at the sight of a long shadow that moved below. She gasped, her shaking legs slowly moving her away from the window. The shadow became larger and larger as its owner emerged from the depths.

Red snake-like tentacles, thicker than some of the oldest trees she'd seen in the forest, slithered up, breaking the water's surface and shooting skyward with astounding speed.

She stumbled backward at the sight of them, falling to her back. Mari scrambled to her feet, her trembling hands reaching for one of the many vials of water-breathing potion in her pocket. She downed the liquid just in time for the ship to lurch sideways, sending her back to the floor.

Desperate to find her companions and get to safety, she hauled herself upward using the captain's desk and lunged for the door.

When she was only feet away from the handle, the sound of breaking glass filled her ears. One of the tentacles had busted in through the window on one side of the room and back out through the window on the other side before finding its way back down to the water. The wet pulsing arm blocked the door completely.

Mari only had a moment to scream before a deep groaning sound shook the very air around her. An instant passed and water began to flow in from the broken window panes, quickly filling the cabin.

It's going to sink the ship! Mari realized. And, worse yet, she was trapped.

"Cylan!" She shouted, "Help me!" Though she could barely hear her own voice over the bellows of the creature and the roar of the rushing water.

Eris, she had only a moment to pray, *please don't let me die. Not yet.*

The water was up to her waist now, and the ship tilted forward, nose-diving into the ocean. The captain's treasures—that sat on shelves along the wall that rose as the ship sank and would soon be totally above her—began to fall into the water. A wooden chest, strengthened with metal bars banded around it, was one of the last things to fall, though Mari didn't see it.

The chest fell directly into Mari, knocking the breath out of her. Her body went limp as she sank below the water, an odd calm and cold darkness overwhelming all of her senses.

It seemed as though it were only a moment later when her mind started to slowly come back to her. Her thoughts were muddled. The feeling in her fingers and toes came back to her first, and they were shockingly warm. She couldn't exactly orient herself, with her eyes still closed, but she could feel her breathing coming evenly, the air around her dry.

Mari began to take deeper breaths, moving her body slowly. She realized she was lying on her back. Her eyes crept open to a dimly lit space and she found that she was tucked into a bed. Cautiously, she sat up, blinking a few times before the blur of sleep left her vision.

"You're awake." Cylan's voice pierced through her confusion.

Mari whipped her head towards his voice, instantly regretting the movement. A wave of dizziness overcame her, and she fell back against the pillows with a groan.

The dizziness was fading though the very walls around her seemed to move. She blinked, focusing her vision enough to see that the walls *were* moving. Or, rather, the schools of fish that swam outside were moving.

She was in a square room. Two of the walls—the one to her right and the one in front of her—and the ceiling were made entirely of glass. As if she were in a reverse fish tank, the ocean that surrounded her teemed with life and color and movement, while she sat in a warm, dry bed with a fire burning in the hearth carved into the sandstone wall to her left.

"We're alive?" Mari knew it was an odd question, but those were the only two words her lips could seem to form at the moment.

Cylan scoffed lightly, a playful smile on his lips. "Of course we're alive. And we're in the Sunken Palace."

"But..." Mari stammered, "the tentacles...the ship; it sank."

"Of course," Cylan repeated, sounding impatient, "how else would we get to the *Sunken* Palace? How hard did you hit your head, exactly?"

She reached up, wincing as her fingers brushed across a tender spot on the side of her head.

"You're telling me," Mari said slowly, her head throbbing, "that everything that happened... You *knew* a giant creature was going to *sink* the ship?"

"Obviously."

Cylan stood, coming to rest his hand on her head. The pain began to dull from a vision-shaking pounding to an almost unnoticeable ache.

"Feeling better?"

"If you cared about my feelings," she pulled away from him, "you would have prepared me for that *monster.*"

"Don't forget I'm cold and unkind." Cylan quoted the words she'd spat at him the night before. "Just trying to live up to your opinion of me, Mari."

Mari had opened her mouth to speak when Maelin rushed through the door, quickly curtsying to Cylan as he sauntered toward the open threshold.

"Oh! Ma'am, you're awake." Maelin smiled, "Thank the Goddess."

Cylan paused at the door, turning to call over his shoulder, "You were never in any danger."

Though Cylan was gone, the anger she felt toward him was beginning to sober her up, the last of her confusion fading away. Mari sat further up in her bed, able to think more clearly.

The frustration she felt was weak, a deeper emotion teased at her conscious mind. Though she didn't have an exact name for the feeling, she was beginning to associate it with Cylan's presence. When he was around, a fog came over her mind and her thoughts centered around him. Usually, it was paired with annoyance or frustration around what he was doing, his reactions, his words, his voice, the way his golden eyes shone...

She shook her head to clear the thoughts, though doing so only made her head throb. At least the pain was something better to focus on.

Maelin sat on the edge of the bed, carrying Mari's backpack. In her other arm was a garment bag. Mari didn't like the looks of it.

"We've made it to the Sunken Palace, as you might have already noticed, ma'am. Here, Princess Brynn resides and she's invited us to a reception over dinner, so I hope Prince Cylan's healing magic has made you feel more like yourself. I've brought some *appropriate* dinner attire and I'd appreciate it if you wouldn't fight me about wearing it."

Mari sighed, stripping the covers back. "I don't think I have any fight left in me today, Maelin. You win."

21

WHINING & DINING

Surprisingly, Mari didn't hate the dress that Maelin had put her in. It was long, fitted until it loosened at her waist, and it was a deep green. The flowy bottom half and long sleeves that went far past her hands were made of a translucent fabric that flowed through the air the way seaweed might float in the water. Fitting for an underwater dinner, she supposed, though it left no way to attach her dagger to her hip.

Maelin hesitated at the door to Mari's room, looking back sheepishly. She reached into her pocket, pulling out the small familiar vial that contained the water-breathing potion.

"Ma'am, the Sunken Palace is... well, *sunken*, save for a few specialty rooms like this one. Our journey to the dining room will be short, but you will have to swim."

Mari took a lungful of the warm dry air in her room and held out her hand to retrieve the vial from Maelin. She tossed the slimy liquid down her throat and sighed heavily.

"I may not know exactly how to swim," she squeezed her hands in front of her to stop them from shaking, "but I'm not going to let a little thing like that stop me once I've already come this far." She hoped that staying positive would get her through the fear that loomed over her like a constant shadow.

Maelin's face brightened, a mixture of relief and joy melted on her face, "that's the spirit, ma'am!"

The two girls walked out into the dry sandstone hallway, where there were a few more doors that presumably led to more bedrooms. To her right, the sandstone walls ended and beyond the threshold, the open water of the dark blue ocean was magically restrained from pouring into the hall.

They approached the edge of the water. In the short distance, over the sandy sea floor and past the exotic plant life teeming with varieties of fish, Mari could see yellow lights within more sandstone structures that spiraled up towards the surface. She held out her hand, dipping it into the ocean. A chill traveled up her arm.

Mari chuckled nervously, "I don't know why I thought it would be warm."

Maelin smiled sadly, "The warmth of the sun has a long journey before it reaches the palace, though I think that's the way the people of the Dominion prefer it." Maelin held her hand out, and Mari grasped it tightly, "Shall we go, ma'am?" Maelin smiled when Mari nodded, "I'll be by your side the whole way."

Maelin took the first step, gently pulling Mari along beside her. Mari entered the cold water with a gasp, followed by a moment of shock as she realized she was breathing effortlessly, *underwater.*

As they shuffled across the seafloor, kicking up small clouds of sand as they went, Mari took a few more experimental breaths. Her anxiety waned a bit as she accepted that she was completely fine. Despite being slower than normal moving through the water, and not being able to see quite as far ahead of her as she would on land, Mari felt a feeling of calm here on the ocean floor. She focused on the light in front of her as they approached the Sunken Palace.

Fish swam around them gracefully, disappearing into the darkness beyond as they continued on their paths. Bubbles floated up towards the surface here and there, where playful young merpeople chased them happily, racing to see who would reach them first.

Before she knew it, they were standing at the entrance to the Sunken Palace. Two merpeople were guarding the door, their silver tridents reflecting the light coming from the doorway. Wordlessly, they moved aside, allowing Mari and Maelin to move across the magical threshold and into the dry entryway of the palace.

Mari gasped again upon moving into the dry air, though it was more of a reflex than an actual need for air. The transition from water to air was going to take some getting used to. Although she was breathing with ease, she did find that being dripping wet in an evening gown was quite annoying. Now a puddle was forming around her and Maelin's feet, and her neatly pinned hair was drenched, clinging to her forehead and cheeks. Mari wiped the excess water from her eyes, turning to look at Maelin.

The little Fae was concentrating silently with her eyes closed, her hands clasped in front of her. Steam began to rise from her cherry blossom skin, her maroon curls drying quickly. Mari looked down and saw that the same was happening to her; the dress that was only a moment ago heavy with ocean water began to lighten and loosen from her body.

When they were most of the way dry—the thicker parts of their hair and dresses were still a bit damp—Maelin let out a sigh, stumbling backward a step.

Mari reached out to steady her, "Are you alright Maelin?"

Maelin gave a brave smile, though her eyes were still showing signs of weakness.

"I am sorry, ma'am, that I am unable to dry us fully. My magic is not as abundant as I wish it were."

"Maelin," Mari's tone teetered between scolding and concerned as she steadied Maelin and started down the hallway, "I would rather be a little bit wet than have you faint while trying to dry me off."

"You cannot be soaked with ocean water for dinner with Prince Cylan and Princess Brynn, ma'am. It is my honor to do what I can for you."

Mari was silent as they made their way through the curved sandstone halls, lit by magic fire torches. The holes in the sandstone walls, like windows out into the ocean, were using the same magic as every other threshold in the building to keep the water out. Mari wondered if these holes would allow a stray fish or merperson to fall into the castle. Or perhaps, only certain thresholds allowed entry.

The thought was only in her mind for a moment, as a more present sense of guilt settled within her at the thought of Maelin using her life energy to attempt to make Mari more comfortable. Mari was used to being independent, used to dealing with a few more inconveniences than the typical girl, but what Mari wasn't used to was being a burden.

They were hardly halfway through their trip and already Cylan had had to heal her twice with his magic, and Maelin had not only literally carried everything, but was now using her own magic to make Mari more comfortable. What other burdens would fragile human Mari put on her companions as they continued?

She was pulled from her moment of self-pity as they approached a tall archway with two stoic guards on either side. From the room beyond, the smell of seafood filled the hallway. The light from a woodless magic fire that burned in the hearth warmed the space. In the middle of the room, a long dining table, adorned with freshly prepared food, had places for only three guests, and two of them were taken.

Cylan sat with his back to the fire, lounging lazily in his high-backed chair. He had just set down his goblet and was laughing loudly. A large smile was plastered on his face; a sight rarely seen.

Next to him, in the chair at the head of the table sat a young female—whom Mari could easily assume was Princess Brynn— reciprocating his smile.

The first and most noticeable feature of Brynn's was her wings. Shaped and colored like the fins of a shark, they protruded from her back and did not move, opposite to the way that Thorsten's monarch wings had constantly fluttered. Mari imagined they were useful here under the ocean, and could easily picture Brynn gliding through the dark waters with grace, her long, raven hair and nearly see-through maroon dress flowing ethereally behind her.

Their laughter stopped as Mari approached. Maelin left her side and went to stand near Leo, who was keeping watch from the wall. One of the palace servants, a nixie female, held out Mari's chair for her. She sat, whispering a quiet hello to her dinner companions.

"Oh." Brynn sneered at Mari, her golden eyes appraising Mari from head to toe. "Interesting."

Mari looked over to Cylan, confused at Brynn's reaction. Cylan only peered into his goblet as he swirled the liquid inside.

"Is she not to your liking, sister?"

Brynn sighed, the look of disgust plain on her face. "I expected more. As far as humans go, this one seems rather plain."

Mari stifled a shocked gasp and instead focused her attention downward on the baked fish that had been presented before her. She gathered herself just enough to paste a smile on her lips before meeting Brynn's sharp glare.

"I'm sure many pale in comparison to your beauty, your highness." She said politely, adding, "It seems that you and your brother have both been gifted with striking features as well as the same delightful, pleasant disposition." She finished by taking a sip from her goblet, briefly noticing the smirk on Cylan's lips.

Brynn scoffed, "Sharp wit for a girl with such a dull face."

"Let's put away the claws, shall we?" Cylan sat forward, taking a bite of the greens on his plate, his fish untouched. "Now, my favorite sister, tell me, why are Fae from across the continent reporting that ships are being destroyed when they sail in your waters?"

Brynn shifted in her seat, fidgeting with the choker around her throat. An oval pendant, boasting the same royal moon and sun emblem as Cylan's ring, was attached to a silky maroon ribbon pulled taut and tied behind her neck. For a moment her shark-fin wings twitched as Brynn gave Mari one more pointed look before picking up her drink. The glare in her face lightened from disgust to annoyance as Cylan continued.

"Harmony between the kingdoms is important, you know. Wrecking everyone's ships is not exactly making people think kindly of the Dominion."

Mari hadn't realized how starved she had felt, and how thirsty. She finished the first goblet of wine and the nixie that had assisted her with her chair was ready with the carafe to fill her cup once more. It was sweet and tart and paired perfectly with the fish that had been prepared for them.

"We don't think kindly of land dwellers at the moment either." Brynn tossed a bone from her fish over her shoulder, not meeting Cylan's gaze, "The *Datalis* was stolen from the palace, and we know it was taken by someone with a ship, meaning it was not someone who resides in the Dominion. Henceforth until we find that artifact, we will be sinking every ship and searching the wreckage." Her face crumpled though her beauty was still undeniable, "Our efforts have not proved fruitful thus far."

Mari took a bite of her fish, her mouth watering at the first piece of meat that she'd had since she'd come here. She looked across to Cylan, watching with petty excitement at his growing frustration. He set down his goblet roughly, sloshing some of the liquid over the edge and onto the table.

"Is there a reason that you didn't report this sooner?" The muscle in his jaw twitched, which seemed to happen each time he was biting back his anger.

Brynn squirmed, looking uncomfortable. Her youth finally showed through her adult facade then, her voice turning whiny and pitiful as she lowered her chin. She looked at Cylan through her long lashes and spoke again, like a little girl manipulating her big brother for a favor.

"Cy Cy, you know how daddy gets when he's angry," she made herself smaller in her chair, her lower lip jutting out slightly, "I don't want him to find out. Please tell me you'll help me get it back."

Mari raised her eyebrows, throwing back the last gulp of her wine and holding out her cup for another refill. *This* was the Unseelie leader of the Water's Dominion? Only a few minutes into their dinner together, Mari could already see that Brynn was nothing more than a spoiled teenage princess, used to getting what she wanted and acting however she wanted with no consequence. Surely "Cy Cy" wouldn't fall for that act.

There was silence for a moment as Cylan thought. Mari cleared her throat, unfazed by the dagger-sharp glare that Brynn shot her way.

"So, what is this Data-thing anyway?"

Brynn gritted her teeth, malice dripping from her every word, "Even with your tiny eyes you may have noticed that from down here we can't see the stars—if there were any to see—and the sunlight is weak, therefore our magic is weaker. The *Datalis* was a gift from Etaldin himself to his people in the Dominion. The *Goddess*," she spat the word, "neglected those of us down here when she gave the stars to the people of the land. Etaldin captured a small portion of that celestial magic and encapsulated it in the *Datalis* for all who reside in the Dominion to have some magic of their own. Without it here, at its perch on the top of the palace where its light can radiate throughout the Dominion, my people suffer."

"*Datalis*," Cylan spoke over his drink, "translates to The Dominion's Star."

"Mm," Mari nodded, feeling a bit lightheaded as she started on her fourth goblet of Faerie wine, "yeah that sounds important."

Cylan sighed, "Brynn. We will aid your search."

Mari hiccuped, "We will?"

"Is she always this stupid?" Brynn scoffed.

"Sixty percent of the time I am less stupid, for sure." Mari chuckled, the heat in her cheeks adding to the warmth rising from the wine in her belly.

"If you weren't my favorite brother's ward," Brynn leaned in closer, "I'd let Octavias have you for a snack. You remember: he's the large, red, tentacled creature? Though I do usually feed him a higher quality diet, it would be okay to let him have a bit of junk food now and then."

Cylan struggled to hide the smile on his face as he stood, "We will head out first thing in the morning. For now, I think it's time to get Mari back to her room."

Mari wobbled on her feet as she stood, "Oh but I think we were just starting to get along!"

Cylan steadied Mari with one hand on her arm and another around her waist. "Lovely to see you, my sister."

"Next time," Brynn stood, "let's dine alone."

22

WRECKS & RELICS

The glimmer of dancing sunlight flashed across Mari's face as she opened her eyes the next morning. Her head ached dully as she sat up, though she was immediately distracted by the view in front of her.

When she had arrived the night before, the waters were dark and cold. This morning, however, the sunlight illuminated the Dominion, quite literally shining a light on the vivacious world that existed beneath the waves.

Various sandstone buildings of the palace grounds were much more visible now, as were the wide array of sea life and foliage that seemed to cover the space outside her window. Coral in various colors and shapes jutted up from the seafloor, while little fish and even some small merpeople swam and hid in the structures. At the furthest expanse of her vision, Mari could see a field of seaweed, where a few kelpies grazed happily. Bubbles formed and burst all around and rays of sunlight danced in the currents.

For a moment, Mari felt a pang of sadness at seeing so much beauty all at once. If she had let her fear keep her from taking this step on her journey, she would have missed out on such a mystical and beautiful place. She only had a few minutes to sit with that feeling before Maelin entered, holding Mari's clothing.

"Oh, good morning, ma'am! I am glad you're already awake. Prince Cylan has quite the day planned for the four of us," she reached in the pocket of her skirt, pulling out a handful of vials, "and I've acquired enough potions for us all for several hours of underwater searching!"

Mari gratefully took her clothes and went to stand behind the changing curtain.

"Maelin, I didn't know you were so excited to explore the Dominion."

"Oh," Maelin sighed gleefully, "yes, ma'am. It's been a dream of mine ever since I was a little Fae. I've read stories about the adventures people have here. The treasures, the unknown depths, the sights, and the colors!"

Mari smiled to herself as she finished the last buttons on her vest before drinking a vial of the potion and tucking a few more vials into her pockets. Normally she'd clip her dagger to her hip but today she decided to put it back into her pack; not only did she not need any extra weight in the water, but she didn't want to risk the dagger rusting either. When she emerged from behind the curtain, she found Maelin holding a tray of food.

"I've brought us a quick meal before we are to go, ma'am. Though, I don't have to tell you that Prince Cylan is rather... eager, to set out."

Mari rolled her eyes, "That's a polite way to say he's impatient and already waiting for us, right?"

Maelin blushed and smiled sheepishly, holding out the tray for Mari to take. Mari deliberately took her time eating the bread and honey and

Faerie fruit that was provided to her, savoring every bite. Maelin had finished her food in record time and was getting more anxious with every slow bite that Mari took. Though Mari enjoyed the thought of Cylan having to wait on her, she felt she should spare the poor girl's nerves and finish up her plate.

The two of them found Cylan and Leo in the courtyard. Mari tried to say hello, but her words only came out in a bubble that floated up toward the surface. Confused, she looked to Maelin, who smiled apologetically.

Then, a voice, second to her inner voice, appeared in Mari's mind.

I apologize, ma'am. I should have told you sooner: the potions only give you the ability to breathe underwater, not speak underwater. Those of us with magic will be able to communicate telepathically, though you won't be able to respond.

A third voice and an odd mental chuckle then filled her thoughts. She recognized it quickly, for even Cylan's telepathic voice held an irksome tone.

A blessing, really. He smirked over at her.

Mari rolled her eyes and scowled back at him. This would be a long day, that much she knew for sure.

She watched in annoyed silence as Leo signaled someone behind her. Mari turned to see a pair of mermen herding a quartet of sea animals towards them. This was the first time that Mari had seen a merperson in the daylight, and if she could have exclaimed, she would have done so.

Their tail fins, long and muscular, glimmered in the sunlight. Shades of red and orange mingled together along the length of their tails, while their top halves, skin and muscle, and bone, were very human-esque save for the fins that protruded from the backs of their forearms and the gills that were etched into their necks. Their hair was long and floated behind them as they ushered a sea turtle, a dolphin, a sea lion, and a small tiger shark in front of Mari and her group.

These will be our transportation for the day, ma'am. Maelin explained, gently stroking the sea turtle's shell.

Cylan locked eyes with one of the mermen, clearly having a conversation that Mari couldn't hear. They both nodded once, and the mermen swam off. Leo positioned himself next to the shark, and Cylan gravitated toward the dolphin. The energetic sea lion swam in happy loops around Mari. She sent up a bubble-filled laugh, petting it gently on the neck when it came close by.

Grab hold. Leo instructed. *We will ride until we find a wreck, then search it thoroughly before proceeding to the next.*

When each of them had a grip on their animals, the four of them swam upward and then away from the palace. Though their speed was limited, they were moving along faster than Mari would have ever dreamed of moving through the water herself. Soon the structures and plants began to fall away behind them and they were in the middle of the open ocean.

Mari looked down and noticed a shipwreck crumpled in the sand at the same time that Leo did. He signaled for the group to go down.

Your rides will need to surface for a moment. He explained, *release them and float down. They will join us again shortly.*

Mari did as she was instructed, releasing her grip from her sea lion's neck and watching as he swam gracefully upward with the other animals. She started to sink slowly towards the wreckage. She blew out the air in her lungs and began to sink much faster, catching up to Cylan and Leo who were already halfway there. Maelin was close behind her.

As they approached the ship, it was clear that this one was freshly sunken judging by the lack of algae or other sea life that hadn't found their home in the broken wood. This ship was split in half; the wood around the middle splintered and compressed as if something—Mari imagined monstrous tentacles—had wrapped around the boat and squeezed.

The four of them made their way into the gaping hole in the middle of the wreck. Suddenly, Mari wished that she had asked what the *Datalis* had looked like before she could no longer speak. It seemed impossible to search for something when you had no idea of what to look for or where to look. Mari assumed it would be a rather small object if it was stolen on a ship and not yet found. She wondered if the word "Star" in its translated name referred to its physical resemblance to a star and not just because of its magical properties. Perhaps none of her ideas were near the truth. She would only truly know when she found it.

The group separated, all doing their best to search each nook and cranny that the relic could have possibly fallen into. Mari had found her way into what appeared to be the captain's quarters. Most of the furniture was already broken open and anything else that hadn't been tied down seemed to have been scavenged. Still, she took her time double-checking every space for something star-like and important-looking.

After she'd found nothing but a tarnished spoon and an old, broken compass, Mari felt a movement behind her and turned to find her sea lion friend had returned. She grabbed hold of him and they quickly made their way to the others.

A few hours, another vial of water-breathing potion, and multiple wrecks later, there was still no sign of the *Datalis*. Mari's stomach grumbled with hunger and her annoyance at being unable to communicate with those around her was growing exponentially.

Mari and her sea lion were a few feet behind the others; her ride was also tiring of the journey, it seemed. A glint of light caught her eye, like a reflection off of a mirror, and she looked downward.

The sunlight only illuminated so far down, and the sea floor was deeper in this part of the Dominion. Below her, in the murky, dark blue water Mari could make out the shadow of a wrecked vessel. She signaled for her sea lion to take her further down and it obliged. The others were moving slowly enough that she was sure she would be able to catch up to them quickly after she took a peek through the small ship.

It looked to be a much simpler boat than the others they had explored; not a grand vessel with large sails that had plenty of room for cargo. Surprisingly, this ship was mostly intact; even its one sail, though shredded, was still attached to the mast that leaned slightly to one side. The obvious sign of its demise, a hole the size of Mari herself, was easy to spot on the side of the ship. Every inch of the wreckage was coated in a thick green-gray slime, indicating that it had been here for quite some time.

She dropped down onto the slippery deck, pleased to find only one small door that led to the inside of the ship. At first glance, there was nothing that looked as though it could have been the source of the light she'd seen. Nevertheless, it was a small enough ship that it would be a quick and easy search.

The chill of the ocean water coupled with the eerie feeling that came from being alone in a place where a few unlucky souls found their final watery resting place, was enough to have Mari looking over her shoulder every few moments and watching each step she took very closely.

Something was different about this wreck, though she couldn't tell what it was exactly. She made her way through the cracked open door, avoiding touching as much of the slimy algae as possible. As her body crossed the threshold, she saw something move in the corner and she froze with her eyes wide, trying to see through the shadows of the room.

As quickly as she could manage, she started to back away through the doorway. A current of water caught her from behind, dragging her further into the room. Her heart was beating quickly, dread pulsating throughout her body as she scrambled backward to no avail.

An instant later, the water rushed around her. It was moving; Mari could feel it whirling around her though she remained in place in the middle of the floor. Suddenly, she felt very wet and heavy. She blinked, realizing that the water in the room had vanished and she sat on the slime-covered floor of the vessel's cabin.

Rotting wood and the overwhelming smell of decay and sea life filled her nostrils. She swept her hair out of her face and looked around in a panic. Her eyes darted over where she had seen the shadow and she stared, open-mouthed, as a figure approached her.

It was tall, broad, and very human-esque. Slowly, it moved toward her, though Mari could not see its legs—after the outline of its hips only more shadow flowed around it. Like the shadow it moved within, there was an opaque quality to the creature's body, as if it were only a projection or a hologram.

As it came closer, Mari was shocked to see its resemblance to a human man. A bushy beard, eyebrows, and long hair obscured most of the man's face, though Mari could easily tell he wasn't smiling. The specter floated closer, his well-worn and holy coat and hat hung from his lifeless figure.

He tilted his head slightly, like a dog examining a small creature it had just discovered.

"A human lass," his voice, heavy with the rumble of a Scottish accent, echoed not only throughout the cabin but throughout her mind, "was the last thing I would expect to find here."

"I can go," her voice shook, "I have friends, they are waiting for me... I—"

"But then," his airless lungs still managed to heave out a sigh, "ye would not get what ye came for."

Mari stared at him, her eyes narrowing. Her chest heaved with panicked breaths, though she told herself if he were going to hurt her, he probably would have done it by now.

"Are you a man?" she asked.

"Once." He floated towards the desk. When he set his hand on top, it fell through the wood. When he pulled it back out, he held a metal object.

"Now, wi' the cursed magic of these seas, I have become something else. Something less."

Mari stared at the object he held. He turned it over and a glow came from between the cracks where each of the many sides converged in the middle. She stifled her gasp as the realization came to her. *The Datalis.*

"My name is Marianne," she said gently, "my family called me Mari."

For a moment the man looked sad. "I dinna have a name anymore. The sea claimed it when it claimed my body. I am now a draugen, one of many nameless seafarer souls trapped in these waters for all of eternity."

"What could you have possibly done to deserve a fate like that?" Mari flinched as the draugen tossed the *Datalis* up carelessly, catching it in his other hand.

"I fell in love."

Mari was silent as the draugen floated around her, the *Datalis* casting a sliver of bright yellow light around the room.

"So long ago…time escapes me now…I was brought to this realm and taught many of the Fae the art of sailing and fishing. I missed home, missed my brother and the lass I had my eyes set on." The draugen's ghostly gaze seemed to be focused on something far away; perhaps the memory of the life he was stolen from.

"She had fiery red hair and a voice that could make any man swoon. One day, I saw that hair again, when I was out showing a pair of Fae brothers a few good knots. She was out in the water, beckoning me to come to her. I went to her that day and every day thereafter for months. Unfortunately for me, she was betrothed to another and he was the jealous, vengeful sort. Aye," the draugen ran his hand over the back of the broken old captain's chair, "he sunk my ship, filling my lungs with water and cursing me to this non-existence. I thought, surely, my lass would come find me." He locked eyes with Mari, "she never did."

"I'm so sorry," Mari couldn't think of any words that might soothe a soul that had been so dejected for so long. "Can I…is there anything I can do?"

His hollow chest jolted upward with a lifeless laugh. "I used to miss 'er. Now, there is one thing I miss more: Earth. I miss the dirt and the trees and the sunlight. I'd give anything to live one more moment in the fresh air."

In the blink of an eye, he was an inch away from her face. Mari gasped, scrambling to put distance between them. He opened his mouth showing a rotten-toothed smile as his eyes searched her face.

"And ye," he held out the *Datalis*, "ye came for this, haven't ye? When this fell to my ship from the heavens I thought surely it must be my chance to escape this hell. Instead, it's proven to be naught but a useless hunk of metal. I suppose it doesn't work unless yer one of *them*."

"I—I'm not one of them either," her brain scrambled for something to say, coming up short.

The draugen's smile widened, mischief and joy tangled together on his face. "Exactly. Ye have something I want, human lass. I will give ye this," he tossed the artifact in the air once more, pointing it toward her once he caught it, "if ye give me a memory of yers."

"A memory?" she whispered.

"Aye!" The draugen shouted, "Aye, a memory. Conjure up in yer mind the best memory ye have of yer home. A bonny summer's day. Show me that which I have been so long wi'out. I will claim it as my own and think fondly upon it o'er the course of eternity. Surely losing a single memory is a small price to pay."

Mari hesitated. She thought for a moment, trying to see what harm this could possibly do her. Sure, losing a memory seemed like an intimate violation, but unlike this draugen, she would be able to make more memories. She could do him this kindness. Mari took a deep breath.

"Will it hurt?"

The draugen shook his head, "I suspect I may be the one to feel pain, lass. The pain of longing and heartbreak. But ye will be just fine."

"Okay," she sat up straight. "I'll do it."

Slowly, the draugen moved to hover in front of her. With a skeletal hand, he reached out, placing the tips on Mari's forehead. It felt as though he was holding ice, but Mari put the thought out of her mind and closed her eyes.

Shortly after Mari had moved to Eastport, she had bought her bike. She loved to ride, loved to feel the wind in her hair and across her face. She may have been alone, may have been haunted by a curse, but on her bicycle, she felt as unburdened as the birds that flew through the air above her.

After a particularly rainy morning, the sun finally came out and Mari ran to her bicycle. She tore down her driveway and found her way to a long and secluded packed-dirt path through the forest. She had no destination in mind; her only intention was to enjoy the afternoon.

The trees were fuller and greener than ever having soaked up the sweet warm rain. The smell of petrichor and wet earth surrounded her, filling her with peace. Sunshine glistened on the droplets left behind on the verdant foliage. Birds sang and bathed in the puddles. Mari couldn't help but let out a deep, joy-filled laugh, smiling as the sun warmed her face. That was the moment she realized that Eastport would be her home until the end; a feeling of joy she hadn't felt in a long time.

But then the image in her mind faded. It was as if she'd been in a sealed room and had opened a window. It felt like a gentle breeze had blown in, lifting dust off of the old furniture. And with that breeze, the thought and the dust were gone. She couldn't recall what she'd been reminiscing on no matter how hard she'd tried to grasp at that breeze.

She opened her eyes to the ghostly face in front of hers. She wasn't sure if what she was seeing was real, and even though the draugen's face was mostly transparent, Mari would still swear that a single tear was rolling down the man's cheek.

His eyes opened as well, and without a word, he held the relic out to her. She looked down at the object as she grasped it with care.

"Thank—" She looked up expecting to find the draugen still floating there, but she was alone.

Mari?

She heard Cylan's voice in her mind, though it was a bit muffled with him being so far away. She had been away a lot longer than she'd originally anticipated and now her companions had come back to look for her.

The *Datalis* was not large, though it still did not fit in any of her pockets. She tucked it snugly in between her vest and her shirt before heading for the cabin door. Mari swam out into the water, looking for her sea lion though it was nowhere to be found.

She took a breath, and another, her chest feeling heavy as she looked helplessly around her. The last water-breathing potion she had taken was starting to wear off, her lungs struggling to siphon the oxygen from the water. Flailing her arms and legs around, Mari made some progress towards the surface, though it still felt miles away.

Above her, the sunlight beckoned, taunting her as it danced through the water. A trio of shadows moved. Without being able to speak, she would never be able to get their attention. Panic sped her heart and her arms as she failed to swim further up. Her short time in the water had been enough to get her used to leisurely floating around where she needed to go, but it hadn't been enough to teach her to swim efficiently.

Mari opened her mouth, precious bubbles escaping. It felt as though she were breathing through a straw. Her body screamed in defiance, craving more oxygen than it was getting.

One of the shadowy figures above broke from the group and began to descend towards her. Hope filled her belly, giving her the final push she needed to hang on and reach out, grasping Cylan's hand.

Without a word, he understood the reason behind the panic in her eyes and rushed them to the surface. When her head broke through the water's embrace and cool air enveloped her head, Mari gulped in a precious breath of air.

She heaved the air into her lungs, coughing as a bit of water followed while the waves jostled her around. Cylan held her upright, supporting most of her weight.

"Mari," his voice was tight, though with annoyance or concern, she couldn't tell, "what happened to you? Are you alright?"

Maelin and Leo surfaced a few feet from them.

"Ma'am!" Maelin's wet head bobbed as she swam closer, "Oh I was so worried about you! Thank Eris that Prince Cylan found you before your potion ran out completely. Here," she peered down through the water as her hands worked below the surface, "I've got...oh no." Her eyes widened as she met Mari's gaze, "Oh, ma'am, I don't have any more potions on me. They are back at the palace and..."

Cylan looked around as if searching for something out in the open water they floated in. For as far as Mari's eyes could see, there was only blue water and blue skies.

"There is a cave, not far from here, that Mari and I can swim to and wait for you. If you make haste, you should be able to make it back to the palace and back to us before nightfall."

Mari looked to the sky; the orange setting sun was not far from the horizon, but exhaustion was setting in and already Cylan was supporting most of her weight. She wasn't sure how much farther she could go.

Cylan looked her in the eyes, his face only inches from her own. "Take a deep breath and we'll be there before you know it."

"I don't want to go back under," she shook her head, fear settling back in.

"We have to Mari. I can't support you here on the surface forever," his dolphin surfaced beside them. Cylan ushered Mari over to it and she wrapped her trembling hands around the animal. Cylan wrapped his around hers, their warmth radiating up her arm.

"Deep breath," he instructed, his voice steady and calm.

The will to survive gave her the last bit of bravery that she needed to take the deepest breath that she could. An instant later, the dolphin was racing under the waves like a torpedo, launching them downward and forward. Her lungs protested though she could see the caves that Cylan had mentioned. They were close. Only a second longer.

Her chest shook, bubbles of air finding their release from her lips as she struggled to keep it in. Just as she could no longer contain it, her breath coming out in one large blast, the dolphin surfaced in the air pocket of a large, rocky cavern. Once more Mari gasped in the air, collapsing to the rock below her.

Cylan helped her to sit up against the wall. He held his hands out, moving them over her body, the glow of his magic warming her skin and easing the burning in her lungs. As his hands hovered over her chest, he paused, staring at the abnormal bulge there.

Mari smiled wide, her breathing easing as she reached inside her vest, wrapping her hand around the *Datalis*. She chuckled at the sound of Cylan's gasp as she pulled the relic out.

"I don't think you'll be surprised to hear that this wasn't simple to get." She chuckled.

"You little human," Cylan smiled, turning the *Datalis* over in his hands, examining it closely, "how you continue to amaze me." He stood, helping her to her feet.

She sighed, "And you continue to come to my rescue." Their eyes met and she held his gaze. "Thank you."

Cylan nodded once in acknowledgment, "You will have to tell me the story behind this," he tucked the *Datalis* in his vest, "as we walk."

He directed her attention to a tunnel that led deeper into the cave behind them. Mari agreed and decided to begin her story shortly after the part where she was sucked into the ship by the draugen. She left out her complete and utter terror, of course.

23

DESIRE & DOUBTS

"**Y**our selflessness saved the Dominion, you know."

She blushed at Cylan's sincerity, "It was an easy choice to make. Though I wish I could remember exactly what I gave up..."

"That's just it," Cylan went on, "none of us could have given that draugen what it was he was after. You, and only you, had recent memories of the *D'ashil* world to give to him. I'm starting to believe your arrival here was anything but an accident."

Mari knew from her sparse Fae language lessons with Maelin that *D'ashil* meant "human". She wondered for a moment what the word for "Faerie" was. She was about to ask him when they turned, their path opening up into a large cavern, unlike any place Mari had ever imagined.

The cavern was large and round with holes in the stone scattered randomly from floor to ceiling. Some of the holes let the water from above flow through, cascading down in waterfalls of ocean water that filled luminous blue pools below. The last rays of golden evening light from the surface shone in from the holes above them where the magical barrier held back the water, offering a window to the ocean beyond.

The light refracted through the water windows sending shimmering rainbows throughout the cave.

"When Brynn first came to rule over the Dominion, she was just a terrified little child," rainbows reflected off of the sharp angles of his face as he smirked back at her, "don't tell her I told you that."

He took a few more steps into the cavern, continuing his story, "Together, she and I found this place and I showed her there was beauty here too, where the two worlds met. The Dominion isn't simply made up of the wicked creatures and the cold, empty water they inhabit."

Mari softened, finally relaxing after their recent ordeal. "I can see that you really care about your sister. Maybe you do have a heart after all," she teased, gently smacking his shoulder.

He caught her hand, pulling her in close.

"I wanted to say," his breath tickled her face, "that I'm sorry for being unkind. I just… don't know how to act around you, it appears."

This close to Cylan, Mari could hardly breathe. Her thoughts were more muddled than they usually were and she wasn't sure what to say. She knew this moment of vulnerability, this glimpse past Cylan's thick armor, was her chance to open up and tell him how she had been feeling. She searched for the right words as his golden eyes, the color of the setting sun, searched her face.

All she could manage to whisper out was a simple, "Thank you."

Cylan didn't release her hand but put it down by their sides. His half-lidded eyes moved their focus to her lips before hungrily darting back up to look into her eyes once more. Mari felt the heat rising in her skin, her bottom lip quivering in response.

"Mari." Cylan's other hand reached up to graze his fingers along her cheek.

An unfamiliar shiver ran down her spine when she felt the warmth of his skin on hers; the tension in her body continued to rise, like carbonated bubbles begging for release. It was enough to drive her to madness. Her breath came in shallow, nervous pants and her legs shook, but she wasn't sure if they were itching to move closer to Cylan, or run away.

What did she want to happen? Or rather, which instinct should she listen to: the logical one or the emotional one? Surely they weren't both saying the same thing...

As Cylan's head began to lower, her eyes fluttered closed, too scared to see the scene in front of her play out and yet wanting to savor every moment.

"Ma'am?"

Maelin's voice echoed through the cavern and Mari gasped, the jolt of her surprise sending her forward just enough that for a moment her lips brushed against his, their touch feather light and electric all at once.

Cylan released Mari as she jumped back, attempting to collect herself.

Maelin and Leo rounded the corner where Cylan and Mari had just been a moment before.

"Ma'am," the relief in Maelin's voice was nearly tangible, "there you are. Are you two ready to go?"

"Yeah," Mari said, a bit breathless. She cleared her throat and tried again, "Yes. I'm ready."

Her eyes searched for Cylan as she took the water-breathing potion from Maelin and found that he was already headed toward the exit.

He looked back before rounding the corner with Leo, a devilish smile plastered on his face.

"You coming?"

———— ·✦· ————

Nina, I hate starting all of my letters like this, but I have so much to catch you up on. It's been one unexpected turn after another over the past few days. And I have never been so excited at the thought of seeing dirt in my life.

Mari absently toyed with the necklace around her throat. She remembered the first night she'd been at the castle and discovered that Cylan had left it in her room for her. He'd disgusted her at the time—his arrogance and his sneer alone were enough to drive her to anger in a matter of a few seconds.

And now...

When she'd proposed this journey with him she hadn't known what to expect, but still, even in her wildest imagination, it wasn't *this*. It wasn't shadow demons in the forest or giant sea monsters sinking ships and it certainly wasn't nearly kissing him in a magical underwater rainbow-covered cave.

She took a break from scribbling furiously in her journal to peer out of her room's window. The sea beyond was black with night, though a warm yellow light shone from above the main section of the Sunken

Palace. Like a lighthouse beam, the *Datalis* was shining brightly back where it belonged.

When Mari had brought it back just a few days ago, Brynn seemed a bit less annoyed than usual. Mari decided to decipher Brynn's slightly less pronounced frown as thankfulness. Mari supposed she was lucky to only be scowled at instead of the dagger-like glare she'd been getting from Brynn previously.

They had extended their trip in the Dominion by a few days to relax and take some time to teach Mari how to swim. In hindsight, this would have been a useful lesson before their shipwreck-searching journey, but nevertheless, it would be a useful skill to have.

Here, away from Eristald and his looming duties and overbearing king father, Cylan seemed to be able to drop the tough-prince facade. Here, he was a different man. Carefree and kind; Mari saw Cylan laugh more these last few days than she had in the weeks that she'd known him.

Her pencil paused on the page, ready to write the next thought that popped into her mind, but her hands seemed to be stalled with fear of the words that threatened to come out.

Nina...what if I stay?

Mari took a deep breath and let the words flow. Maybe this way she could finally start to make sense of the emotions that had been flying around her head like ping pong balls.

Despite the few near-death experiences—which, for the record, could have found me back home too with this stupid family curse—things have been kind of nice here. I've truly felt more alive in this last... how long have I even been here? A month? More? Either way, I've seen so much beauty and magic and have had such unique experiences that I worry if I came home after all of this, life in Eastport would be simply...unsatisfying.

Her mind skipped then to Alek and wondered if he was okay. He'd done and risked so much for her when she first stumbled into the Faerie Ring. Along with Fyodor, Rae, and Lyna, the four of them had been better friends to Mari than she could have expected, or deserved. If it was true what Rae and Lyna said, that Alek was in trouble... Well, the guilt of not being able to help him in his time of need was enough to bring tears to her eyes.

She wiped them away before they dripped onto her paper below. Her only comfort was knowing that if she and Cylan succeeded in their quest to bring the stars back to the Realm of Faerie, it would be helping her friends as well.

After taking a sip of the strange yet sweet herbal tea that Maelin had brought her, Mari finished her letter to Nina.

At the risk of sounding dramatic, I have to say, I feel a sort of fire igniting in me. I just wish I could tell what started it. It could be the sparks from our adventure so far; the excitement and wonder all around here would be enough to fan even the smallest of flames. I have a feeling though, that the real arsonist might be—

She couldn't bring herself to write the final word. It was only a name. Five letters. But still, she was afraid. Afraid of what accepting this truth might mean. How one simple sentence with one simple name at the end could bring the thought one step closer to reality. With this singular truth, the trajectory of her life could pivot so sharply.

Was she ready for it?

The pencil moved across the page, its soft scraping noise suddenly louder than a train.

—The real arsonist might be Cylan.

24

WANTING & WAITING

The magic fire crackled in her sandstone hearth. The sealife outside her window was calm and the night was peaceful. She'd had plenty of time to work out her thoughts and had even begun copying the map of the realm into her journal when her bedroom door creaked open.

"Maelin?" Mari sat up straighter in her bed.

Cylan crept into the room, slowly closing the door behind him. Mari blinked a few times before letting out a small, "Oh."

"My arrival is usually not such a disappointment," he smirked.

Mari quickly closed her journal, suddenly embarrassed by the private words she'd written about him just a short while before.

"I'm not disappointed," she attempted an encouraging smile, patting the bed next to her. "I just wasn't expecting you, that's all."

"You weren't?" His smile turned goading as he stalked closer.

"Should I have?" Her words were soft and breathless as he stopped directly in front of where she sat on the bed.

Without another word, he leaned forward, hovering over her. She laid back, instinctively creating space between them and instantly regretting that space. Cylan wasn't phased. His hands settled on the bed on either side of her face and his smile faltered, a more serious expression taking its place.

He lowered his face to hers, stopping only a fraction of an inch away from touching her. When he spoke, his lips brushed hers, sending a shiver of longing down her spine.

"May I?"

She nodded, and as her head tilted up, their mouths met. A burst of heat spread from her lips across her face and as Cylan's kisses moved down her jaw and throat, the fire spread there, too.

Caught up in the growing wildfire of longing and excitement, Mari didn't notice when the heat started to become uncomfortable. The tingles of warmth had turned to lashes of pain, the fire that was Cylan was consuming her, melting her, and soon she would be nothing more than a pile of ash and—

Mari sat up in bed, the morning sunlight shining innocently across her face. Her breathing was borderline hyperventilating and she was sweating profusely. The page she'd been sketching the map on was smudged from where her cheek rested on it as she slept moments before.

It was only a dream.

The thought first brought her comfort and her breathing finally began to calm. Then, a wave of disappointment crashed over her, settling in a pit in her stomach. Mari groaned, throwing aside the covers and sliding from her bed.

It was too early for such emotional whiplash, she told herself. They had a whole day's journey planned to leave the Dominion on the way to their next kingdom and now she'd have to travel beside him, all the while remembering how real his lips had felt on hers... even if it had only been a dream.

But, it hadn't *only* been a dream, she reminded herself. Just a couple of days ago, they had nearly shared a kiss, though neither of them had mentioned it since. Still, she couldn't be the only one feeling this tension and experiencing such torment.

A knock on the door startled Mari. She dropped the clothes she'd been shoving unceremoniously into her backpack.

"Good morning, ma'am!" Maelin's cheery, pink face appeared in her doorway, her maroon hair braided and tied neatly behind her head.

"Oh, you're already dressed! My, you must be excited to leave the Dominion. At least let me help you pack," she chuckled, coming to take Mari's bag, and placing it over her shoulders next to her own small bag, "I don't blame you for wanting to get out of here. I've had my fill of the ocean as well. Here you are, one last water-breathing potion for you, ma'am."

Mari took the vial from Maelin and sighed, drinking the contents quickly. Thank goodness Maelin was able to use a bit of her magic to waterproof her backpack, Mari thought as she handed her notebook and dagger to Maelin to pack away.

"You're right," Mari agreed, heading towards the door, "I'm ready for sunshine, dry air, and trees!"

The two of them discussed the things they were excited to leave behind until they had to enter the water where Mari could no longer talk. They met Cylan and Leo in the courtyard as they had when they were searching for the *Datalis*. This time they didn't have a parade of sea animals to guide them to their destination.

Instead, Mari looked up, seeing an oblong dark shadow floating on the surface above them. She followed the others as they swam upward, towards the shadow. Mari was still a slow swimmer, but the lessons she'd been given and the experience she'd had here in the Dominion had really paid off. Now, with a moderate amount of effort, she propelled herself upward, following not too far below Cylan, who kept peeking back to make sure she wasn't falling behind.

The four of them emerged next to a sailboat. The captain, a tall female resembling a cat in every way besides the fact that she was bipedal, lowered a rope ladder for them to climb up onto.

When they were all aboard, dripping water onto the deck, the captain smiled, turning to Cylan.

"*Indis Hahom;* my prince," she bowed, her accent unusual and heavy, "I am Sahil. It is an honor to have you aboard my modest vessel. My many sincere thanks for convincing the Sea Princess to allow ships in her *wyna* again." Her fur, black with brown and orange patches, seemed to glisten in the sunlight, "My entire livelihood has been ferrying people back and forth from the isles to the mainland. I was worried I would never be able to do so again."

"If you feel the need to thank someone," Cylan turned towards Mari, gesturing to her with one hand, "she is who you must thank. My sister's mind would never have been changed if Mari had not helped."

Mari could feel herself blush as Captain Sahil's tail twitched behind her before she bowed to Mari. "My thanks to you as well, Lady Mari."

It felt beyond strange to be called "Lady" Mari and to be bowed to in such a formal fashion, but Mari tried to take the appreciation and compliment in stride. She smiled back at the captain.

"The pleasure was all mine." As she said the words she decided they were mostly a lie, though the sentiment held true.

A moment later they were off, the boat easily picking up speed as it sailed across the sparkling blue water.

Between the salty breeze and scorching sunshine, with a bit of help from Maelin's magic, Mari was dry in no time. She stood confidently near the side of the boat—a place she would never have dreamed of standing before her adventure in the Dominion—looking ahead across the water.

Maelin was on the other side of the deck, admiring the view, and Leo was talking with the captain. Mari felt Cylan's arm brush up against hers as he came to stand beside her. Wordlessly, they stared out over the water together. They stood close, but barely touching, though for all of the heat and butterflies his proximity was causing her, they might as well have been making out right there, in front of everyone. Mari could take the silence and the tension no longer.

She pulled out her map and tried to orient herself, partially for something else to focus on besides the intoxicating smell of pine and incense coming from Cylan, and partly because she was curious where they were headed. She could see a small island to the left of them, and further to the right, the continent loomed. A tall, ominously smoking mountain of some kind was becoming more visible in the distance as they sailed closer.

Mari cleared her throat, "Is that the volcano in the Fire's Territory there? Is that where we are headed next?"

Cylan shifted his weight from one foot to the other. His eyes and fingers focused on peeling a section of chipped paint from the railing in front of them. "Next we'll be headed to the southern Indigo Isle. There's a portal ball there that will take us to the Kingdom of *Niha*—the Kingdom of Air. The beautiful and serene Airy Reach."

Alek sighed, tired of waiting and sick of sitting on this cold, hard rock. He was using Etaldin's seemingly limitless magic to levitate ten or so pebbles, swirling them around each other in a lazy infinity symbol before changing their shape to resemble a butterfly, and then a leaf. The air around the stones was tinged purple, the color that Etaldin's magic presented itself as.

He was cold and tired, and he missed his friends. He missed his cozy cob house and wondered when he'd see it again. He vowed the next time he set foot into his home, it would be with Mari at his side.

How miserable she must be, and scared. Prince Cylan was an eccentric ass at the best of times, and Mari was a gentle soul, warm and kind. Surely she was going mad having to travel with him across the realm.

The thought of her reminded him why he'd endured sleeping in the dirt under a starless sky, eating only what he could forage or steal with Etaldin's magic from unsuspecting passersby. In the short while he'd known her, he'd been consumed by thoughts of her. He wondered, had she been thinking of him as well?

Focus your thoughts, my son. Etaldin's voice rumbled in Alek's mind. *They may be drawing near any moment now if the word from the loyal merfolk is to be believed.*

Alek rolled his eyes, resting his head on the cold boulder he was hiding behind. He had had enough of lurking and waiting and receiving messages from Etaldin's Unseelie spies. Etaldin's approach was turning into more of the "set a trap and wait" method, while Alek wanted to dive out with his magic and take Mari by force. After their failed offensive attempt with the demons in the forest, Etaldin said he wanted to wait for the *right* moment while Alek felt that any moment could be the right one if they just *tried*.

Etaldin, privy to all of Alek's private thoughts, began to chide Alek for his lack of patience when the sound of crunching gravel filled the air.

"Wait," Alek said, though speaking aloud was more of a habit than a necessity when speaking with Etaldin.

Etaldin was quiet, for once. Alek listened intently, using his magic to enhance his hearing. His ears perked up at the sound of Mari's voice approaching, his heartbeat fluttering faster than pixie's wings.

"If there are portal balls that can just transport you anywhere with a touch of a finger, why have we been traveling on foot this whole time?"

Alek expected to hear the typical arrogant tone Cylan typically used when he spoke. Instead, Alek found himself confused at the steady and calm explanation he heard.

"Each portal ball can only go to one place that is predetermined. It cannot just take you anywhere you want. There are only a few portal balls in the realm, and this is one of them."

Alek felt Etaldin chuckle. There were not many things that could send a shiver of fear down Alek's spine faster than Etaldin's joyless laugh, for nothing good ever came afterward.

The prince has not familiarized himself enough with Unseelie magic to see the hex we've placed on the ball. Once she's separated from the others, we will let the wisps do what they do best and then we'll be there to take her.

"To *save* her, you mean." Alek corrected, eager butterflies tickling his stomach.

He was so close. Only a little while longer and he'd be the hero, swooping in to save Mari and take her home.

Alek could see the four of them clearly as they climbed the stone steps that led to the pedestal where the portal ball sat. The portal ball itself was beautiful, perfectly round, and glowing with a blinding white light. Though, today the glow was tinted violet; an aftereffect of the hex and hardly noticeable to the untrained eye, Etaldin assured him.

Together the party of four stood around the ball, hands outstretched and ready to grab hold and be transported. For a moment so brief that Alek wondered if he might have imagined it, he saw Mari look at Cylan, her deep brown eyes hesitant and questioning before a gentle, encouraging smile stretched across her perfect lips.

Unmistakably, and to Alek's growing dismay, Cylan smiled back.

25

SNOWFLAKES & SPIRITS

The Mari from a few weeks ago would have been much too nervous to just grab onto a portal ball without asking a million questions first. She would have wanted to know what it would look like; would it be like watching a movie stuck in fast-forward as they zoomed across the land? She'd have asked about what it would feel like; would it hurt? Should she close her eyes or hold her breath?

But today, she was the Mari that had overcome her lifelong fear of the water. She'd survived demons in the forest and helped a dryad and traveled countless miles across a strange world.

She was beginning to realize she was more than just scared and careful. She was brave and resilient and hopeful, too.

With only one encouraging look from Cylan and his promise of "see ya on the other side," Mari reached out and placed her hand on the glowing orb.

The illumination from the orb grew brighter the instant her fingers made contact. White light consumed her vision and she instinctively shielded her face with her arm. Where a moment ago she had felt sturdy ground beneath her feet and a solid portal ball under her hand, she now felt open air.

The feeling of plummeting hit her as her insides rose to her chest and her limbs flailed in the freefall. She couldn't scream, though the fear was certainly building within her. Disoriented and anxious, she wasn't sure how much more of this she could take when the brightness finally began to dim and her body landed in something soft and cold.

She sat up quickly, blinking to let her eyes adjust to the much darker area she found herself in.

"Cylan?" Mari called out, shivering in the cold wind. It was a drastic temperature change compared to the tropical island they had just been on.

Mari stood, calling out once more, "Maelin? Leo?" She wrapped her arms around herself, to brace from the chill.

It was clear she was alone, but where was she?

Thick snowflakes flew through the air around her and at least a foot of it had accumulated at her feet. The landscape, what she could make out of it, was rocky with sharp, ice-covered peaks that emerged from the blanket of white. The raging clouds above covered the sunlight, casting a foreboding shadow on the already monochrome wasteland.

"Hello?" She called desperately, though her voice was consumed by the wind, "Is anyone there?"

She took a step forward, her limbs already growing numb from the cold. Despite the fact that she was without a map, an idea of where she was, or an idea of where she was headed, Mari kept moving forward. She whimpered, shivered, and tripped over unseen objects under the snow, but she kept moving forward. Even as her repeated cries for help were swallowed by the storm, she kept moving forward.

I am brave, resilient, and hopeful. She repeated her mantra like a prayer as she trudged forward. *Brave. Resilient. Hopeful. And, cold. Very, very cold.*

With a grunt, as her boot came in contact with a rock that had been lying in wait, Mari fell forward. She threw her hands out to catch herself as she dove into the snowbank, landing only inches away from a large boulder.

Mari's scream of frustration was carried away with the gale as she pulled herself to a sitting position, resting against the boulder. She couldn't feel the tears that she knew had to be freezing as they ran down her numb cheeks.

"Is this it?" She sobbed to the sky, "*This* is how the curse gets me in the end?" She pounded her fists against the ground, "of all the things I survived so far, the *snow* is going to kill me?" Mari nearly laughed at how ridiculous it sounded.

She'd heard freezing to death was one of the better ways to go. Supposedly, in the end, the pain of the cold vanishes, and you become so warm that you finally drift into your eternal sleep. Though, she'd learned long ago that you can't truly believe every story you hear.

Mari was staring into the nothingness of the storm around her when a tiny flicker of color popped into existence a short distance away from her. It was a cheerful purple color, growing larger as it moved toward her, sputtering like a candle flame.

"Hello?" Mari called out, scrambling to her feet, though she could no longer feel her legs, "Hello, can you help me? I need help!"

As she and the purple flame neared each other, Mari could see that it was attached to the head of a small, white creature. The little Fae stood only a foot or so high and had three small ovals on what Mari assumed was its face; two glowing red eyes and one gaping, black mouth. The flame burned steadily on its head despite the wind, and Mari could feel the heat from it. Greedily, she took a step closer, soaking in the warmth.

"I'm lost," she told the little Fae, "and I'm cold and afraid...can you help me out of this storm?"

Though it did not appear to be able to speak, its little purple flame flickered in response, and the Fae began to walk—well, more like *hover*—across the top layer of snow as it headed back the way it had come. It turned once to make sure Mari was following.

Pure stubbornness and the will to stay alive was all that she had propelling her every labored step. Every inch of her was numb and stinging with cold. The hope that had abandoned her in the snow a minute ago had returned, but not with much vigor.

Through the haze of the falling snow, a large dark edifice rose up before them. As they came closer, Mari was relieved to see it was a cave that the snow had not found its way into yet. With the final bit of strength left in her frozen limbs, Mari launched herself into the open space where the wind finally stopped pummeling her.

"T-thank you," Mari said to the little candle-like Fae, huddling closer to it to keep warm.

As she looked around the small, domed space, several more purple flames flickered to life, their tiny white bodies appearing under their flames a moment later. Surrounded by countless pairs of eyes and a comforting purple glow, the cave was beginning to warm up and Mari's body was starting to thaw.

"I don't know what I would have done if you hadn't found me," she smiled at the small faces staring up at her. She looked out at the snow, yawning as a sudden tired feeling began to creep into her mind. "I wonder if my friends are looking for me."

The tingling sensation in her hands and feet brought on from the cold had subsided, though it was quickly replaced by a growing heaviness. Concern tugged at her thoughts and she did her best to ignore it. She'd only just found relief from the panic and fear and wanted to relax for a moment, but the nagging feeling of worry wouldn't go away.

She looked up through heavily lidded eyes and saw that the flames of the creatures had grown, their red eyes growing brighter as they moved closer. With every inch they gained on her, the heavy, draining feeling grew stronger.

Somehow, instinctively, Mari knew the little Fae were doing this to her. As their flames grew larger and their eyes glowed brighter, she could feel them draining her energy, and she doubted they were simply trying to lull her into a restful slumber.

"Stop. Let me go," she tried to yell but her voice only came out as a tired mumble.

Mari ordered her legs to move, begged her arms to drag her away from the cave. Panic rose within her as they stayed still at her sides; like dead limbs at the end of a fallen oak.

Her mind rushed through a hundred thoughts per second, trying to find a solution, when Mari remembered something that Maelin had said, shortly after they'd first met. She'd said that Mari's parents were surely waiting for her in *Inohryil*—the Otherworld—and that they would be reunited someday.

If Mari died, here in the Realm of Faerie, would Eris welcome her to the afterlife? Would she really see her parents again? Her uncle? Though she'd worked so hard for so long to escape death, the thought of what might happen afterward was comforting.

Then, as blackness crept in at the edge of her vision, another thought came to her. A tanned face with golden eyes. A cocky yet endearing grin followed by a snarky comment and an intoxicating laugh. She may have loved ones of her past waiting for her after she was finished with her life, but she couldn't get past the nagging feeling that there was more waiting for her in her future.

Instead of fading, the vision in her mind grew stronger as her body grew weaker. The purple-flamed creatures were winning the battle for her life, and she knew there wasn't anything she could do about it. She held onto the picture of him, though it began to morph and change in front of her. She saw pine trees that rose impossibly high and pools of blue water surrounded by rainbows that danced along rock. She saw ball gowns and crowns and a pair of black feathered wings that blocked out the ominous purple glow of the flames around her.

As her eyes grew too heavy to keep open, and her body began to feel like a long-forgotten piece of her, it seemed as though she were rising from the ground and soaring through the sky wrapped in a warm embrace. She finally felt safe, happy, and relieved.

If this was what dying felt like, she supposed it wasn't so bad, after all.

26

CONVERSATIONS & CURSES

When consciousness found Mari, the fear she had felt before blacking out came rushing back like a river escaping a broken dam. She froze, willing her body to be as still as a statue.

Afraid to open her eyes, she focused on her other senses to determine if she was safe. She was shivering, but she didn't feel cold. To her right, a wave of heat radiated and blossomed around her. Her mouth was dry and she craved a glass of cool water. She could smell wood smoke and smell food cooking somewhere nearby, reminding her of backyard bonfires in the summertime.

Her fear was subsiding slowly, her bravery returning just enough to begin to allow her eyes to flutter open.

"Oh," the relief in the simple sound was undeniable. "Thank Eris."

Maelin sat close to Mari, her usually excited and happy expression now melted with worry and concern.

"You're awake, ma'am." Maelin moved closer, helping Mari sit up and resting her back against a few pillows. "How do you feel?"

"I—" her voice cracked and she cleared her throat, trying again, "I'd like some water, please."

"Right away!" A second, unfamiliar voice called from further away.

As Mari searched for the voice's owner, she was able to take in her surroundings. She was sitting on a cot, next to a large fireplace that burned actual firewood and wasn't the scentless magicfire she'd been starting to get used to. Everything looked cozy and inviting, with pillows and blankets that were strewn about the furniture of an open living space. The building itself, which Mari quickly gathered was someone's home, was made of fallen logs, their golden color dotted with darker brown splotches at random intervals. The room was lofted, though Mari could not see what was beyond the railing above.

Across the space from them was a kitchen area and standing over the island in the middle of it, was a female Fae. She was stunning, with glossy, cropped black hair. Mari couldn't help but stare at the luminescent wings that unfurled behind her, the same colors and shape of a luna moth.

She brought over a steaming mug and smiled at Mari, her golden eyes sparkling like two tiny suns. Her robes, a cheerful shade of butter yellow, hung loosely over her thin frame. As she came closer, Mari could see the robe was pinned together near her shoulder with a broach that had the royal family crest—a half sun and waning moon—etched into the metal.

"I am Princess Hanli, Cylan's oldest younger sister," she chuckled briefly at her choice of words and offered the water to Mari, sitting down gracefully beside her, "and this is my home, where the four of you will be staying during your time here in the Airy Reach."

Mari took a sip, sighing at the relief the warm tea brought to her sore throat. When she spoke, her voice remained quiet but steady.

"What happened?"

"We got separated, ma'am, in the portal."

"It is very abnormal for the portal ball to take a traveler somewhere other than its intended destination," Hanli explained, a confused look on her perfect face, "so abnormal, in fact, that this is the first time it has ever happened."

Mari shook her head lightly, surprised when she didn't feel pain in the movement. "Strange things are happening all over the realm, it seems." She exchanged a glance with Maelin before looking back to Hanli, "We believe it's Etaldin's doing."

Hanli sucked in a breath, "Etaldin? In the Mistral Summits? Eris' light is so strong here. I would have never thought, in my lifetime, something like this could happen..."

They were all quiet for a short while, the crackling of the fireplace the only sound to be heard. In the silence, Mari was able to focus long enough to realize it was only the three of them in the home together.

"Where's Cylan?"

Hanli's face fell even further. "He said he had to... take care of some things."

Mari turned her confused face to Maelin who only sighed, wringing her hands lightly in her lap.

"He and Leo have gone to deal with the spirits, ma'am," Maelin spoke softly as if the words saddened her as she spoke, "the ones that harmed you."

"They do not know any better," Hanli said quickly, "it is only their nature; what they are meant to do. Though I am glad they did not succeed in your case, Marianne."

"What were they?" Mari wondered aloud, her curiosity outshining her slight shock at being called by her full name.

"Willow wisps," Hanli stood, pacing as she spoke, "they are spirits that reside on the far side of the mountain. Since the beginning of time, the wisps have been leading lost souls deep into their lair to consume them, or, as they see it, to end their suffering."

Mari shuddered. "Spirits, lost souls... it all gives me the creeps."

"Oh but," Hanli's tone perked up, "not all spirits are so malevolent. No, you see, most inhabitants of the Airy Reach are spirits in a way, for the path over the summits is the final leg of the journey that all must take before finding rest in *Inohryil*. The majority of them are only passing through, searching for peace, not looking to cause mischief and harm. Come," Hanli extended a hand to Mari, "if you are feeling well enough, let me show you."

To Mari's great surprise, she did feel well. Had Cylan used his healing magic on her before he left? She stood, testing out her limbs and stretching the stiffness away. She was alive, she was safe, and she was ready to continue onward. Mari took Hanli's hand.

Together, they stepped out of the cabin's front door and onto a long, covered porch. The air outside was crisp and cool, like a delightful October afternoon and not a monstrous January blizzard like Mari had experienced before.

Hanli's cabin was perched in a spot that seemed made especially for her. Surrounded by rocky cliffs and tall evergreens, the mountaintop had the most beautiful view of the sunset. Like a watercolor painting, a mixture of pinks, oranges, blues, and purples flooded the sky and tinted the clouds.

Nearby, a round pond sank into the mountain, spilling over the edge of the escarpment and disappearing into the mist below. In awe, Mari let Hanli guide her closer to the pond where a section of the mountain jutted skyward. They followed the rocky path upward. With each step they took, the wind blew more and more until it was so fierce that it was becoming difficult to breathe.

"This is the highest peak of the mountain."

As Hanli spoke, the wind responded, instantly stopping as if a door had been shut. A chill ran down Mari's spine, the sudden eerie calm evoking a sense of concern. She turned to see Hanli, arms open wide, taking in the last of the sun's rays.

"If the wind falls silent, she is listening to you." Hanli smiled sweetly at Mari, gesturing to the open sky around them. "Speak!" She ordered cheerily before adding in a warning, "She already knows everything about you, so never lie."

Mari hesitated, stepping closer to the peak. She could feel an energy there, expectant and curious, like a crowd waiting for the person on stage to begin their speech. Mari looked out over the land, green and full of life, and could even see the Dominion on the blurry horizon. She turned back to Hanli.

"What do I say?"

"That, I cannot answer for you. I can tell you this: the spirit of *Niha* can give life to your words. Make them meaningful." Hanli chuckled fondly, "and, like many a strong female, she has a strong temperament.

Make sure to always speak nicely to her; you don't want to be on her bad side!"

The wind picked up for a moment, tousling Hanli's robes playfully. Hanli only laughed harder, raising her hands to allow the breeze to slide through her fingers.

Mari smiled back, watching as the wind—full of a life of its own—continued to tease Hanli, caressing her skin, tossing her hair, and gently tornadoing around her. Mari turned back to the cliff and took a deep breath. There were only two things she could think of that had the most meaning to her, now more than ever. Perhaps the spirit of the *Niha*, the air, connected to Eris and overseeing the entire realm, may be able to give her guidance on the things most important to her. A gentle touch of wind tickled Mari's lips, practically begging her to speak.

"Please," Mari whispered, her words carried away by the breeze, "help me break my family's curse and bring back the stars to the people of the realm."

The once gentle breeze became a strong gust, whipping her hair and clothes around wildly. Mari turned back to Hanli, worried that she'd done something wrong, but Hanli only smiled.

"The wind has become my friend in the years I have been in the Airy Reach," Hanli spoke loudly to be heard over the roar of the wind. "I have learned a lot about her and she does not open up to many of us as quickly as she has seemed to open up to you." For a moment Hanli looked wistfully out over the land, "I have truly found my place here, unlike some of my other siblings who cannot seem to grow where they have been planted."

Mari wanted to smile at her, but the burdens she still carried weighed heavily on her heart and mind.

"How will I know if the wind will give me the guidance I've asked for?"

Hanli's hair blew aside and her expression went still, as though she was listening to someone whisper into her ear.

"She tells me you seek to break a curse." Hanli's tone was calm as she reached for Mari's hand, "Come. Let me take you to a most sacred place."

Hanli's grasp was gentle and reassuring as she led Mari past the log cabin and down a set of stairs carved into the mountainside. The path wound from the east side of the mountain to the north, then to the west where they disappeared behind the waterfall. Hanli stopped close enough to the falls that the mist they created began to coat Mari's skin and clothes.

She turned to Mari, a gentle excitement flashing in her liquid gold eyes. Hanli took both of Mari's trembling hands in her own, speaking with a smile of pure happiness and joy.

"When Etaldin cursed Eris' creations with his magic long ago at the beginning of our world, Eris was able to save a lucky few from his powers."

Mari recognized this as part of the story that Alek had described to her during the play she'd watched soon after she'd arrived here. A pain in her chest blossomed at the thought of his kindness and friendship. She didn't have time to dwell on the feeling as Hanli continued.

"Eris gathered up the last of her precious *D'ashil* in her loving embrace and brought them here to the Airy Reach where Etaldin's magic had not yet spread. Behind the Lah Waterfall here, she found a cavern and conjured a pool of *wyna* from the deepest depths of the mountain below. She bathed her *D'ashil* in the spring, protecting them from Etaldin's curse and ensuring that no magic could ever touch them. Then, she opened a portal to a new world—your world—and sent them safely through."

Mari's heart was racing with anticipation. Hanli couldn't speak fast enough as the words fell from her lips.

"The spring still holds so much of her essence, Marianne. Now, you too must bathe in the blessed mountain waters. They will break any and every curse, no matter how powerful."

Mari focused on Hanli's eager and beautiful face. The roaring noise of the waterfall melted into the background as her beating heart and hurried breathing filled her ears instead.

Was this really it? Was this the moment she'd dreamt about for years? Could she walk into that cave, only a few feet away, and walk out free of the curse that had taken her whole family from her?

"Hanli," Mari's voice shook, even as she shouted over the rush of the water, "I'm..." She stopped, searching for words that didn't come. Hanli touched Mari's face, a motherly gesture.

"Absolutely no soul that enters those waters with a curse leaves with that curse," she smiled brightly, "it will work. Bare yourself to the Goddess by entering her waters in your most natural form as you once entered this existence in the waters of your mother's womb. I will wait here."

Mari took a deep breath, her feet carrying her forward; a mixture of blind faith and unrelenting hope leading the way. She rounded the corner behind the falls and stopped. The small rocky area was illuminated by blue magic firelight dotted along the perimeter of the space, casting a serene glow on the scene before her.

Only a few feet of a rocky path stretched out before her until the ground dipped inward to a pool of cerulean water, still and smooth as glass. A statue of Eris, similar to the one she'd found in the temple in the Goddess Pinery—pure white with long silky hair and a gentle smile—was carved into the wall overlooking the water below.

Mari slowly removed her damp clothes, lying them neatly beside her and gently placing Cylan's necklace on top of the pile. She shivered as the cold, misty mountain air enveloped her naked body, but she was sure this was the right thing. After all, this was her most natural state and the state that she had been in while she swam in her mother's womb, as Hanli had said.

She would have expected to feel embarrassed or unsure in a situation such as this, naked and alone in a cave. However, deep in her bones she felt at peace, closer to Eris than she'd felt before, and ready to give herself to the Goddess completely.

Was it really this simple? Mari stared at the reflection of her plain face in the calm water with hope nearly strangling in her throat. After everything, all this time, a small dip in a pool of magical water and it would all be over...

Mari dipped her foot into the water, surprised to find that it was unnaturally warm. A ripple danced along the water's surface. She took another step, disturbing the water again. Without any further hesitation she dove in, submerging herself in the spring from head to toe, a wave splashing up along the edges of the pool.

Under the water, she opened her eyes and fought the startling feeling that typically would have made her gasp. There, in front of her, the water shimmered and twisted, forming a vision of her past. She saw faces before her. Smiling, happy faces that she hadn't seen in far too long.

Her father stared back at her, and her uncle, before they morphed to take the shape of her grandparents. The charred remains of a home, a mangled car, a flat lining heart monitor, the symbols of their lives lost flashed before her. The painful memories tugged at the last of the air in her lungs, constricting her chest.

Mari recognized her own face in the features that appeared before her next. The face of a woman, with chocolate brown eyes and long, chestnut hair smiled up at her. A face that Mari had only seen in photos, though nevertheless a face that felt like home and love and comfort.

As if she had been covered in oil, a black substance oozed from her body, swirling in the water around her. She knew she needed to go up for air soon, but she was mesmerized by the inky cloud that dissipated into the blue water.

When she could wait no longer, Mari surfaced, her head bursting through the water as she gasped for breath. She tread the water there for a moment, allowing her eyes to readjust to the light. The last of the black substance dissolved, leaving her alone in the pool.

Alone, and reborn, and in the deepest place of her soul she could feel it was true; she was finally curse-free.

Mari slowly re-dressed, a weak disbelief and joy muddled in her heart. The warmth of the waters had faded from her skin and her body trembled in the chilly air. She went out to face Hanli, who was waiting as promised.

Hanli rushed over to support Mari's shivering body, her wings wrapping around them to offer a bit of heat to Mari's soaked frame. Hanli only smiled and did not need to ask how it had gone. She looked at Mari knowingly, and Mari nodded.

"Let us get you in front of the fire once more."

On their way back up the steps, Mari left a trail of water on the rocks behind her. Hanli sighed and hugged her closer. She seemed not to care that she was getting wet as well.

"Cylan tells me that you all are traveling the realm to quell any disturbances in the kingdoms, and earn the Goddess's favor." She smiled kindly, clearly trying to distract Mari from the overwhelming cold rattling through her body. "But there is no trouble here. No conflict for you to fix. The Airy Reach only heals and brings peace. My brother seems to need a lot of peace but he is too stubborn to let it in."

Mari snorted, forcing words through chattering teeth, "You're t-t-telling me. He's got to b-b-be the most stubborn person I've met."

"It seems as though you are very important to him," Hanli said softly.

"I d-d-don't know why." Her words were nearly a whisper.

"Cylan has a long way to go on his journey to becoming a worthy King of the Realm, but I believe that you are helping him towards that goal in more ways than you might realize. After all, I cannot think of anyone that Cylan has unfurled those black wings of his for in quite some time."

Mari stopped a short distance from the cabin. Hanli's words brought back the memory of being swept up by what she'd thought was a giant raven. She'd been delirious and close to death at the time, so she'd let it slide over her like the hallucination she thought it had been. Now, Mari could see the memory through clear eyes. She turned to Hanli.

"Cylan saved me?"

Hanli nodded, "The moment he arrived and realized you were gone, he launched himself into the sky, willing to fly all night until he found you. But," she paused, searching Mari's face, "perhaps you should discuss that with him."

Hanli nodded toward the doorway where Cylan leaned against the frame, watching them with concern in his golden gaze. Hanli helped Mari to the porch before disappearing inside, leaving her alone with Cylan.

Mari allowed him to help her inside, silence between them. He seemed to understand what had just happened, handling her tenderly. Her suspicions were confirmed as he sat her back on her cot by the fire and leaned down next to her. The firelight made his eyes swim like pools of lava as he spoke.

"Hanli took you to the Goddess Spring, did she?"

Mari nodded. An odd sort of embarrassment settled over her at discussing a moment so personal. She stared down at her hands, unable to meet his gaze.

"And, Eris lifted your curse."

It wasn't a question, but Mari nodded anyway.

Cylan sighed, though there was no annoyance there, only relief.

"You are safe, warm, curse-free, and surrounded by those who care for you." He stood, wrapping a blanket over her shoulders, "all that is left for you to do is rest now. We can talk later."

27

LIMITLESS

Mari fell asleep there by the fire, waking up hours later in a dark and quiet house. The endless fire was still burning, a new log recently added. She had fully dried off, and someone had laid a light blanket over her as she slept. Though she still felt physically tired, her mind was wide awake, racing through thoughts and emotions unfamiliar to her.

She stared into the fire, watching the wood blacken and crumble into red and orange cinders. The vision of her family, mostly her mother's foreign yet all too familiar face, was stuck in her mind. They were all happy, despite their fates. They hadn't had the opportunity to escape the curse, but she had. And, she did.

As the ominous inky cloud had detached itself from her and dissipated into nothingness, dissolved by Eris' magic, she felt lighter, more clean, and pure. No longer did she feel the anxiety and worry that had hung over her like her own personal rain cloud. No longer did she have to wonder if today was the day the curse would take her.

Now, as her mind eased and years of fear began to melt away, a new question entered her mind. A question that she had not once thought to ask.

Why?

Why had she and her family been cursed in the first place? Who had cursed them and when? Had it been an Unseelie Fae that had ventured to her world one day and randomly—with a touch of unluckiness on her family's part—cursed them just for its own sick enjoyment? Or perhaps there was a bigger story behind it; an ancestor of hers had become cursed long ago and it had only carried down their bloodline.

Mari had spent so many years simply grieving and avoiding the curse and the tragedy it had left behind, that she'd never thought about its origin or purpose—if there had been a purpose at all. Perhaps certain questions may never be answered. Besides, did she really want to know? Maybe she should just continue to move forward, accepting the gift of freedom that she'd been given and never looking back.

She sighed, rolling over on her cot to put the fire behind her. She gasped, sitting upright when she saw she was not alone in the cabin.

"Cylan," she sighed, her heart still beating quickly from the scare, "I didn't know you were here."

He stood from his seat, carrying two clay mugs full of steaming liquid, and came to sit on the floor next to Mari's cot.

"Couldn't sleep," he said handing her a mug, "Leo snores. I made some tea instead."

Mari took the mug, grateful for the comforting drink inside. She thanked him before taking a sip of the honey-sweetened tea.

The burning logs continued to crumble and settle in the fireplace, sending up sparks that crackled and burst. Mari and Cylan sat in comfortable silence. The wind howled outside, blowing steadily across the mountaintop. Mari shivered, an ominous feeling passing over her, though she couldn't say what caused it.

Cylan reached out, grabbing her hand, "Something wrong?"

She didn't pull her hand away, though she was anxiously aware of every place his skin was touching hers. She smiled politely, trying to shake the feeling.

"I think I just need some air." When she tried to stand, his grip tightened. She paused, her head whipping back.

"*Onhma,* not now," he pulled her back down, past her cot, and onto the cushions on the floor beside him. "Unless you want to get carried away with the dead. When the wind sounds like this at night," he paused, his long pointed ears twitching as he focused, "she's carrying a group of spirits to their next home."

This time when Mari shivered she wasn't sure if it was her response to ghosts and spirits surrounding the cabin, or the tension she was feeling between herself and Cylan.

She was painfully aware of the small distance between their bodies and could think of little else besides trying to maintain that space. Any closer and all rationality would leave her immediately. Her mind flashed back to the memory of their near kiss in the caves, and her all-too-realistic dream a few nights afterward.

"So we're off to Fire's Territory next?" She tried to keep the conversation light. Mari knew there was much for them to talk about, but wasn't ready for discussions of broken curses, winged saviors, and near-death experiences.

He glanced at her sideways. Could he hear the tremble in her voice? "Yes."

"It's our last stop," she continued, suddenly afraid of awkward silence, "do we go back to the palace after that?"

Cylan sighed, settling further back into the pillows. He was only wearing his undershirt and a loose pair of pants. It was the most at ease that she'd seen him. His shirt rode up slightly, exposing the tanned skin of his stomach as he stretched. Mari's breath hitched.

He noticed that, turning to examine her a bit more closely. She could practically feel his gaze, like the gentle touch of curious fingers, as his eyes raked over her body, her hair, her face, lingering on her lips.

"Let's just focus on getting through Thorne alive before we make plans for the future."

"Thorne?" She pulled herself into a cross-legged sitting position, folding her hands tightly in her lap when the urge to brush a hair from his face twitched in her fingers.

"The capital city of the *Rinah* Kingdom—the Fire Territory. My brother has an overly extravagant palace there where he sits on his throne finding pleasure in terrorizing his people. You're going to love it there since you love terrorizing me so much."

Mari couldn't help but snort in disbelief; his comment catching her off guard. "Oh? It's *me* terrorizing *you*?"

His brow lifted with his interest and his lips pulled up in a confident smirk. Cylan leaned forward, setting his mug down beside him and shifting his weight to his knees before falling to his hands.

"Do you feel *terrorized*, little human?" He crawled closer to her, a lion stalking its prey.

Mari felt her eyes widen involuntarily and she leaned backward, supporting her trembling frame with her hands behind her. She couldn't speak as he positioned his body over hers. Though, even if she could have formed coherent words, she knew that she'd betray her rational, stubborn side by saying, *"Come closer."*

"You're shaking," Cylan whispered, his breath hot in her ear.

His nose nuzzled her neck, moving slowly down to her shoulder where his lips caught on her skin. Mari was mortified when a small moan escaped her lips, causing Cylan's mischievous smirk to deepen into a truly devilish smile.

He glanced up into her eyes then, his tone taunting, "Are you afraid of me?"

"Cylan," she breathed, unable to vocalize anything she was thinking. Why was she fighting this? She couldn't think of a good reason. Right now, at this moment, everything she had been secretly dreaming about was within her grasp. She only had to reach out and...

Mari leaned forward then, and Cylan's body responded. He fell backward as Mari's hips straddled his, her hair falling into his face. Here, above him, she felt more in control.

"Why did you save me?" She whispered down at him. "You continue to save me. Over and over...it would be so easy to let me go."

His eyes darkened. An instant later their lips were crushing against each other, their eyes fluttering closed in sync.

She was only vaguely aware that there were others in the loft above them as Cylan's hands greedily grabbed at every curve of her body. The thought of anyone else quickly faded away when his hand cupped her breast and she let out another involuntary moan. Her face lifted skyward to steal a breath as he covered her neck in kisses.

It was just the two of them here in the firelight; wordless, breathless, limitless.

A noise of impatience broke free from Cylan's throat. In one swift motion, he effortlessly lifted Mari, shifting their combined weight so that she was lying on her back and he was between her legs. She couldn't help but let out a nearly hysterical giggle as satisfaction and anticipation ravaged her body. Cylan smiled against her lips.

She looked at him then as he pulled back, breathing heavily. In the yellow glow, his amber eyes seemed to dance with a flame all their own as they absorbed every inch of her face, silently asking permission to go further.

"Do you want to stop?" she hesitantly asked, reaching up to run her hand through his tousled hair, her fingertips brushing across the pointed tips of his ears.

He leaned into her touch. "Do you?"

She responded with a kiss, relief flowing over her when he kissed her back, silently acknowledging that he understood completely.

Rain pattered on the roof. Thunder soon followed, and the fire in the hearth continued to crackle. The old wood of the house creaked, and someone somewhere was snoring. Part of Mari hoped these noises were drowning out the moans and sighs and gasps that she couldn't seem to control.

Even the sound of roaming spirits outside couldn't muffle everything, though, and when the moment came when Mari felt she was about to completely fall apart with satisfaction, she buried her face in Cylan's shoulder. He held her tightly as they both collapsed into the pillows below, a tangle of sweaty limbs and hot breath.

"I saved you," Cylan whispered into her hair as he kissed her gently, "for purely selfish reasons."

Mari smiled as the fire warmed her face and she closed her eyes. It wasn't long before sleep claimed her and, for the first time here in the Realm of Faerie, Mari felt truly at peace.

28

END OF THE ROAD

This has been a fruitless journey. I believe a change in our plan is long overdue.

Alek's legs buckled underneath him. He sank down to the black volcanic rock that covered the streets of Thorne. Etaldin's voice, which had been much like an annoying whisper in his ear, now turned to a vicious roar that shook him to his bones.

The goblin messenger that had just delivered news of Mari's safe arrival in the Airy Reach scrambled away, seeking safety further in the city. Alek wished more than anything that he could follow the goblin, but as Etaldin's rage grew, Alek could feel that he was losing control of himself.

"It's not my fault!" Alek countered, "Your demons couldn't cross the water to find Mari and your spies in the Dominion were useless. Not to mention it was your plan to let the wisps capture Mari. Prince Cylan found her before we did, and that's not something I could help, either. If you'd just let me try one of my ideas for a change—"

His voice caught in his throat, his limbs shaking, as Etaldin spoke again.

It is time for you to take a backseat.

Alek gasped as a weightless feeling came over him. Terror flooded every sense of his being, though he could no longer feel the pounding of his heart or the rise and fall of his chest. His limbs weren't responding to his attempts to move them and when he heard his voice fill the air around them, he realized he wasn't in control of the words that came out.

"Flesh and bone feel better than I remember, even if this body isn't exactly as large as I had hoped my vessel would be." His legs took a step forward, and another, no matter how much he protested. His mouth smiled with each movement, then, Etaldin lifted Alek's hands so that his magic elevated him above the ground.

Alek screamed inside, fighting with all of his inner strength but to no avail. Was this really the end of the road? Alek didn't want to believe it, but as he struggled he began to fade like fog burnt away by the full force of the sun.

Etaldin was in total control of Alek's body now. It felt as though Alek's consciousness was nothing more than an uncontrollable mist, centered right behind his own eyes. He could still feel Etaldin's presence, as they shared the same body, but Etaldin's was stronger now.

Now that Alek was the one inside Etaldin's mind, he realized he had a front-row seat to all of Etaldin's thoughts and plans. The deepest feeling of dread and despair settled around him as he discovered the ulterior motives and truth that Etaldin had been hiding from him.

What a fool he had been, to trust an Unseelie God! How could he have been so naive to think he had been the one in control? That he was doing what was best for Mari? Etaldin made it clear to him now, with a savage sense of gloating and arrogance, the full extent of Alek's mistake.

"Yes," the God laughed through Alek's mouth, "now you know the truth, stupid boy. Though it will do you little good, trapped as you are."

Mari woke the next morning to the smell of food in the air. The fire had finally dwindled overnight and the warm, gentle rays of early morning sunshine filtered through the cabin's many windows.

She was alone on the floor, though the pillow beside her was still warm. Mari sat up, scanning the room for Cylan.

Almost everyone was there, rummaging through the kitchen to find their breakfast. Hanli was absent and Mari briefly wondered where she was before her thoughts were redirected to where Cylan and Leo sat. The pair were deep in conversation. The words *Thorne* and *danger*, and *keeping Mari safe*, floated across the room. Mari studied the back of Cylan's head, smiling now that she knew how it felt to have her fingers twisted in his curly hair.

Maelin had filled two wooden plates with berries, nuts, and—surprisingly—eggs, and was headed towards the living area.

"Good morning, ma'am," Maelin walked a plate over to where Mari sat on the floor. "Eat up now, for we will have a lot of walking to do to get to the next kingdom." She nodded her head towards the side table where her leather backpack sat, "Your things are still packed, secure, and neat."

Mari set down the plate, reaching for Maelin's tiny hand. Maelin's soft pink features curved into a gentle smile as she asked, "Is everything alright, ma'am?"

"I just," Mari began, a feeling of joy and gratitude overcoming her, "I'm really thankful that you've been here with me, Maelin. I couldn't have made it this far without you."

"Oh," Maelin's violet eyes shimmered and she squeezed Mari's hand tighter, "this has been my pleasure ma'am. A journey of a lifetime. Without you, I'd be back with my parents at The Good Inn, up to my elbows in soap and scrubbing the floors!"

Maelin chuckled. Mari laughed as well, picturing fragile Maelin with her bucket and scrub brush on the floor of a dirty inn. The picture was too detached from the reality of the dainty and elegant Fae sitting next to her.

Mari's life had been mostly friendless until she'd found herself in the Realm of Faerie and had met some of the most selfless, genuine companions. With the thought of her friends back in Eristald, memories surfaced of the bazaar and the little cob house that she'd called home for a short while.

She shook her head, refusing to let the thought of Alek make her sad. Her heart had never been more full of love, friendship, and hope than it was right now, and she intended to hold on to that feeling as long as possible.

Once they were finished and Maelin had gone to ensure everything was packed and tidied away, Mari went to get her things from the side table and slipped on her boots.

She opened the pack, looking at the few belongings she had acquired over her time here. The dryad's gift—a perfect flower, preserved for all time—sat tucked into a pocket of its own. She picked up the small orb, turning it over in her hands. Mari placed the trinket in her pants pocket so that she could have more space to look through the rest of the pack.

A change of clothes and her journal with the map tucked neatly inside were resting at the bottom of the bag. Mari wondered, running her fingers along the spine and the pencil that was growing smaller, how she would accurately capture her time in the Airy Reach. How could she depict the feeling of the wisps draining all that was left of her, or the indescribable feeling of the Goddess Spring, her visions there, and being freed from her curse?

A few more descriptive words came to mind next, as the recent memory of her and Cylan's shared moment made a heat flush through her stomach and chest. In the moments between roaming mouths and hands, part of her had been waiting to wake up, expecting it all to be a dream. Thankfully, she never did.

"Good morning," Cylan appeared behind her, his hands gathering her hair and moving it aside so that his mouth could nuzzle her neck.

She turned, unable to hide the beaming smile on her face even if she'd wanted to.

"Good morning," she replied.

Cylan looked over her shoulder, his eyes focusing on her backpack. He reached around, grabbing out the dagger that Mari had been given in the temple at the beginning of their journey. He examined the dagger, unsheathing it and studying the blade.

"I nearly forgot Eris had gifted you this." He murmured, "What a treasure it is."

Mari took it from him, the weight of it heavier than the metal in her hand. She hadn't forgotten about it, though she tried. The words inscribed on the dagger resonated loud and clear in her thoughts. *A blade that will leave only one. Defeat my greatest enemy, o' wielder of Eris' Fury, no matter the cost.*

She took a deep breath, looking up at Cylan, "I had prayed to Eris for the opportunity to help the Fae of the realm in any way that I could." She scoffed, sheathing the blade once more and sliding it into place on her belt. She'd learned her lesson when she'd kept it in her pack. From now on, it stayed on her body at all times. "I had hardly expected the prayer to be answered, let alone have that answer be a weapon that was meant to be used to defeat Eris' greatest enemy."

"Hm." Cylan made a soft noise, reaching his fingers up to her throat and running them across the chain that hung there holding the pendant he'd gotten her. "For your sake, I hope you do not have to use it. But, Mari," with gentle fingers, he lifted her chin to look at him, "you must be brave enough to do what Eris has asked of you if that need ever arises. Do not forget all that she has done for you, bringing you here and lifting your curse. And, of course, bringing you to me." He smirked, kissing her softly before releasing her chin.

She rolled her eyes and made sure her tone dripped with playful sarcasm, "And what a gift you are."

"Don't forget it." He chuckled, closing her pack and handing it to her, "Now, let's get going."

Hanli met them outside to say farewell, "May the starlight watch over you, dear brother, and your companions. I pray you are able to earn Eris' favor and bring the starlight back to us."

"Continue to pray, Hanli. I fear we'll need all of the support we can get."

The four of them—a hopeful human girl, a determined Fae prince, a gentle handmaiden, and a half-orc warrior—descended the stone stairs on the southern side of the mountain. What a unique group they were, Mari thought, with all of their differences and their strengths. Could they really be the ones to succeed in this quest and return the starlight to the realm?

The descent was easier than Mari had anticipated when they had been at the top staring down upon a seemingly endless length of steps. Still, the journey down the mountain took several hours and by the time they reached the bottom, Mari's legs felt weak.

They paused for a quick lunch at the bottom of the mountain where a long ravine stretched out before them to the west. To the east, Mari could only see a vast expanse of rock and sand. They had made good progress, but the end of the road seemed an eternity away.

They were in the Zephyr Ravine, Mari recalled from her map. A narrow, rocky path that cut through the mountains. A thin river trickled through the ravine and would lead them towards Fire's Territory if they followed it westward. Stubby plants grew up from cracks between the rocks and remained close to the ground.

Large statues, the detail of them worn away by time, stood randomly along the ravine as far as she could see. They varied in size, some no larger than a small dog, others as tall as a house. Their bodies were sturdy and wide, and their limbs—two legs and two arms each—were carved in various positions to show some of them walking or reaching skyward, immortalized in movement. Their heads and faces were indiscernible, just rounded rocks on top of the bodies with hardly any neck to support them.

As they finished up their meal, continuing onward, Mari looked over to Cylan, who refused to walk more than a few feet away from her.

"Who put these statues in the middle of this place?"

Cylan chuckled, though not impolitely, "They put themselves there. If we hang out until nightfall you'll see where they move to next."

"They are trolls, ma'am." Maelin added, "The morning sunlight turns them to stone where they stand, but when the first moonbeam hits them, they'll come alive again."

Mari winced as she passed one that towered over her by at least ten feet, imagining the damage one of them could do, "Guess we wouldn't want to be around when that happens, huh?"

"Trolls are quite gentle giants." Leo, who was walking only a few paces in front of them, surprised Mari by speaking up, "In my experience, they are more afraid of you than you are of them."

Mari glanced over at two smaller troll rocks that looked to have been frozen in the middle of playing a game of tag. She smiled, "I'd like to meet one, one day, I think."

29

THE ETERNAL ONE

They continued to walk, sometimes in silence and sometimes filling the space between them with idle chit-chat. Mostly, Mari's mind darted between thoughts of Cylan and what their futures looked like, and if those futures intertwined.

She remembered Alek telling her that Fae don't love in the same way that humans did, but what exactly did that mean? Either way, was that what this really was? Love? It was too soon to tell to exactly what depth their feelings for each other ran, but there was clearly a connection worth exploring.

Mari stifled a laugh at the thought that popped into her mind next. She thought, if someone had told her when she first met Cylan that the two of them would be civil, or friendly, or *intimate* together, well she would have found that more unbelievable than any of the mythical creatures she'd encountered.

Yet, here they were, walking so close that their arms touched, sharing small, knowing looks that made Mari blush and smile. She'd seen the attitude that Cylan carried with him like a shield, but she'd also seen and appreciated the reality of the person behind that shield. Despite all of the things she'd discovered that she liked about Cylan, there was still one glaring hole in the plan for her future.

Was she still planning on going home once their journey was done? At first, this hadn't been a question but the only logical option. Of course she had to return home, return to safety and comfort and a world that she knew. Mostly, she still felt that way. However, a prince with a pair of golden eyes and raven black wings was beginning to make the idea of a second option feel more real.

Mari's focus snapped back to reality for a moment. She noticed that the sun was beginning its descent in the sky and in the somewhat near distance, Mari could see the end of the ravine.

"We will soon be near the Boiling Springs," Leo announced. "There, the river turns and becomes too deep and dangerous for us to cross on foot. We must find the bridge and cross it to get to the Yellow Lizard—a tavern where we can stay for the night before continuing on to Thorne in the morning."

Mari sighed, relieved. Her feet and legs had walked more today than they had in her whole life. She hadn't wanted to complain, but the blisters on her feet were beginning to become unbearable.

The roar of the rapids was heard long before they neared the section of the river that cut straight across their path. The water moved viciously as it raced downstream. It was clear that without the bridge Leo had mentioned, getting to the other side would be impossible.

Mari looked down the length of the river for a bridge, but what she found instead made her heart sink. A few yards away, the remnants of a bridge that had been torn in half sat on the other side of the riverbank.

The side that Mari's group was on, was devoid of any structure. She turned to Leo, who had noticed it as well.

"What do we do now?" Mari was tired, her feet ached, her stomach rumbled, and if she looked closely enough, she swore she could see the smoke from the chimney of the inn in the distance.

"We must find another way across," Leo said simply, though his voice was beginning to show his exhaustion as well.

Cylan and Leo pulled out their map to find an alternate route. Mari's eyes wandered further down the river, where the water poured from a cavern in the mountains. Next to the cavern's opening, a sign hung with black letters painted in the unfamiliar Fae language.

Mari grabbed Maelin's hand and began to walk towards the sign. "We're going to keep moving for a minute, we'll be right back!" Mari called to Cylan.

"Don't go far! We'll have a plan thought up soon enough." He didn't sound optimistic.

"Maelin, what does that sign say?"

Maelin squinted and after a few more feet, she said, "It says that the hot springs are located inside the cave, ma'am."

"Hot springs?"

"Yes, ma'am. This area is known for its relaxing hot springs, but–"

"That is exactly what I need right now." Mari interrupted her. "Let's go, just for a moment."

"But ma'am, the sign also says..."

"Unless it says something about complimentary refreshments, I don't wanna hear it!" Mari smiled at Maelin who was looking increasingly uncomfortable. "Loosen up, Maelin. Dipping our feet in the nice, hot water will be blissful!"

Maelin nodded, though the worry line between her thin eyebrows stayed deeply creased.

As they approached the entrance to the cave the river calmed, still flowing steadily but without the terrifying foamy rapids. A few more feet inside the cave the river disappeared into a hole in the wall, where the water must rise from underground.

The warmth and humidity of the air in the cave were soothing, like a sauna. In front of them, the path forked into four separate carved-out sections, each with signs above them. Voices, laughter, and the flicker of magic firelight emerged from three of the four paths. The fourth cave, while more dimly lit, was quiet. For Mari, the choice was obvious.

Mari held tight to Maelin's hand as they entered the fourth cavern. With every step they took the humidity increased, the steam obscuring their vision. Perhaps this particular spring was too hot, and that was why no one had been in it. Still, they'd come all this way and Mari was going to see for herself.

The path ended in a rounded half-circle surrounded by steaming, bubbling, opaque water. Mari bent down to remove a boot, hoping to test the water with her toe. As she did, the water surged.

Mari froze halfway to her boot, watching the water. The thought that it might have just been a large air bubble crossed her mind until another surge came, and another, small waves lapping onto the rock at her feet. She took a step back. Something was clearly in the spring. Something large.

"Ma'am," Maelin's voice shook, "I tried to tell you, the sign warned that we might possibly encounter—"

Water sprayed across them in a hot mist, causing Mari to stumble backward into Maelin. The two girls gasped as the creature rose from beneath the waves with a groan. It touched the cave ceiling before coming back down, landing with a thud that shook the earth beneath them.

At least half of its long, red, serpentine body was still under the water, but its front portion, with its two legs, wide as tree trunks, and head the size of a bus, was resting on the rocky floor before them. Behind it, two large veiny wings encompassed the full width of the cave, curling in towards its body when they could not outstretch any further.

"A dragon." Maelin finished, her voice a whisper.

Mari's eyes were wide as she fixed them on the dragon. "You didn't think to mention that?" She hissed.

"You told me you didn't want to hear it, ma'am. I—"

"Hello there," the dragon spoke, its forked tongue flicking quickly in and out of its sharp-toothed grin. "What brings such a small human and its Fae pet to my hot spring?

"I'm sorry," Mari bowed a bit, as she backed away, "we didn't mean to disturb you. We were just leaving."

"Stay!" Its tone was polite but left no room for arguments. The end of its massive tail surfaced, falling across the path behind them, and blocking their exit. "I insist."

The dragon's head tilted down toward them and Mari's heart nearly stopped. It was hard enough to breathe as it was with the humidity in the air, and her increasing panic was sure to make her pass out if she didn't get control of it soon. The two large nostrils positioned perfectly at the end of its elongated snout flexed as it took in their scent.

"You're working for *her*." It sneered.

"I work for no one but myself," Mari said defiantly, her hand reaching out to hold Maelin's shaking arm.

"I can *smell* her on your skin. Her essence follows you."

"Who are you talking about?"

"The *Goddess* that banished dragons from her land long ago. I chose to reside here in the God's land for he welcomes all. Besides, the hot water is euphoric." He sank a bit further beneath the waves, "Why are you here?"

Mari saw no point in lying. She and Maelin were trapped here and unless she could get on this dragon's good side, they might end up as his dinner. The thought shuddered through her as she spoke, willing her voice to remain steady.

"We are on our way to Thorne. To see Prince Xerxes."

"Ah," the dragon's deep voice rumbled, "Give him my regards. He's always been a friend of mine."

"What is your name?" Mari asked, attempting a formality that felt a bit foreign to her, "So that I may deliver your message properly."

"How many dragons do you think there are?" He laughed a thunderous noise that reverberated off of the stone walls. "I am Zayndru, The Eternal One." His large round eyes moved down to Mari's lower half and then narrowed, "what is it that you have in your pocket, human?"

Mari reached into the pocket that bulged out at her hip. Slowly, she pulled out the dryad's gift which faintly glowed with a pale green light.

"Where did you get such a thing?" Zayndru leaned in, his tongue fluttering to taste the air around her.

Mari winced but stayed calm. "It was a gift. From a thankful dryad in Beryl's Grove."

Zayndru purred, a deep noise rumbling from within him. Mari couldn't help but be amazed at the sheer size of him. One bite from those powerful jaws and... well, at least it would be a quick death.

"What you may not know, human, is that below these waters I have sunken my horde of treasures. What I have never had in this collection, however, is a thing such as that. What will you take as a trade?"

"What if I don't want to trade it?" A stupid question, she realized as soon as it left her lips. She braced herself for his reaction.

Zayndru was an icy, terrifying calm as he responded with a hint of enjoyment in his tone.

"Oh I will have it, that's not the decision to make here. The decision you must make is if you'd like to walk out of here, or not."

Mari thought of Cylan and Leo outside and wondered if they had figured out a way ahead. Perhaps they would come looking for her and Maelin soon. She took a steadying breath before responding.

"I would ask for something that will get my companions and me across the river and into Thorne."

Mari took a step forward, prying her hand free of Maelin's. She dropped the dryad's gift at the edge of the stone walkway. Zayndru's clawed hand reached out from the water to claim his prize.

A moment later, as the orb sank beneath the water, Zayndru emerged from his hot spring and bent down in front of Mari and Maelin.

"Hop on, small one."

Mari hesitated, looking back at Maelin, her worried pink face softening slightly. She nodded in understanding before walking forward. The girls used Zayndru's outstretched arm to help them climb up onto the dragon's back between his wings. His scales were warm and hard as the rock around them.

Once they were in place, Mari closest to Zayndru's head and Maelin grasping Mari's waist from behind, Zayndru began to move. His serpentine body undulated, moving like a wave as he rose from the water, his wings slowly beating. With an impressive amount of dexterity, Zayndru deftly maneuvered through the narrow passageways and out into the blueish blanket of dusk that had settled on the land.

Mari could see Cylan and Leo, walking toward the cave they had just exited. They froze as they saw Zayndru launching through the air towards them, their eyes wide and mouths agape. Just as they turned to run in the other direction, Zayndru dipped down, positioning his clawed hands above the two now-running males. The hands secured around their bodies, lifting them into the sky like a crane in a claw machine.

Mari looked down as they thrashed against the dragon's vice-like grip and couldn't stop the laugh that burst from her at the sight of their shock. Then, realizing their efforts were futile, they looked around and up, noticing the girls atop the menacing creature. Mari hadn't thought it was possible that anyone could look as confused, terrified, and disbelieving as they did at that moment. With a mischievous smile, she waved down at Cylan.

As Zayndru soared across the darkening skies, Mari looked down watching as the world fell away beneath them. The land was quickly changing from sparse greenery and sandy earth to blackened rock and barren, burnt trees. Soon, the world below them was a scene from a black-and-white film. Greys, blacks, and ash white covered the desolate wasteland that was Fire's Territory.

Huts, built from a leathery material and stark white bone, were scattered along the land and made up small villages. The people of this land, though appearing small from Mari's current vantage point, were broad-shouldered and various shades of green, red, black, and gray. A few looked up as the dragon's shadow passed over them, blocking out the rising moonlight, though they remained indifferent at the sight of him.

Soon, Thorne volcano began to rise in the distance, smoke and a warm red light emanating from its core. In its shadow the largest city she'd seen yet expanded across the blackened earth. Some buildings were huts like the leather and bone ones she'd seen, others were made of scraps of darkened wood or stone, though they all appeared to be run down and neglected.

Along the eastern face of the volcano, a palace was carved. Smooth black stone, dark as the starless night sky, had been added to the carved rock. It reflected the silver moonlight, rising up like grand swords along the tops of turrets. Bricks of it were speckled along the walls of the palace, enhancing the shadows that clung to the rock. Along the base of the mountain, shielding the dark palace from reach and view of the city below, a wall of the onyx stone rose and curved in a perfect semi-circle.

Zayndru flew over the wall, landing just beyond it at the foot of the mountain. He released Leo and Cylan a few feet from the ground where they tumbled in the dust. His great shoulder lowered, allowing Mari and Maelin to slide off effortlessly.

The dragon's catlike yellow eye examined her for a moment before, with one strong beat of his wings, he launched himself into the sky without another word. In the middle of the movement a scale the size of a dinner plate flew off of his back, landing at Mari's feet.

She bent down to grab it. The scale was warm to the touch as if it had been sitting out in the summer sun. Palace guards, two enormous toad green orcs, had begun walking toward them. She quickly moved to tuck the scale into her backpack. She might not know everything about the realm and the magic bestowed on its creatures, but she could guess that owning a dragon scale from the last dragon was something special and didn't want the guards to see or take it from her.

Cylan approached her, his hair and clothes ruffled and windswept. He bent to whisper in her ear, his tone serious but still holding a hint of a smile.

"We'll be talking about that surprise later, dragon rider."

Leo stepped forward to greet the guards. If Mari had thought that Leo was large before, he now looked like a horse standing next to a pair of elephants.

The orc on the left barked out two short words that Mari did not understand, holding their maces at the ready. Leo held one hand up in greeting, the other rested gently on the sword at his hip. He spoke back with them in their native language. With an unhidden disappointment, the guards huffed a sigh and turned to lead the four of them into the palace.

30

ONYX & ISOLATION

The palace was a dark and empty place, with ceilings so high that they were hidden in shadow. Magic fire sconces, too few and far between, only did so much to light the way. Perhaps most notably, there was no furniture or decor; only the rock of the volcano and black stone lined the walls and floors. And, to Mari's dismay, the stairs were seemingly endless.

The orc guards led them up several flights of stone stairs, their footsteps echoing in the darkness. Even her welcome in the Water's Dominion was better than this. At least there had been a dinner prepared for her, even if the company was less than desirable.

Finally, with Mari's calves screaming in protest, they arrived at a pair of tall onyx doors that the guards easily pushed open. Inside was another long and empty chamber, save for an extravagant high-backed throne with three red velvet steps leading up to it. The throne, made of dark brown wood, was carved with ornate designs and cushioned with the same red velvet as the steps. In its seat, sat a bored-looking male that Mari could easily assume to be Cylan's brother. Prince Xerxes.

"Little brother," Xerxes purred like a wildcat eyeing its prey, "I wasn't expecting you until tomorrow."

Cylan held fast to Mari's hand pulling her alongside him as he stepped forward, but not past Leo.

"Xerxes. Our sudden arrival was," he shot a sideways glance over to Mari, "unexpected for us as well. However, we are here now, and thank you for your hospitality." Mari saw a muscle in Cylan's jaw clench as he forced out the last words.

"Oh," Xerxes straightened and stood slowly. His wings were batlike, dark as night, and massive, with three peaks on top of each and a longer one at the bottom. With his long-legged stride, he closed the distance between them quickly, "I am nothing if not hostile. I mean, *hospitable.*" He chuckled at his own attempt at humor. "Who is this that you cling to so fiercely, little brother?"

Xerxes's smile was dazzling, his white teeth a perfect contrast between his sun-darkened skin and dark lashes that shaded his molten gold eyes. Although all of Cylan's brothers and sisters looked very similar in their coloring and features, Xerxes looked so similar to Cylan that Mari felt she was seeing a vision of what Cylan might look like in another decade. He was a bit taller and more muscular than Cylan was, and ten times as arrogant, which Mari wouldn't have thought possible.

"Your name?" he inquired. With a long-fingered hand that was adorned with the same family ring that Cylan had, Xerxes bent at the waist and secured Mari's hand in his. With his head angled downward, he locked eyes with Mari through his lashes and brought her hand towards his mouth for a kiss.

"I am Mari." She said, nearly cringing at the echo her voice made in the room.

He held his lips there a moment too long and Mari barely resisted the urge to snatch her hand back from him. Cylan stiffened beside her, not relaxing even as Xerxes released Mari's hand.

"*Mari.*" Xerxes groaned in delight as if he'd just taken a taste of his favorite dessert, "She smells delicious. Which reminds me, you all must be starving after your journey from those dreadfully cold mountains. Come," he made his way to another set of doors to their left. A second later he snapped his fingers and they slid open with a vibrating groan.

Here, with the heat of the volcano around them, there was no need for a large fireplace in their dining room. Instead, the outermost wall was gone, leaving only thick pillars to hold up the mountainside. Between them, Mari could see out over the blackened city where small fires burned, dotted in between buildings.

The long wooden table sat in the center of the space. It was adorned with more food than any of them could ever eat in a night. The spread before them was steaming hot and included many things Mari would have eaten back home; meats of every kind, roasted, grilled, and stewed, with other filling foods like potatoes and pasta and breads.

Her mouth watered but her heart faltered. After being here for so long, she began to realize that any number of those delicious meats on the table could have been a Fae person and not simply the animal it had appeared to be. Here, in this kingdom, they wouldn't care much if the meal they hunted was not truly an animal.

They sat, goblin waiters bringing over wine and filling their plates. Mari politely accepted the food, but kept to the potatoes and vegetables she'd been served and pushed the meat aside.

Xerxes sneered as Maelin and Leo took their seats. Mari even heard a grumble from the servants, their gazes locked on her pink and green friends.

"You dine with your staff?" Xerxes did not hide his look of disgust.

"We dine," Cylan said with a clear effort to stay calm, "with our friends. Though, I wouldn't expect you to understand considering, well, that you don't have any."

Xerxes snorted, turning his attention to Mari, "So, Mari dearest, tell me," he sliced off a bite of seared steak, popping it in his mouth before continuing, speaking around his food, "How are you enjoying your time in our realm so far?"

A polite question. Mari saw no harm in answering though the tension in the room still made her cautious. "I've had a wonderful time. Let's hope that holds true while I'm here." She took a sip of her wine.

"Charming," Xerxes said, unimpressed. "When I received Cylan's letter announcing his tour of the realm, and with a human companion, no less!" Xerxes continued to stuff his face with meat and wine, "I thought, what a stupid idea, trying to bring the stars back. Your *Goddess* abandoned you all long ago. Time to move on, I'd say."

Cylan hadn't touched his food, instead never taking his eyes off of his brother. "And, as our people grow weary, dying and continuing in a miserable state of existence, you'd have me, what... watch from my throne and do nothing?"

"I didn't say that, did I?" Xerxes leaned back, holding out his goblet for more wine, "No, no, I just meant that seeking out your Goddess is a pointless effort and that perhaps you should be looking down more Godly avenues. You know, I hear Etaldin is alive and well, here in the city! Perhaps, I should track him down and invite him to tomorrow's dinner?"

Mari nearly choked on her wine, looking to Cylan for a response. He was pale, though his steely expression hadn't changed. "If Etaldin truly is here, then we should not be." He started to stand, shoving his chair back with a loud scrape on the stone floor.

"Oh don't be so sensitive, baby brother." Xerxes rolled his eyes and Cylan sat back down. "If anyone at this table has a right to be in a bad mood, it is myself. I did not choose to be banished to a fiery wasteland to oversee a bunch of imbeciles." He threw a meatless rib bone at the head of one of his servants, striking her between the eyes. She hardly flinched. "The only thing they have going for them is their love for mischief and violence."

Everyone had stopped eating but Xerxes. The room fell silent as he finished his dinner. After wiping his face with his napkin, Xerxes stood, his wings spreading outward for balance.

"Allow me to show you to your room for the night." They all stood, following him for a step before he stopped in his tracks. He turned back to them with a look of annoyance, "I was speaking only to Mari. The staff here will escort the rest of you in a moment."

At Mari's shocked stare, Cylan nodded once. "Xerxes and his staff all know you aren't to be harmed." His voice held the strength of the Crown

Prince that he was. Mari was proud of him, though the pit of worry and fear still held steady inside her. "Go with him."

"Don't worry, little brother," Xerxes' smile was venomous, "I'll keep her close."

"I will be there shortly, Mari," Cylan called after her.

Mari forced herself to follow the wolf leading her further into its den. As they traveled through the echoing halls of the palace, she tried to maintain a safe distance from Xerxes and kept her hand on the hilt of her dagger. She doubted she would be a match for his strength and magic, but she wouldn't go down without a fight if that's what it came to. He'd been civil so far, but it was clear that he couldn't be trusted.

"You know, beautiful girl, I think you may very well be the first human to be in this palace. Well," he paused, adding with a sickening grin, "as a guest, anyway."

"An honor." She said dryly.

Xerxes chuckled, slowing his pace to walk next to her. He outstretched his wing, wrapping it around her shoulder.

"Too bad the walk to the residential wing isn't longer," They turned a corner, entering a hall lined with multiple sets of tall black doors. "I was hoping to find out what a human could possibly have to offer the people of Fire's Territory, besides being the entree of a delicious meal."

Mari glared at him. She had never so quickly formed such a strong and distasteful opinion of another living being. Xerxes was crude, entitled, and clearly sadistic. No wonder he'd been the one chosen to lead the most dangerous and Unseelie kingdom in the realm.

They'd come to a stop in the middle of the hallway between two sets of doors. Xerxes gestured to the pair on their left.

"Your staff may use this room," he took a step closer to the one on the right, "and yours is here."

She stepped away from him, her back brushing against the door, her hand searching behind her for a handle or knob of any kind.

"Well, thank you for dinner and the unnecessary personal escort but—"

"I see the way my brother looks at you." His eyes raked lazily over her frame. He leaned closer, one hand bracing himself on the door above her. His scent of smoke and spices filled her nostrils, "Surely you're not satisfied with that sad excuse of a..."

She cut him off, her hand finally finding the cold metal handle, "If you'll excuse me, I have the future king meeting me in my room soon." She turned the handle, taking a step backward as the door opened. Xerxes stumbled forward as the door moved out from under his hand.

Mari smiled, "I'll be sure to let you know how *satisfied* I am in the morning unless you hear it for yourself through the walls tonight."

Shocked silent, for perhaps the first time in his life, Xerxes only stared, his eyes a mixture of frustration and amazement, as she closed the door in his face.

Mari sighed, sinking down against the door. No wonder Cylan had been so hesitant to come here. She'd been in Thorne for a couple hours and already she could tell that this was a terrible place to be. Despite the warmth of the volcano, the chill of the dark unwelcoming atmosphere was already beginning to feel suffocating.

The room before her was elegant and overly extravagant. The bed, wardrobe, desk, and chairs were all carved from mahogany. They, along with the curtains that covered a window along the furthest wall, were adorned with gold paint, embroidery, black metal accents, and red velvet upholstery. The magic fire chandelier that hung in the center of the room cast a dim and sensual glow.

She stood, exhausted and ready to sleep for days. She undressed down to her shirt and underwear, leaving on the necklace that Cylan had given her. Mari wished she'd had the opportunity to bathe the day's travels off of her.

She crawled onto the bed, setting her backpack next to her on the floor. She kept her dagger on the nightside table, just an arm's length away. Only a moment later, the doors to the bedroom opened and Cylan stepped in.

He looked as weary as she felt. He walked toward her, undressing just as she had, and sat on the edge of the bed.

"Are you alright?" He asked, his tired eyes searching her face.

Mari nodded, "Are you?"

Cylan sighed and shrugged. "I'm worried. We've come all this way and not a single star has appeared in the sky. This could be our last chance to bring the stars back and in a kingdom so far detached from Eris, I don't like our odds."

She reached out and rested a hand on his shoulder, "We'll find a way."

Cylan stared at her hand. He looked up to meet her gaze. His eyes were wide with an emotion she hadn't seen on his features before. Uncertainty.

"I don't want you to think... just because of what happened in Hanli's cabin... that you're obliged to share a bed with me now. I'll have to insist on staying in the room, for your safety and my peace of mind, but I can request another bed if you'd like."

Mari blinked at him, though her response came quickly. "No," she slid over, pulling the covers aside, "I want you here."

Cylan lay beside her and she curled up into his embrace. His intoxicating pine and incense smell still lingered on his skin despite the day's events, and Mari inhaled deeply. His hands rubbed soothingly along her body, caressing her into a peaceful slumber.

An unknown length of time later she woke up, her stomach rumbling. She looked over at Cylan's slack sleeping face and smiled. He snored ever so lightly, his breathing deep and steady. Carefully, Mari untangled herself from Cylan and slipped on her pants. She grabbed the dagger from the table and headed for the door.

She opened it slowly, peeking out to see if the hall was clear before creeping over to knock on Maelin's door across the hall. Her groggy pink friend answered a moment later, yawning and holding a magic fire lantern.

"Ma'am?" Her voice was deep and raspy, "Is everything alright?"

Mari smiled sheepishly, "Sorry to wake you. I was just hoping you might walk me to the kitchen for a snack? I don't want to go alone." Her stomach rumbled as if on cue.

Maelin smiled and stepped out, looking back once at a loudly snoring Leo sprawled across one of the two beds in their room.

"I'd be happy to ma'am. It's hard to sleep very soundly with the roar of Leo's breathing. I could use a moment of silence."

Linked arm in arm, the two girls headed back down the hall towards the dining area and kitchen. Voices traveled out from the room beyond the cracked kitchen doors; a lively conversation taking place. Mari and Maelin stopped short, clinging to the shadows along the wall to listen.

"Etaldin should have chosen me to possess instead of that wimpy little elf." The sound of a belch and a bang on a table made Mari jump. "I don't even think that scrawny boy will be strong enough to harness Etaldin's true power, once it's fully restored."

"Etaldin doesn't make mistakes." Another voice spat back, nasally and sharp.

"Besides," a third says, the deep timbre of his voice nearly rattling the walls, "once the boy has built the magic back up enough, the dark one is able to fully assume his body. It won't matter what condition it's in at that point."

Mari, breathing heavily, held tighter to Maelin. They remained frozen in place, unable to stop listening.

"Our God is one step closer to taking control over the realm," the nasally one said excitedly. "Imagine how glorious it will be when Unseelie can roam free!"

"Why stop with just this realm?" The first belched again, "I hear the human world has a lot to offer."

"You idiot," the deep voice barked out, "of course that's his plan. You think Etaldin has been trying to help that clueless, white-haired lover boy get this girl for no reason? He needs a human sacrifice in order to enter the human world."

Mari's stomach flipped, all thoughts of food vanishing from her mind. Maelin's mirrored expression of fear sent a shiver down her spine.

"Alek," Mari whispered in horror.

Maelin grabbed Mari's hand, dragging her back down the hall towards her room.

"Hurry, Ma'am. We must tell Leo and Prince Cylan."

31

INEVITABILITY

The sun was rising by the time everyone had assembled in Mari's room to discuss what the girls had overheard. In any other kingdom, hints of early morning blue would be starting to lighten the horizon. Here, the sky was a constant cover of grey clouds.

Leo and Cylan were animatedly discussing their next course of action—even Maelin chimed in from time to time. Words were being thrown around like, *Gather the rest of Eristald's army* and *evacuate Mari from the city now.*

Mari hardly heard them. She sat on the edge of her bed, numbly staring at the Goddess dagger she held in her lap.

Defeat my greatest enemy, o' wielder of Eris' Fury, no matter the cost...

Eris's greatest enemy. Etaldin. *The Goddess has entrusted you with a grand responsibility,* the blue Fae had told her once the dagger had appeared in Mari's lap. A grand responsibility it may be, but an impossible choice.

This was *Alek,* after all. Kind and sweet—if not a bit overbearing at times with only the best intentions—Alek was the first person in this world to give her a chance. He extended a hand of understanding and care when she'd been her most alone and afraid. Apparently, he'd even taken the most drastic of measures to try to find her, and it'd landed him in the place between Eris and her oldest adversary.

Despite her hesitations and objections, Mari knew in her heart how this would have to end. The inevitability of it was suffocating and yet, the certainty of it was almost reassuring.

"I've got to talk to Alek's friends." Mari's voice came out quieter than she'd anticipated. She blinked her eyes into focus, raising her head slowly. No one had heard her. She cleared her throat, forcing herself to speak again.

"I have to speak with Alek's friends back in Eristald." The three of her companions were silenced and staring at her with bewildered expressions, "Can you summon them here?"

Cylan tilted his head inquisitively. "I could," he said slowly, "but if you need to speak with them so urgently, we can use the scrying mirror at the palace here. I can request that they be escorted to the scrying mirror at Eristald castle."

Mari nodded slowly. "Thank you. I'm going to need to tell them what I have to do. I need them to know...that I had no choice."

"Ma'am?" Maelin took a concerned step towards her but it was Leo whose eyes fell on the dagger in Mari's lap.

"Madam," he said formally, "if you think you're going to be able to kill a God with a dagger like that... I regret to inform you that it will not be so simple."

Cylan caught on quickly. He strode across the room, gently taking the weapon from Mari. He studied the blade, reading the engraving aloud for everyone to hear.

"'A blade that will leave only one. Defeat my greatest enemy, o' wielder of Eris' Fury, no matter the cost.'" Cylan paused, handing the dagger back to Mari, "The choice is no longer ours to make. Eris has entrusted Mari with this task and," he knelt and held Mari's tearful stare, "I do not believe that the Goddess would have bestowed such a gift on someone who was not capable of using it."

Less than one hour later, Mari and her companions had been escorted deeper into the castle where the Scrying Mirror was secured. Magic fire light glinted off of the black stone walls of the small space. Hung directly in the middle of the furthest wall was a floor-length ornate mirror. Its frame was golden, carved with a galaxy of stars and moons and suns. As they approached, the reflective surface blurred and rippled like calm ocean waves. A second later they were no longer looking at themselves, but three confused and concerned faces.

Mari's breath came out in a huff, tears stinging her eyes once more as she stared at Lyna, Rae, and Fyodor. She was holding on to her dagger—Eris' Fury—hoping she may be able to draw some personal strength from the magic of the weapon. So far, it wasn't working very well.

"Hi, guys," Mari said slowly, as she would if she were trying not to scare off a wild animal.

Their eyes locked with hers, shock on their faces. It was Fyodor who spoke.

"Mari, you're alright!" Then he paused, adding, "Right?"

She didn't get a chance to answer him before Rae spoke up, "Alek," her voice quivered, "have you found him?"

"Is he alright?" Lyna's ears twitched nervously.

Mari took a shaky breath, "Actually, that's what I wanted to talk to you about." She hesitated, looking them each in the eyes individually before continuing. She looked between Lyna and Rae, "What you two told me, in Earth's Provence, about Alek being in trouble... I'm sorry to say you were right. I—" her voice cracked. She looked to Cylan for help.

Cylan nodded, stepping forward, "We believe your friend Alek has misguidedly trusted Etaldin himself and has, somehow, become the vessel for the God's spirit." Cylan didn't flinch as Alek's friends gasped, fear freezing their eyes wide, "We also believe that he's no longer himself. He's completely enthralled by Etaldin and together they intend to take control of the realm, and other worlds as well."

"You're going to save him." Lyna nodded, willing truth into the words, "aren't you?"

Leo stepped forward this time, "the only way to save your friend is to release him from his suffering."

"You mean..." Fyodor's face was grim.

Mari held back a sob, lifting Eris's Fury to show them the blade. "Eris has given me this weapon. It is the only thing in existence that could defeat an evil like the one that's consumed Alek." Mari took a deep breath, "I—I have to..." she couldn't bring herself to say the word *kill*, "I have to use it on Alek."

Everyone was silent for a long moment, taking it all in. Rae wiped her tears, her iridescent wings trembling behind her. Acceptance settled over them slowly, like a gentle breeze.

"This isn't the kind of life he would want." Rae sniffled.

Lyna nodded, "he would want you to save the world, no matter what."

"And, as strange as this may sound," Fyodor's ears sagged, "he wouldn't want anyone else to wield that blade but you, Mari. He really cared about you."

"I know," Mari choked out between the sobs that she could no longer hold back.

"May the Goddess be with you, Mari." Lyna's voice faded as the image blurred and disappeared.

Mari turned away, not wanting to see her tearful, red face staring back at her in the mirror. Cylan followed closely behind her, flanked by Leo and Maelin.

"You know," Xerxes' voice echoed throughout the dim hallway. Mari turned to find him lazily leaning against the wall. He'd been waiting for them. "Dear old dad could still change his mind. He could still choose his firstborn, his eldest, the son whose *birthright* it is, to take his place on the throne of the realm."

"Xerxes," Cylan said, his voice strained and tired, "now is not—"

"Unfortunately," Xerxes continued, ignoring his brother. He stalked away from the wall, towards Mari. "He'll never have the chance if Etaldin comes to power and claims the realm as his own."

"What are you saying?" Mari's voice was hard. She didn't have the energy to play his games.

"I'm saying," Xerxes stopped a few steps away from Mari, holding her steady gaze, "I want to help you."

"Help?" Cylan scoffed, "I didn't know that word was in your vocabulary."

"Keep it up," Xerxes spoke between gritted teeth, "and I'll show you just how extensive my vocabulary is."

"Enough," Mari said. "How do you plan to help us?"

Xerxes' grin was the epitome of mischievous, "I'll deliver you to Etaldin myself," he held his hands up to show his innocence when Cylan and Leo took a step towards him. He quickly added, "At which point you'll have the chance to use that fancy dagger of yours to deliver the killing blow."

Mari flinched at his words, her voice a whisper, "How do we find him?"

Xerxes barked a laugh, "Dear human, there isn't a thing that happens in my city without my knowledge. I know exactly where Etaldin is."

32

ERIS' FURY

Mari stared at the thin white gown draped across the bed. She had undressed, save for the thigh sheath she'd been given for Eris' Fury, but couldn't bring herself to slide the dress onto her body. Apparently, this was a gown similar to the one that Eris wore in the few pictures and statues of her. Xerxes had said that Etaldin would appreciate the theatricality of it, during his "performance."

Cylan came up behind her, gently wrapping his arms around her mostly naked frame. She shuddered under his touch as his breath tickled her ear.

"Are you afraid?"

She nodded.

"I believe in you, Marianne Dawson." He kissed her neck all the way down to her shoulder. His lips lingered there, whispering, "I will forever be in your debt, my beautiful human girl, for saving the people of my realm."

Mari took a shuddering breath. "What if I fail? What if," she turned to look at him, their faces inches apart, "what if when the time comes, I can't do what needs to be done?"

Cylan's citrine eyes bored into hers, "You will. I will be there, in the crowd, and I will lend you my strength. As will all of Xerxes' army that will be there too. And Leo, as well." He took her face in his warm grasp, "You can do this."

She leaned forward, crushing her body and her lips against his. Their hands grasped and held each other close, savoring the moment together in case it was their last.

A glint of red caught Mari's eye as she broke away. She took a step toward her backpack that hung open slightly, exposing the dragon scale she'd tucked away.

Cylan followed her gaze, reaching down to grasp the scale, "Ah, so Zayndru left you with a very special gift, did he?" Cylan took the scale, holding it up to Mari, the width of it completely covering her chest.

He pressed the scale to her breasts, and she gasped at the warmth of it. Before she could ask what he was doing, Cylan used his magic to mold the scale to her body until it wrapped around her torso like a second skin.

"Dragon scales are the absolute strongest material in our world," he explained, "Now, I'll be a bit more at ease, knowing you will be safer." he sighed, "Right, well, let's get you dressed."

Xerxes had told them that Etaldin was planning a performance of sorts, near the top of the volcano. Etaldin had sent an official invite to the palace which was addressed to Xerxes alone. The letter informed him that in order to show his true loyalty to the Unseelie God, he would have to deliver Mari to be sacrificed at the public announcement of his return to the realm.

Xerxes' plan was to do just that, but with Mari's dagger hidden carefully and with several dozen of his most loyal soldiers hidden in the crowd in case things went awry.

"I do wish, more than anything," Cylan said, sliding the dress over Mari's head, "that there was another option. I can't stand the thought of sending you in there, alone."

The silky gown perfectly concealed Mari's chest plate and dagger. She turned back to him, her bare feet easily sliding across the cold stone floor, "but now that we know what Etaldin has planned," She said, hoping that saying it aloud would make her feel more confident and reassure Cylan as well, "we have the upper hand. This could be the only chance we get to be close to him while his defenses are down."

A knock on the door made her jump, Cylan's hands on her hips were the only thing steadying her.

"It's nearly time," Xerxes drawled from outside, "wouldn't want to be late, would we?"

Cylan swung open the door. "Brother," he said, his voice holding none of the usual venom towards his older sibling, "You'd better keep her safe. Please."

Xerxes nodded once, his expression serious. He broke into a devilish grin, looking past Cylan at Mari.

"Ready?"

It felt wrong, having Xerxes' arms wrapped around her back and under her legs, but it was the best way for him to hold her as he flew them up to the top of the volcano. His hands roamed where they were not welcome on her backside, and she slapped him across the face.

He only chuckled, and said, "Good girl. Keep hitting me; you'll want to look like you're being delivered against your will, so perform like your life depends on it. Because it does."

Hot anger rose in Mari's chest, amplified by the heat of the dragon scale breastplate. She looked down, seeing an enormous, undulating crowd below them. The crowd chanted in a language she did not know, stomping in unison with their words. They were all facing the same direction, towards a rocky ledge ten or so feet above them where a Fae male stood, arms outstretched as he smiled down at them.

Alek.

Mari's heart sank as she took him in, his white hair clean and perfectly styled atop his head. His clothes—a long purple overcoat with golden embroidery—were open at the front to expose his black leather armor. Her stomach threatened to purge its contents, but she took a deep breath, doing her best to will away her body's human response to terror and panic.

"Now." Xerxes' voice was unnervingly gentle.

Mari thrashed in his arms as he landed with a jolting thud behind Alek. She swung at his chest, her hand landing a blow on his jaw, leaving a thick pink scratch behind on his perfect skin. He growled, tossing her to the ground.

"My lord," Xerxes said, bowing his head and taking a step backward.

The crowd's chanting stopped, the sudden silence sending a fresh wave of cold fear through her bones. Alek—Etaldin—turned, a sickly satisfied smile on his lips. A deep chuckle rumbled in his chest, and when he spoke, it was and was not Alek's voice all at the same time.

"Ah, at last we meet." He looked up to Xerxes, "You have done well, my son. You may leave us. Join the others, if you'd like," Etaldin swept his arm out over his acolytes below, "enjoy the show." Xerxes silently obliged, the breeze from his wings tousling Mari's hair and dress.

"Alek," Mari's voice cracked as she knelt on the stone, gravel digging into her knees, "Alek, are you in there?"

He took a step forward, his predatory stare locked on her, his mouth set in a thin line. He leaned down, so near her that Mari could see his once black irises were now a glowing sickly purple.

His fist made contact with her face and she cried out, falling to the ground. Her ears rang with the impact, her teeth rattled in her jaw. Between her shock and the crowds cheering, she barely heard Etaldin when he spoke.

"Your role today, *D'ashil*," he spat the Fae word for *human* out of his mouth as if it were poison, "is purely symbolic," he smiled with an icy malice, "Perhaps a better word would be, *sacrificial*."

Mari refused to give him the satisfaction of showing her fear. She spat blood that was pooling from her split lip and screamed at him, "Alek! I know you're there! Alek, come back to me!"

This time, Etaldin ignored her, turning back to his adoring crowd.

"Today, my children," he held his arms out wide, the pose of someone who had no doubts of their safety and power, "is the beginning of a new era! The era of the Unseelie!"

The crowd chanted and cheered, their stomps reverberated throughout the mountain.

Mari crawled forward, looking out over them. Hundreds of green, red, gray, and yellow faces jeered and screamed at her. Dark elves, orcs, goblins, and others she could not identify made up the sea of Unseelie before her, and somewhere in that crowd, she reminded herself, her companions and Xerxes' army were there. Hope and fear swelled in her chest in equal measure.

"Alek! Don't do this," her voice barely rose above the roar of the crowd and yet, Alek's ear twitched, his head slightly turning back towards her. Her heart soared and she called out desperately, "Fight him! Fight him, for me!"

"Silence," Etaldin ordered, though not with the same vigor as before. When he looked back at her, the purple glow in his eyes faltered for a second. She continued to scream at him; she screamed until her throat was raw. The small bloom of hope continued to grow in her chest as flickers of the boy she knew shined through.

Etaldin continued his speech, the warm wind blowing his coat around him like a grand cape. He was the picture of power, the very essence of evil. Purple mist shimmered around him, pouring from his open hands.

"The *Seelie*," he spit the word, "would have you all believe that you're as weak as they are, reliant on a pathetic Goddess' *starlight*," his voice dripped with venom, "but I alone created magic! It is the power of a *God* that flows in your veins, and I will give you the strength you require, the magic that is your birthright!"

His purple mist rained down on the Fae below, sinking deep within their skin, and energizing them even more than Mari would think was possible. The tempo of their pounding feet and fists spiked upward, their screams were deafening.

"With our extraordinary power, why stop with this world? We should extend our reach to other worlds—*all* other worlds! Tonight," he looked back at Mari hungrily, "I have just what I need to make that happen."

"Alek," she sobbed, rising and taking the final step forward that she needed to reach forward and grab his hand, "Alek, I need you."

A look of disgust splayed across his features and he ripped his hand away. Mari fell forward, catching herself with her hands on the rough ground. Blood seeped from the cuts on her palms.

"Tsk, tsk," Etaldin tutted, "we can't have you wasting any more of that precious human blood of yours," he motioned swiftly to someone standing behind her.

She had no time to turn before vice-like arms wrapped around her and the stench of rotting meat and garbage overwhelmed her. One of Etaldin's orcish warriors had her pinned against his monstrous torso. She tried to flail, but his grip only tightened, restricting her chest.

Mari gasped for breath, sickened by Etaldin's gleeful smile. The orc grunted behind her, his rumbling laugh vibrating Mari to her bones.

"You promised to protect me!" Mari screamed despite her small lungful of air. "I believed you, Alek, I trusted you!" she gasped, her chest struggling to expand beneath the orc's arms, "I still do believe in you, and everything you've done, Alek, I know you tried your best but—" her body ached as she struggled, "you can't give up now. I still need you, Alek, you can still save me!"

A flash of pain entered his eyes then. His knees buckled and he dropped to the ground. He was fighting Etaldin. Alek was still in there, alive and fighting an all-powerful God. Fighting for her. Mari pushed past her shock and continued to scream his name.

"Alek, Alek, *Alek!*"

A wet sound filled her ears unexpectedly as hot liquid splattered onto her. The orc that held her stumbled backward, dropping her to the rock below. She glanced up in time to see his lifeless body falling towards her. Mari scrambled backward, narrowly avoiding being crushed by the creature as it crashed to the ground, an arrow protruding from its skull.

All at once, chaos erupted below. Her saviors who were scattered among the crowd burst into action; shooting arrows and swinging swords into the unsuspecting Etaldin loyalists.

Between the surprise of the ambush and Alek's persistence, the old God was stunned just long enough to give Alek a chance to take back control of his body for a heartbeat.

Mari gasped, clutching Alek's shoulders. The purple around his irises sputtered away like an extinguished flame.

"You must do it," he gasped reaching out to stroke Mari's cheek, "it's okay, Mari. This is the only way I can protect you now. Do it; this is your only chance. Do it!"

She pulled the dagger from her thigh. The breeze quickened, loosening her braided hair. It fell, spilling all around the two of them like liquid chocolate as she rose above him. Tears stung her eyes but she blinked them away.

"I'm so sorry." She whispered, choking on a sob.

Inside of her, the fear, the guilt, the pain, and the sadness were all stripped away as she gazed into his struggling face. Left behind was the lone and roaring flame of her anger. Her rage. Her *fury*—Eris' Fury.

Never before had Mari felt such raw seething and hatred. It burned over thoughts of all that the curse had taken from her; her family, her childhood. The flame engulfed the images coursing through her nightmares of Unseelie magic and tortured humans that never had the chance to return home. It scorched the memory of being dumped in a strange land and welcomed by a beautiful elvish boy, embraced by his friends, now being forced to betray him in the end. The rage left her reduced to cinders and wholly, fully, broken inside.

Alek's eyes closed as he relaxed with a deep, peaceful breath. She positioned the blade in between his ribs as Leo had instructed her to do. With one fast and strong movement, Mari plunged the dagger up and into his heart.

The breath he'd just taken came out in a huff. He fell backward, bright green light pouring from his wound. His eyes met hers a final time. The look of calm and adoration sent Mari into an uncontrollable sobbing fit. Despite this, a smile turned the edges of Alek's lips upward, blood dripping down his chin.

The sobs overwhelmed her. She dropped the blood-soaked dagger and buried her head into the hand of hers that was not slick with Alek's lifeblood.

At the sight of the Goddess' green light that burst from Alek's chest rising to the sky like a pillar of goodness and hope, the Unseelie in the crowd scrambled to retreat. The emerald light washed over Mari like a soothing wave, extinguishing her flame of pain and anger.

A hand touched her shoulder gently, before two arms wrapped around her, lifting Mari to her feet.

Cylan's grasp was firm. He supported her full weight while she sobbed, crooning in her ear, "It's over now. You're okay. You're safe. It's over."

"Heal him" she begged, her bloody hand staining Cylan's shirt where she clutched it.

He shook his head, an immense sadness in his eyes, "this is a wound that even my abilities can't fix."

She heard Leo approach to collect Alek's body to take home for a proper funeral, as she had insisted, but Mari couldn't bring herself to look at them. Her beautiful Fae Prince gathered her up in his arms, cradling her like a small child.

To her great relief, his wings unfurled, beating with a calm strength, as he flew her away from the place that would haunt her nightmares.

33

STILL HERE

"Our journey is over."

Cylan sat in a chair across from the bed where Mari had just woken up. She sat up weakly, realizing they were back in their room at Xerxes' palace. Cylan continued, staring blankly across the room at nothing in particular.

"I set out from Eristald only wanting to please Eris; to please my realm. Who would have guessed that we would have ended up being part of a much bigger battle?" His eyes blinked, coming back into focus.

He stood, moving to sit on the bed. "And here you are, the human girl who saved us all. I owe you my thanks, on behalf of the Realm of Faerie"

Mari sighed, chuckling, "I had only wanted to save my cat." The memory spilled from her mouth as she remembered that day so long ago when she chased Hank right into the faerie ring, "That silly beast is the only reason I'm here in the first place."

"You're right. I do owe him my most heartfelt gratitude for bringing you to me." He ran his hand across her cheek.

She leaned into his touch, tears stinging her eyes and spilling over onto her cheeks.

"Cylan," she sniffled, grabbing his hand from her face and holding it in her lap, "now that my curse is broken and our journey is over...I think it's time for me to go home." She said the words reflexively, her original goal still stuck in her mind like residue from an old bandage. Even as the words left her lips, she knew she didn't feel as deeply about it as she had before.

"Why?" He leaned forward, pulling his hands away from hers to cradle her face, "Why can't you stay? Stay here. Stay with me."

Mari began to cry harder, sobs heaving from her chest, "I don't belong here, I don't—"

Her words were cut off as Cylan crushed his lips against hers. She melted into that kiss, wishing that her heart wasn't breaking.

"You're wrong," he broke away, still close enough to whisper against her lips, "this world needed you. It will never be the same now that you've been here."

He stood with a growl of frustration, his tone rising with anger though she knew the anger was not towards her.

"Even so, with everything we've done—we haven't brought the stars back! I don't want this whole journey to be for nothing," he turned back to her, "let me at least bring the realm a queen if I can't bring them back the *Indis*."

She scoffed, her sobs slowing and her tears starting to dry, "as if your Unseelie will accept that."

"We'd be a perfect balance," he knelt at the side of her bed grasping her hands in his. His eyes were bright as sunlight as he gazed up at her. "We could usher in a new era where Fae and humans can both live and thrive together. I can open the portals back up, our economy can thrive with human influence... I don't think I'll be able to do any of that without you, though."

"How long have you been thinking about this?" She chuckled, freeing a hand to wipe her face.

"An embarrassingly long time," he assured her with a smile.

"Cylan. There's something else."

"There's nothing else. Nothing else but this love we share."

"That's just it," she sniffled, "Fae can't love the same as humans, can they?"

His brow furrowed, "That has been said before, yes. but tell me," his golden eyes burrowed into hers with a ferocity that made it impossible to look away, "What is love if not the ache in my chest when I see you hurt? What is the feeling that nearly overcomes my soul when you're near, bringing with it the blinding urge to touch you, kiss you, feel your warmth radiate around me? Tell me it is not love when I find myself smiling with my whole body after seeing a hint of a smile on your lips." He stroked a tear that had fallen down her cheek, "Perhaps when they said our love was changed by magic it was not diminished, but strengthened beyond human comprehension."

She kissed him again, the salt of her tears on her lips. A knock on the door interrupted them and they broke away slowly, Mari hiding her tear-swollen face from whomever stood in the doorway.

"Enter," Cylan spoke, clearing his voice.

An elvish servant opened the doors, with a scroll in hand. Cylan took it and upon reading it his face fell, his eyes widening and mouth going slack. He looked up at Mari, his tight fists crumpling the paper.

"It's my father. The king is dying." He straightened, controlling his expression, "We must go back to Eristald immediately."

She jumped out of bed onto wobbly legs. Unsure of what exactly to do next, she only stood there, staring at him. His eyes ran up and down her figure. He sighed, his gaze stopping at her throat.

"There's one more thing I have to tell you," he moved closer to her, his fingers brushing the bare skin of her collarbone. "As you know, my mother loved to visit the human world. However, she hated having to travel to a portal to do it. She wanted a way to go back and forth as she pleased even if she was not close to a portal."

He gently grasped the ball of the necklace between two fingers, his voice so quiet it would have been impossible to hear him if she'd been any further away. "So, she crafted the smallest portal ball, and encapsulated it into a necklace."

Cylan looked up to her then, a sad smile on his lips. "If you really want to go back to your world, just open my mother's necklace. That's why I gave it to you in the first place."

Mari froze, stunned, as he placed a slow and gentle kiss on her lips before turning and exiting the room, calling over his shoulder to her.

"I'll meet you downstairs in the carriage. Maelin and Leo will already be waiting for us."

The door clicked shut behind him and Mari gasped for breath. Her heart pounded in her chest like a drum; her hand reached for the pendant that hung above that steady beat.

A portal ball. But, not just any portal ball: it was one that would send her to the human world, and all she had to do was open the necklace. Her mind reeled with the realization that hit her like a train.

I've had one this whole time? He gave this to me on my first night and I could have gone home whenever I wanted?

She knew she could have sat there for hours mulling over this information, but there was a much bigger issue at hand and there wasn't any time to waste. They had to get back to Eristald, and quickly.

With next to nothing to pack, it took her only seconds to ensure her bag was filled with her handful of belongings before dressing back into her travel clothes. She didn't give her mind a moment to roam and she didn't look back at the dark palace filled with Fae that would rip her apart if given the opportunity.

She hurried over to the extravagant carriage attached to a team of horses with hair so black that it held a blue tint. She smiled up half-heartedly at Maelin who sat atop the carriage with Leo by her side, holding the reins. She reached up to open the door, happy to find Cylan was already inside, waiting for her.

"You're still here." He stared at her, the tension in his face instantly melted away with relief.

She crawled in, sitting directly next to him. As she rested her head on his shoulder, she whispered up to him.

"I'm still here."

34

ENDINGS & BEGINNINGS

Dear Nina, The carriage ride back with Cylan was calm and silent. It wasn't a silence filled with awkward or tense feelings, but instead a silence of two people just happy to be near each other and soaking in the moment. We both knew so much would change once we arrived back in Eristald, but for a few hours longer we could just be Mari and Cylan, together.

We arrived at the castle at the same time as the other four royal siblings. Together they made their way into their father's room to sit by his deathbed. All I could bring myself to do was pace outside the door. As I waited, I couldn't help but let my mind roam.

Could I really stay here, in the Realm of Faerie? It's not like there would be anything I would be leaving behind but... to be a queen?

Is that something I am actually capable of, or something I even want?

Mari paused writing, thankful for the warm cozy bed she was nestled in. She stared at the paper in front of her, the last few pages left of her journal, and pictured her life back in her human world.

She could see herself holding Hank in her too-stiff bed, watching a movie on her laptop—but, of course, she could never watch fantasy movies again; they would never compare to her journey. She pictured taking a walk in the forest on a warm afternoon and realized she'd never be able to forget the night they'd spent riding under the moon in the forest here.

She'd make friends in her new hometown, and they'd go to the beach to swim in the ocean now that she knew how, and the whole while she'd be conscious of the fact that the golden evening sun would be the same color as Cylan's eyes and the dark sand where the waves soaked the shore the same color as his skin.

This world, Cylan, and her journey were things she'd never be able to leave behind, even if she wanted to, even if she tried.

She picked up her pencil, which was now only about an inch or two long with no eraser on the end.

It didn't take long for the door to the king's bedroom to open again. Xerxes and Hanli stood to the left of the doorway, Brynn and Thorston to the right. It was strange and yet made perfect sense to see the four of them—so different and so similar—standing together. I looked further into the room and found the face I was looking for.

Cylan knelt at the end of a large canopied bed, where gray dust covered the sheets—the remnants of the former king. He stood and as he made eye contact with me, my heart faltered. When he closed the distance between us, each of his siblings—even Xerxes—dropped to their knees as he passed them. The guards posted outside the door did as well. I flinched as the guards clanged their weapons on the ground. Shouting in unison:

"Hail King Cylan. May his reign bless our lands."

His siblings echoed the chant. I couldn't bring myself to move, let alone speak a word. When Cylan reached out to grab my hands, I thought I must have been shaking. I quickly realized though, that my hands weren't trembling, but his were. Without loosening my grip, I did the only thing I could think to do. Slowly, I knelt to bow before him, the new King of the Realm of Faerie.

A knock on her bedroom door had her setting down her pencil once more.

"Hey," Lyna entered, carrying a tray with a bowl of steaming soup and a cup of water. "Thought you might be hungry."

Mari gave the female faun her thanks before Lyna turned to leave the room.

Rae and Lyna had been kind to let Mari stay with them. Cylan had said that Mari would be welcome to stay at the castle, but Mari knew that Cylan would be too busy with coronation plans and whatever else came with becoming the new King of the Realm. She didn't want to distract him, and she wanted to help Lyna, Rae, and Fyodor with Alek's funeral plans.

Alek.

Oh, her poor friend. She still had nightmares of his face, fading from gray to white as the blood left his body through the hole she'd pierced. The hole *she'd* pierced. *She'd* killed him. It was a horror unlike any she'd experienced before.

She found comfort in the fact that he'd broken through Etaldin's control for just a moment, long enough to give her the permission and opportunity she needed to stop the evil God, even if it meant losing him in the process. She found grace in his eyes at the end and understanding in the hearts of his friends. Now, she would just have to find the courage to forgive herself, as well.

The inscription on the metal had said, *a blade that will leave only one,* but Mari had hoped the "one" would be Alek. Instead, the Goddess' dagger was enough to weaken the old God and remove him from his vessel, though Etaldin's spirit did survive, and fled without a trace.

Now, while the Realm of Faerie mourned their king and the end of an era, Mari would stay with her friends while they mourned Alek and the end of his story.

She hadn't had time to tell Cylan what she had decided about whether she was going to stay or go, and she hadn't seen him since the day his father died, which was about a week prior.

When the castle courier showed up with a summons for her to return to the castle, she remembered vividly the last time she had received a summons in Alek's rounded doorway. Her stomach had tightened with fear and Alek had been there to hold her hand. This time, though, her heart soared with happiness at the thought of getting to see Cylan again. She bid her friends goodbye and entered the carriage that was waiting for her.

The carriage rattled along the cobblestones and the bridge across the castle moat and through the tall doors at the gate. It came to a stop in front of the castle entrance. Mari paused a moment, staring up at the grand edifice, taking a few steadying breaths.

Stepping out of the carriage seemed less daunting when she noticed Maelin appear in the doorway with a big bundle of gray fur in her arms. Mari threw open the door and hurried towards them.

"Hank!" She exclaimed, taking the purring cat from Maelin's arms. After giving him a gentle squeeze, noticing he'd put on a few pounds—from hunting squirrels that unwisely crept into the castle garden, no doubt—she turned to Maelin and smiled even more warmly.

"My friend," she said, "I've missed you."

Maelin beamed back at her, "Welcome back, Ma'am. Let's get you over to your dress fitting right away."

Mari blinked, "dress fitting?"

"The coronation ball is tomorrow," Maelin explained, gently grabbing Mari's arm and leading her into the castle. "And Prince," she cleared her throat, correcting herself, "*King* Cylan certainly didn't give us very much time to prepare your dress so now it's a race against the clock! Quickly now!"

As they swept through the familiar halls, Mari was on high alert. She found herself looking through every doorway and down every corridor they passed hoping for a glimpse of Cylan. She was so distracted that she nearly ran into Maelin as she stopped to open the enormous wooden doors where the dressmakers awaited her.

After the seamstresses had taken their measurements and hurried Mari away so that they could get to work, she was escorted to her former rooms, where Hank made himself right at home by the fireplace. The bath was steaming and ready for her, while a fruit, cheese, and bread platter was waiting for her on her table.

With a sigh, realizing she probably wasn't going to see Cylan tonight, she bathed, dressed, and ate as the sun set outside and the lonely moon shone overhead. Her fingers traveled up her chest to find the necklace that still hung there. She smiled, chuckling as she remembered how desperate she'd felt to find a portal. Now, Mari was happy enough to know she had the opportunity to travel back to the human world if ever she desired it.

Once in bed, she put her hand under the pillow, surprised to find a piece of parchment there. She smiled as she read Cylan's handwriting.

My beloved, Marianne,

It's been much too long since I've seen you. My mind refuses to focus on anything besides the thought of your gentle touch.

A KING SHOULD BE EXCITED FOR HIS CORONATION AND SUBSEQUENT REIGN, BUT INSTEAD, YOU'VE CONSUMED EVERY IOTA OF EXCITEMENT AND ANTICIPATION I'M ABLE TO PRODUCE.

TOMORROW NIGHT, AT THE BALL, MEET ME IN THE GARDENS.

DON'T KEEP YOUR KING WAITING.

~C

Mari was woken the next morning by the sound of her bedroom door opening. She sat up, groggily watching as several members of the castle staff, led by a cheerful Maelin, bustled into the bedroom.

"Good morning ma'am! Coronation day festivities will begin shortly after breakfast and last until after the ball this evening so I hope you're well rested."

A smile crept onto Mari's lips as she watched her dainty pink friend organize and coordinate the staff around her. She was in her element here at the castle, preparing for a large celebration. Maelin was a different, more confident person than she'd been at the start of their travels, and Mari could relate.

Several hours later, Mari was staring at her unrecognizable reflection in the floor-length mirror. The woman before her was brighter, more energized, and more confident. She held herself with a posture and expression that said, *I am here, bold and unafraid.*

They'd put her hair up in a tangle of intricate braids with golden strands like tinsel weaved in. Pinned perfectly into her pile of hair was a golden circlet with a devastatingly gorgeous green emerald set in the center of it. She admired her white satin elbow-length gloves and her matching shoes before letting her eyes linger on the gown she'd been sewn into.

It fit like a second skin, hugging every curve of her body. The satin was a cream color at the innermost layer with an overlay of shimmery golden gossamer. The gown resembled a star in the night sky, she thought, wondering if she'd earned the right to wear such an exquisite garment. With every movement she made, a mesmerizing golden sparkle amidst swirls of white and yellow caught the light mimicking the sparkle of the starlight.

After an agonizingly long day filled with yard games, mingling, tea and snacks, and tours of the grounds that revealed nothing new, finally, the coronation ball was beginning. The words from Cylan's note cycled through her brain like a caress.

Don't keep your king waiting.

She attempted to dash straight to the back of the ballroom where the entrance to the garden sat wide open, beckoning her outside. She stopped in her tracks when she noticed Cylan appear at the top of the staircase to address the crowd.

Her heart skittered, her breath hitched, but her eyes stayed locked on his presence there. He was a powerful sight to behold, adorned in the same golds and whites as she was, though with a mighty crown atop his boyish black curls.

"Eristald!" His voice rang throughout the ballroom and a chorus of cheers filled the air, "Tonight, I officially take my place as the King of the Realm."

The cheers grew louder, and Mari smiled brightly; the energy buzzing around her felt electric on her skin.

Cylan continued, "I will do all I can to be deserving of your adoration and support. And as your king, my top priority will always be for the health and happiness of all who reside within the Realm of Faerie." He paused, eyes scanning the crowd. Was he looking for her? "It is my greatest hope that all four kingdoms within this realm may enter a new era of peace, collaboration, and prosperity."

When his speech was over and the music resumed, Mari watched as Cylan descended and went out to the garden, his guards standing at the door to ensure no one followed him.

After dodging the other partygoers and nearly knocking over a Fae waiter with drinks on a platter, Mari finally made it to the tall glass garden doors where the guards stepped aside only for her.

She ran down the empty hedge lane, the full moon illuminating her path perfectly. The white moon flowers bloomed all along the edge of the in-ground fountain where she found Cylan sitting on the bench facing away from her. He was the image of a starlight king under a still starless sky.

"Cylan..." her heels clicked on the stones and her dress hissed as it drug behind her. At the sound of her voice, Cylan sprang from his seat, closing the distance between them with just a few of his long strides.

She thought her heart might truly burst as he pulled her close and buried his face in her neck. She inhaled the scent of him while he trailed kisses up the length of her neck, exhaling with a moan when he reached her lips.

"I'll go mad," he said between kisses, "if you try to leave me. You're my *Y'nilsa*—My soul's smile." He held her at arm's length, his eyes searching hers, "the thought of a lifetime without my *Y'nilsa*... Mari, have mercy on me."

A hysterical giggle bubbled through Mari's smiling lips, "You're lucky, my king, that being merciful is a core trait of mine."

He pulled back, a look of confusion furrowing his brow and causing his jaw to sag slightly. Had he really expected a different response?

"Are you saying you'll stay?"

"There's no way I could go back to that mundane, colorless, cold world. Not when I'm clearly meant to be here, to be with you." She looked up into his eyes, the color of bottled golden starlight, hoping the sincerity she felt sparkled through her gaze, "The Goddess truly gave me a gift when she brought me to the Realm of Faerie. How could I throw that blessing away? Throw this feeling away?"

Even through his shock, Cylan's smile was brighter than the moon and sun, and stars combined. He whirled her off of her feet, spinning gleefully as the rest of her giggles flew from her chest.

The slow-tempo music filtered out of the open window, swirling around them in the warm breeze. Their embrace turned into a sort of dance, where Mari rested her head on Cylan's shoulder, and closed her eyes.

Today officially marks the end of one journey that I never imagined I'd go on, she thought with a small pang of sadness. The sound of Cylan's heart beating under her ear and the familiar smell of his favorite pine cologne brought a smile to her face. She sighed, her heart warming as the next thought entered her mind.

And the beginning of an even better one.

EPILOGUE

"**A**re you ready, ma'am?" Maelin adjusted Mari's crown so that it rested perfectly atop her curls.

Mari smiled and nodded, fidgeting with the new ring she wore. The metal was as silver as moonlight and the band that wrapped around her finger was as simple as the starless sky of the realm. The ring was more than just a piece of jewelry, though. With the official royal family crest carved into the top of it, this ring symbolized that she was officially Faerie royalty.

Today, her first official decree as Queen of the Realm of Faerie was being announced and celebrated. Soon, she would walk alongside her king and together they would re-open the first portal to the human world. The first of many portals that would allow humans to roam freely between their world and the realm.

Of course, there would be more strictly enforced rules this time around. Mainly the laws would be regarding the Unseelie treatment of visiting humans and the expectation that all humans had to come of their own free will.

She made her way to the carriage, Maelin trailing close behind. The trip was short as the carriage headed north of the city to a place she'd been eager to finally visit. Maelin's family business, The Good Inn, had been a popular place for human visitors once upon a time, so what better place for them to come to first upon their arrival in a new land?

Cylan had commissioned a grand one-of-a-kind door to be erected near the beautiful stone inn with a thatched roof. The door loomed over Mari now as they stood at its base, addressing a very large and very excited crowd of Fae from every kingdom in the realm.

"And now," Cylan spoke, his voice steady, "my queen and I will be the first to travel to the world of the *D'ashil* through this very portal!"

The crowd cheered, and chanted, "Hail Queen Mari, hail King Cylan, our *Indis Hahom!*"

The sun had taken its nightly journey under the horizon, the deep blue-black of dusk enveloping the darkening sky. Warm magic fire light filled the windows of The Good Inn, where Maelin stood in the doorway, wrapped in her parent's embrace. Heart filled with joy and excitement, Mari looked up to send a silent prayer of gratitude to Eris, and she gasped, reaching for Cylan's arm.

There, directly above them, a single star twinkled.

The crowd noticed their king and queen's stares and lifted their eyes skyward as well. Cheers of joy mixed with disbelief erupted through the forest as millions of tiny stars blinked into existence. One after the other, stars of all colors and sizes sparked to life and, like electricity in the air, Mari could feel the magic of the Goddess return.

Mari laughed softly, turning to Cylan, "It makes perfect sense now; How could we not see it before? Eris was saddened when your father closed the portals and—"

Cylan smiled brightly, finishing her thought, "And all she wanted was for the portals to be opened again." He turned to the crowd before them, raising his voice for all to hear. "What could possibly be a better sign that today's opening of the portal has pleased our Goddess?" One by one they began to look skyward, "May all of your journeys be illuminated by Eris' grace," Cylan's excitement was tangible as he shouted, "as she has seen fit to bring her light to our skies once again."

With the Fae now focused on the stars above, Mari and Cylan slipped away through the portal and back to Mari's homeland.

They appeared in a familiar place outside of the tiny town of Eastport. Mari recognized the narrow alley they'd landed in, the single streetlight, and the tall old oak tree that hung over the road beyond. They weren't far from her former house, and eventually they would go there to grab a few of the things that she wanted to bring home to Eristald, but first...

The town was empty, not a soul in sight. Thank Eris for that, she realized as an afterthought; Mari wondered what someone might have done if suddenly there were two strangely dressed people standing where only a heartbeat ago there had been nothing.

In the distance, she could hear the lapping waves of the ocean, and she could smell its salty brine. The shops were all dark, their doors locked. Mari guided Cylan up to a purple doorway, noticing the paint was a bit more chipped and faded than it had been when she was here last. She'd remembered, with an uncomfortable feeling, that time was passing more quickly here in the human world than it had been back in the Realm of Faerie.

As she knocked on the rattling old door to Madame Zarena's Metaphysical Shop, Mari worried that perhaps the old woman may no longer be alive. After all, she had been in the winter of her life when Mari met her all that time ago.

A light flickered to life in the back of the building and a door opened. Through the shadows of the store, a hunched figure shuffled towards them. Mari's chest loosened at the sight of Serena's smiling face as it appeared in front of them, unlocking the store door.

"Welcome home, child." Serena's voice shook with age, but she smiled brightly.

Mari didn't have the heart to correct her and tell her that this world was no longer a place she considered home. Instead, she leaned in to give the old woman—witch, psychic, whatever she was—a hug.

"I'm sorry that we're here so late," Mari straightened, turning to her husband, "This is Cylan, King of the Realm of Faerie."

Serena started to feebly bow to Cylan, but he only held out a hand to stop her.

"I hear that you are the one to thank for sending Mari to my realm."

The old woman looked close to tears, but Mari spoke up before she could stammer out a reply.

"I came tonight because I wanted to finally offer you your payment."

Mari smiled slyly, remembering what felt like a lifetime ago when she'd tried to pay Serena for the book and gifts. Serena had only said—knowing the journey Mari had been about to go on—*I will only accept payment in the form of stories from your adventures.*

Serena's eyes sparkled and she stepped aside, welcoming them in, "Well I suppose I ought to put on the kettle then, hm?" She chuckled once as they strode past her, "It's not often I get to have tea with the King and Queen of Faerie, after all."

THE END

Acknowledgments

I'm beyond grateful to the following individuals for their contributions to Grasping for Starlight. Without you, I wouldn't have been able to get this book into the hands of the people reading this right now.
THANK YOU!

Nana (Nanna Arts), I am in love with the scene illustrations and character art that you so skillfully created for Grasping for Starlight! You captured Mari, Cylan, and Alek *perfectly*. I cannot wait to commission more art from you in the future!

Natalia Junqueira, your cover art and world map exceeded my expectations. Thank you for your professionalism and for your patience with my edit requests!

Heather Daniel, words can't adequately express how thankful I am for your production of the audio book version of Grasping for Starlight. Not many people out there are able to say they are as kind and talented as you are! I am so grateful that I randomly scrolled upon your video on social media. Thanks so, so much.

Perhaps one of my favorite parts of this whole journey was the privilege of working with my Street Team. Though there are too many of you to name individually, you all are truly amazing! To my **Beta Readers**, thank you; your feedback was invaluable! To my **Social Media Partners** and **ARC Readers**, thank you so much for helping spread the word about Grasping for Starlight. I am confident I would not have found as much success without your help and support!

Kelsey at Flying Pig PR, thank you for your feedback on the story, your ARC services and for sharing your knowledge on social media strategy. Your unwavering support of all indie authors is unmatched and really warms my heart.

Connolly Bottum, this book would still be stuck at chapter nineteen if it weren't for your valuable book coaching services and the developmental edit you provided on the first half of this story. Your kindness and encouragement got me through my writer's block and gave me the motivation I needed to finish this project!

Kerry Murphy, thanks for offering your services on my Threads post! I'm extremely appreciative of your work on my Pronunciation Guide.

A big thank you to my parents, who always contribute to the "struggling indie author fund" and help me make my dreams a reality with their monetary assistance.

My most heartfelt gratitude extends to all of you—my readers. You're the reason I continue on through the doubt, fear, and difficulties that come with being an independent author. Thank you, thank you, *thank you* for choosing my book and supporting my work!

ABOUT THE AUTHOR

Learn more about Livvy on Facebook, Instagram, TikTok, or on her website, livvyhollisbooks.com

Livvy Hollis is a proud independent author with a passion for fantasy and romance literature. At the time of the publication of "Grasping for Starlight," she was twenty-eight years of age, although her interests in both reading and storytelling began early in her childhood. Her inspiration for her work originated from the enchanting stories told by her grandmother during her formative years and the magical ambiance of her native state of Michigan.

Livvy steadfastly intends to pursue her writing and self-publishing endeavors as long as her fingers remain capable of pressing the keys of a keyboard. For Livvy, reading and writing serve as a refuge from the overwhelming pressures of reality. In a world that can often appear harsh and mundane, immersing herself in fantasy romance books keeps love and magic at the forefront of her existence.

ALSO BY

LIVVY HOLLIS

escape. dream. obsess.

The Good Inn: A Grasping for Starlight Companion Short Story eBook

The Cautionary Tales of Curious Souls

In the Shadow of the Lark: Parts One & Two